The Weeping House

The Weeping House
© 2025 by Ellie Johnson

All rights reserved. No part of this book may be reproduced, stored in a retrieval system, or transmitted in any form or by any means—electronic, mechanical, photocopying, recording, or otherwise—without the prior written permission of the author or publisher, except in the case of brief quotations embodied in critical articles or reviews.

This is a work of historical fiction. While the settings and certain historical details are based on real places and events, the characters, incidents, and dialogues are products of the author's imagination. Any resemblance to actual persons, living or dead, or actual events is purely coincidental.

Cover Illustrated by Elliot Williams
Interior Illustrations by Ellie Johnson

Published by
Growlery Publishing House
Jacksonville, Texas
First Edition
Publishing Date: May 25, 2025
ISBN: 979-8-9927131-0-7
For permissions, inquiries, or additional information, please contact:
Growlery Publishing House
P.O. Box 84, Jacksonville, TX, 75766
Printed in the United States of America

THE WEEPING HOUSE

To the Starnes family, who always make room for one more even though their table is crowded.

The Weeping House

Treu
Hanoverian Scenthound

1
The Quiet Man

The quiet man of Mittenwald was unknown to any newcomers, and had, by that measure, made himself out to be a stranger among strangers and friends alike. He was like this, a sturdy man, with little to show for conversation or for sport; well-made, with an overly abundant sense of misery; one found always to be minding his own business. He was never long in town and had no other investment in life to weigh him down.

He lived in a cottage set alongside the Isar River, with a garden of dead shrubs and wilted roses, and an old hound with tired eyes called Treu. The quiet man and Treu oft went walking through the woods, where they espied otters, toads, and frogs among the lilies. Treu had long given up his youthful penchant for chasing toads and was now content merely to be an observer of his once sworn enemy.

The man was known for having a serious way, not prone to idle chatter—not prone to any chatter at all. Though most men nearing thirty are seeking out wives and the bloom of a family, he sought out the silence of his home.

His mother had been a tall, vain kind of woman. She had decided how much she hated being a mother only after becoming one and made that fully known to her son. She was weary of life and weary of him almost immediately.

His father made it evident how he detested her and was much weighed down by that woman's lamentations and self-destruction. As a child, the quiet man knew the sound of his father's wrath more than he knew the sound of his laughter. His father's hand was strong, and he had been rich with the love of drink.

His mother had one day found herself weighted down in the pond, and his father had gone not long after that, forever leaving his son behind.

The quiet man was called Carey, though his Christian name was Hugo Johannes Carey Alsch. His mother had kept tight hold of some Irish ancestry, and, though her family connection was distant, she had retained something so simple as a nickname to remember it by. Despite this attempt at remembrance, Carey was not remembered. He was alone by the age of two-and-ten and made his way steadily through life without ever looking up. There are some people who are weighed down by the large, fancy hats they wear, and in vain cannot raise their head for fear of cervical injury, and there are others who do not look up because they cannot bear to see that they live in a beautiful world and yet feel so miserable.

The quiet man was today carrying a sack of apples, the last falling of the year. Treu clung to his legs. Despite the white whiskers around his muzzle, the hound was less disenchanted by the scenery than his master and was invigorated by the out-of-doors. He was up and down the lane, always looking to Carey, who was far too slow by the hound's measure.

"Do still, Treu," Carey would say, adjusting his grip on the sack of apples-for-peeling. Treu always stirred up a deep sound when Carey spoke to him and held conversation with his master in a way that would have baffled the mind of any logical, reasoning type of person. Carey would speak, and the dog would speak, and Carey, and the dog, and Carey. And so, Carey was not so quiet a man as people assumed. When hounds were concerned, that is.

As he walked along the Isar River, Carey would whistle and perfect the call of a quail, or pigeon, or the rtt-ttt-ttt of a squirrel. He was rather talented at conversing with any that were not of the upright, human nature, and would more often seek out the little things that crawl.

Now, rabbits, and mice, badger, and mole were less communicative than any bird a-tittering, or frog a-croaking, but they did have sound for song. Mice were always peeping, and the badger raucously fending off his hidey-hole was Carey's loudest neighbor.

This is the way with people who keep their head down. As Carey Alsch was not looking (for he hated to look), he was clearly hearing. When he looked, he had seen the back of his father going down the lane, never to return. When he looked, he saw the white dress of his mother making waves in the pond.

He kept his eyes down, and oft knew the patterns in the ground. To him, the passage of time was marked by the wearing out of his shoes.

Following his little trail up the hill, he was in his home before night fell. He did not see the stars come out at night, for he did not look up. He did not know their place, nor the crescent shape of the moon.

He steeped the kettle in the fire, cut soft cheese on the board in the kitchen, where stone overlapped with wood in a roughly hewn counter. Having just taken lavender from the garden, he strung them from the oaken beam overhead alongside dried sage and a variety of mint bushels.

Treu settled near the fire and laid his chin upon the familiar, socked foot of his master. His breathing turned deep and even, and the fire crackled warmly at his back. Treu was used to, and enjoyed, good feelings. It was splendid to be near his master, it was a delight to see the woods, and lovely to play among the hedges. He never felt great sorrow, except when Carey was away where he could not follow.

His master was not this way. Carey was not used to great feelings of goodness and usually held some sort of burden in his chest. There was comfort in reclining near the fire, but he was not warmed; he was instead nearly lacking feeling entirely.

Pulling draughts from his pipe was a pleasure, but he was staring into the fire without thought or sense, rather than blowing pleasant clouds to ascertain what shape they formed. He was not a breathing dragon when he smoked; he was a worn-out man with a worn-out soul.

Now, he was peeling the apples and speaking casually to Treu.

"Fire goes?" he muttered. "I think it needs 'nother log."

Treu was sleeping soundly by this time.

"Shall I fetch it?" Carey sighed, dropping peelings into a wooden tub for later. "If I fetch it, I must put my coat on, my hat, and my woolen scarf. And I shall have to tramp in the snow and make my boots soggy with cold and wet. And then I shall have to dry out my socks on the hearth. It'll not do, Treu."

The dog would have answered, surely, if he was awake.

"Well," Carey said, "once my socks are dry, then the fire'll be low again. And I'll have to fetch 'nother log. And the process'll repeat."

He stared into the licking flames of the fire, not realizing that the kettle was screaming that it was done. Carey was often so deeply lost in thought that no sound could pierce the haze.

"I'd rather sit here," Carey said, "and let the fire die. Build it in the morn. I've half a mind to not stir from this chair."

He set the peeled apples aside, covering them with a board of rough wood so no rot would mar them.

Someone looking through the window would have thought the quiet man of Mittenwald was dead in his fireplace chair for how little he stirred. Though his eyes were wide, Carey Alsch seemed not to breathe. The coals smoldered. Smoke was lazy-drifting over him in waves—some wafting out the chimney in normal fashion. As if carved from stone, some men are stuck in one place and remain stuck there for all the lengths of their lives.

2
Christmas Dinner

Snow soon covered all of Mittenwald like a blanket tucked tightly to the edges of a bed. Pristine and undisturbed, reflecting all the light of the strong sun. The Isar was frigid and swift flowing. It was not fit for playing in or near, or so the parents of the wild children in the village were oft scolding their broods. Red holly berry was double-laden on branches already weighed with powder. They bent and bowed as boughs only do in winter. Such is how winter has dominion over the branches, as fall has dominion over the leaves, and spring and summer dominate the buds.

Carey trudged through the snow, cap pulled low, scarf wrapped up past his ears. His coat edges were flung up against white flurries, and his hands were buried deep in lined pockets. He carved a path behind him that Treu religiously avoided, so deep abreast in snow that he could have been swimming if it was water. The dog was joyously breaking through heaps of white like a ship plows through waves, creating rolls of wake in the deep ocean.

He won a smile from Carey. A rare changing of features on the face of the quiet man of Mittenwald.

"I should rather follow 'ee, and the path you shove aside, Treu." Carey almost laughed.

He was nearing the village, which sat at the bottom of the hill. The road was plowed, likely done by one of the many able-bodied men of the town who had no livelihood aside from seasonal tendings: plowing, raking, pruning, and building.

The Weeping House

Carey paid little heed to the livelihood of other men of the town. He was a leatherworker by trade and always had employment, regardless of the season. In winter, there were boots, and coats, and pants for mending. In summer, quivers, sheaths, and belts. Every nine months he was making little leather shoes, and every now and then taking the shoes of old, dead men, and reworking them for new.

Today, he pulled behind him a sled laden with five pair of little shoes, and two overcoats of stiff hide, not yet worn till supple. They would keep the wearer warm and fetch a price for living. He also had Mr. Remble's bridle, which had worn away at the crownpiece and throatlatch, and had to be reworked.

"Keep on guard, Treu," Carey said, half to the snow, half to his feet, which were covered in a mixture of mud and ice. "There're people in this town who'll take 'ee. And there's people here who'll take my leather without payin'. Mind you keep on guard."

Treu was rather invested in not hearing his master and pleasantly greeted the first who greeted him. A youth known commonly as Miff, who was actually christened Michael. Old dog and young boy cavorted in the fresh snow, one not minding the cold, the other covered in leather and warmed by wool.

"Hello, Mr. Alsch!" Miff stood abruptly when the master of his playfriend walked past. The boy stiffened due to the uncaring attitude of the man passing by. Miff followed Carey through the narrow streets of Mittenwald, keeping a safe distance.

"What've you got today, Mr. Alsch?" Miff was a very kind boy, raised well by parents known by Carey for always needing a new pair of little boots, as Miff had ten brothers and sisters. He was middling among them, and oft left to entertain himself, although he did not mind this on days where Carey came into the village and brought with him Treu, who was by far Miff's favorite playmate.

Carey kept his head down, looking at his feet and the shape they left in the snow.

"Mutti has got a need for new baby shoes, I figure," Miff said. "I got a new sister, called Isolde. I don't much like the name, but I reckon it's a far cry better than Michael, which is not anything like a first name and is in all things like a second name."

The silence was not conversational, not like when Carey spoke to Treu, who answered, though he was a dog. This silence was one of rejection. Carey was a man of many rejections. Not that he plied for conversation. He was the death of most exchanges.

"Well," Miff said, plunging on bravely. "I would ask you to join us for dinner come Christmas. Mutti said it would be awful pleasant if you came by. Don't have to bring no gifts neither. Just y'self."

Carey paused so suddenly that the front hitch of his sled bumped into the heel of his boot.

"I just hate to think of you all alone on Christmas," Miff said. "Well, I guess you ain't alone—you got ol' Treu here. He's good company, I'll say."

Carey nodded, glancing quickly from boy to dog. Miff, he noticed for the first time, had bright eyes of a warm brown color, and a little red nose all disturbed by the cold. He was thin but looked thicker because of the winter coats he wore. He was a boy well cared for, despite having so many siblings.

"I'll stay home." Carey nodded stoutly, not fully meeting the eyes of the child. He always found difficulty where eyes were concerned. He did not like to be looked at or to do the looking.

"But—" Miff was set fully to protestations of the child-kind.

"I'll stay home." Carey was ever so curt.

"I just want you to feel welcome," Miff said. "Mutti said the first thing about bein' Christian is makin' others feel welcome."

"I don't feel welcome," Carey snapped. "I feel like carrying on with my business."

"I just—"

Carey moved on down the lane before Miff could speak further. Treu followed, tail tucked in, with the quiet misery that is a dog separated from its playmate.

The quiet man in old leather and wool made his deliveries without pomp-and-circumstance. The little shoes were indeed meant for Miff's mother. At the back door of the house, he was again invited to Christmas dinner and had a less easy time refusing the mother than the son.

"—but if you change your mind, Mr. Alsch, you are always welcome at our table. I know it's raucous in this house, but joy is spirit and mirth, and we have plenty. We would share both with you."

"Never you mind, Mrs. Reinalz." Carey ducked his head, not looking up from the bottom step. "I'll stay home."

"We'll have roast duck!" the second youngest Reinalz boldly announced, leaning around her mother's skirts.

"And raspberries for sup," another Reinalz declared, as if it were some great prize to know what Christmas feast would entail.

"I—I don't want to come," Carey said. "I couldn't dare bring Treu into the house, and I ain't like to leave him home alone. And I have nothing for cooking to bring."

"You can bring the dog," a young Reinalz said, resisting her mother's persistent shooings-away.

"I'll go now," Carey said, backing down off the clean-swept back steps of the house. The door closed softly, with the sound of gentle admonishments carrying beyond the sturdy wood frame.

3
Cheese and Bread

A shining sun was just reaching its zenith when Carey finished his deliveries. He evaded any other cordialities by hiding beneath a scarf pulled round his nose.

He ate his lunch on a log that had fallen near the Isar. Winter was still, leaving the glasslike surface of the frozen river undisturbed. Carey swept off the log's surface with a gloved hand and ate sparingly of a rye loaf and some soft cheese. A twittering jay landed in the nearest bough of a juniper, angrily sounding the alarm. The quiet man of Mittenwald responded to the jay with a likewise cheerful call, then pleasantly watched the bird show a state of confusion, abandoning its post in a flurry of feathers.

The most Carey Alsch looked up was when he was looking at birds and other natural things. A winter-coated fox traipsed by on the far side of the Isar, listening closely for a mouse or a mole beneath the surface.

Taking a small delight in the flavor of the cheese spread across his bread, Carey was inclined to share some with Treu, who supped generously, fully cleaning any remnants of cheese from his masters' fingertips.

In the far distance of the forest into which Carey peered, a figure was coming close. This one was dressed in long, grey skirts and a muddy-red hood and cloak. It was tied about her neck with a pink ribbon, tangled in with a yellow scarf, fanning scarlet cheeks.

A song rose in the woods, not unlike that of the wind, or of a mournful loon, which glides on the waters in early morning and sings of all things lonesome. She was singing. The figure Carey quietly observed was certainly fascinating.

There were no words to her song, only rising and falling and an almost perfect understanding of the way in which one note may sound pleasant near the others.

Carey had entirely forgotten his bread and cheese, a distraction that Treu took full advantage of as he gobbled up the remainder with all the messy slobber and uncouthness most hounds possess.

A woman bounded along the opposite side of the river, arms laden with forest things. A few sprigs and the odd winter mushroom fell out of her arms, leaving a trail behind her. She moved quickly, spurred either by the cold or by some inner excitement. The latter seemed to be the primary encourager of her movements. She smiled a great deal.

She came close to the frozen shore just opposite Carey, who had not moved. He was not prone to agitation, but his stillness could usually be attributed more to apathy than to any other feeling.

The woman ceased her singing and took up a conversation with a willow hanging over the edge. A few of its tendrilous branches had been captured by the flow of the river, so the willow seemed more bent than any other of its kind.

Carey was ever intent and silent, doing his best at listening to the conversation between woman and willow.

"Well," she said to the tree, "I shall only take a little, because you are held captive by the river. It is a shame, to be held like this for all of the growing you will do. Regardless, I need just a little for my friend."

She took out a small knife from her pocket and set about shaving a thin layer of bark from the tree. The first roll of mottled bark was tucked into her arms, and she went back to her task, being careful to not entirely strip a ring of bark off the tree.

"Dear Isola has just had a baby," the woman said. "And she has these terrible aches and pains. They were so kind to invite me for Christmas, and without having anything else to bring for myself, I thought I shall make her a poultice for her aches. That'll be the thing."

The tree said nothing in return, but that did not deter the woman from regarding it as if were a vibrant, living thing.

"And she is so wonderful, Mrs. Reinalz is," she said happily. "And so many children! I should be glad to come and live in this village. I only wish I had done so earlier. Listen here, stout friend-near-the-water, I shall never go back to the city. Only the country will do for me, until I die!"

Carey Alsch suddenly wondered why he had so adamantly refused Christmas dinner with the Reinalzes. It was obviously no difficult task to inform Mrs. Reinalz of his mistake when going home.

Christmas dinner was quite a lovely prospect.

Barn Owl
Tyto alba

4
Gloom-and-Glump

Any recollection of maidens in forests was lost on Carey Alsch after a few days of winter desolation. He sat mostly in his chair by the fire and was never seen out-of-doors once the sun began to fall behind the trees. His hands were often interlaced and resting on his stomach, with feet splayed out to obtain the perfect, relaxed posture.

Treu had thought to go out and romp in the snow today but had an aching in his right haunch, worsened by his playing with Miff.

The hound was perfectly happy to be curled against Carey's leg and had little else to care about in the world. Hound and master were as hound and master should be, in his estimation.

Carey had set about to perform his nightly staring-into-the-fire habit. This activity usually stretched on into lonely hours of the night. He was tonight plagued by despair of the social nature, wondering what sort of cruel trick had seized him to so suddenly accept felicitations. He would rather spend Christmas alone, though the day was still two months away. He had time to prepare his heart and mind for a great gathering. He wished deeply that he had nothing to prepare for.

"Surely I can still say no, Treu," Carey muttered, tugging at his neat beard. Though he had little liking for the world, or for his fellow man, or for town, Carey Alsch would be known as a neat man. He was always trimmed, walking in cared-for shoes, and wore only his 'least-dusties,' his smartest, least dusty pants.

"Do ye think 't'would be considered a slight?" Carey had not yet ceased his ponderings, though the fire was lying low. "Mr. Reinalz would understand, I suppose, bein' a man an' all. I'm not fit to go out an' socialize. I got nothing clever to say, and I am not good for a laugh. I can call a crow to come and roost." He considered this, his brow set lower over his eyes, weighted heavy with despair. "But who wants a wild man as Christmas dinner guest? No one wants a crow to come and roost, or a gloom-and-glump like me to take a seat at the table. I should have a talk with Mr. Reinalz. Man-to-man. He'll understand."

The next day, Carey took up early and made his way into the village before most folk were awake. Treu was with him, this time following in his master's tracks so as to not exacerbate his injury. The hound was equally happy to be near to Carey as he was to romp in the snow.

Upon reaching Mittenwald, Carey stopped to inspect the town while the sun rose. Preeminent in the morning glow, a domed church spire with green roof and silver steeple—Saint Peter and Paul Kirche. Aside from this, various arches, small gardens, pointed rooftops covered over with brown shingles. All were arranged close to one another, some atop the other, or crowded in beside, so there was very little room to breathe, in Carey's estimation. The streets were cobbled, slanted, and upon bridges spanning the Isar, which ran through the middle of the town proper. A similar, albeit smaller river known as the Lainbach flowed parallel to the Isar on the far side of the town.

Turning away from one of his rare steadfast gazes, he found the Reinalzes' house, with its wide porch and railing, dark beams and pale walls, with baskets in the window for spring flowers. It was modest but obviously large enough for eleven children and two parents.

Carey sat on the Reinalzes' porch and waited for the man of the house to pass by on his way to work. Which was, as Carey had once heard, a career of being the only clerk of town fit for any legal determination. He was effectively the village judge.

Only, Mr. Reinalz was not going to work that day and instead planned to take his whole family to the frozen-over lake outside of town, called Lautersee, which was bordered by the mountain Hoher Kranzberg.

It was a bitter winter day with no shining sun and a stiff winter wind. Carey began to shiver; though wrapped fully in wool and leather, a chill crept over him. He tucked his hands beneath his arms and hunkered down on the steps of the wooden porch. Treu curled against him, offering some of his heavy coat to his frigid master.

"Mr. Alsch!" came the voice of Mr. Reinalz, who was sent out by his wife to collect wood for the stove and thereby heat the whole house. "Whatever are you doing on my porch?"

"I am come to recant." Carey hung his head, tugging his hat low over his ears.

"Recant?"

"Well," Carey hesitated. "I should apologize to this missus. I told her I would come for Christmas dinner, but I am finding myself unable to attend, sir."

"Call me Holt." Mr. Reinalz came and perched on the steps beside Carey. "Are you in need of assistance, Mr. Alsch? May I help, or any of my children, so you may join us?"

"No." Carey shook his head. "I don't like to be among people and I only said I would on a whim. A whim of which I have never had the like in my life, and I wish I had not."

"Sir." Mr. Reinalz's face was drawn up in a grimace, observing the anxious, cold man found on his porch. "Will you come inside and warm by the fire? My wife and I are making breakfast. The children are not yet awake so there'll be no ruckus."

"Can't," Carey said. "My dog, he bain't like to go inside a stranger's house."

The door of the house swung lazily on its hinges, and a warm draft of air scented with pancakes and butter washed over those seated on the porch. Treu decided this was an appropriate time to be entirely antithetical to his master's statements and entered the house of his own free will in search of pancakes.

Mr. Reinalz grinned, his eyebrows rising considerably high above his blue eyes and dark-rimmed spectacles.

"Sorry!" Carey exclaimed, climbing to his feet and charging after his hound. Mr. Reinalz rose slowly and followed, contented with having the lonely man enter his warm, comforting house, one way or the other.

5
Change in the Mind

The Reinalzes' house was everything a house containing ten-and-three people would be. Great curtains covered the windows, cut from a heavy green cloth, that lent a sense of comfort, contrasted with the cold, white outdoors. Pretty paper adorned the walls, following the steps up to the second floor, where shadows still rested and kept the children asleep a little while longer. Candles illuminated the lower hall, which led into the kitchen on one end and a fully furnished blue sitting room on the other. Mrs. Reinalz affectionately called the sitting room her Blue-Rue.

Treu headed for the kitchen, following his nose toward the breakfast that awaited him. He was resolutely set on this quest and not easily deterred. Carey plunged after him, set on deterring. The man endeavored at quietness to keep the sanctity of the home, but his boots were caked with mud and snow, and his leather soles thumped rather loudly.

The dog was beyond the double swinging door before master could catch him, and at the loud exclamation from the woman of the house just beyond, Carey flushed with embarrassment.

He pushed through the doors and was all apologies, bowing and scraping as he gathered up his hound to leave.

"Don't go, Mr. Alsch!" said Mrs. Reinalz, who hefted a great platter of steaming pancakes across the kitchen. "Never mind the dog. He's welcome. Oh, Holt! Holt, come here and help me!" She spoke in the kind of voice a parent knows well, one that is both loud and quiet, a yell and a whisper. Her husband came to the rescue, taking the platter from her.

"No, I'll be going now," said Carey, slowly backing out the way he had come, gripping Treu tightly in his arms, like a shepherd carries a sheep back to the fold. "I'll be going, 'scuse me, ma'am."

"Sit!" Mrs. Reinalz was rather emphatic, and Carey Alsch, who was not entirely used to people, and not at all used to women, sat down.

Treu looked rather embarrassed now and had the cut of eye that dogs have when found tearing into trash, or eating off the table when they know it is not allowed.

Mr. Reinalz stood with the platter of steaming pancakes in one hand, holding a finger to his lips, his eyes alight with great mischief. "Isola," he whispered, "I saw one little ghost on the stairs. Hush, or we shall be haunted, and our breakfast claimed by others before we have partaken." He joined his wife at the counter, where he chose an apron from a clean pile and tied it round his waist.

"I should not have snapped at you like that, Mr. Alsch," said Isola, looking closely at the man seated at her kitchen table. He would not meet her eye and instead studied the fanciful pattern of her beloved tile, which had been lovingly hand-painted by an expectant Isola Reinalz many years ago. They showed the wear of many years and many feet.

Carey Alsch said nothing. He continued to stare at the floor, his gaze now resting on the notch just between his muddy boots.

"Pancake?" Isola Reinalz held a plate with a round flapjack drizzled over with honey beneath Carey's nose. Treu regarded the plate longingly but had learned enough of rebellion and its consequences to not act foolishly.

Something shifted in Carey's eyes. His nose twitched. Having been fully abandoned by ten-and-two, and never properly cared for prior to then, he had never been given a warm breakfast.

He looked fully into the face of Mrs. Reinalz and blinked. She was a sight to behold, with loose curls framing her face, the endings of which were coated in a fine layer of flour, and a smile far too bright for such an early morning. Her skirts and smock were dipped in light blue, which only highlighted the beauty.

Mr. Reinalz was equally as handsome as his wife, with a stern, set brow that did not match his oft-worn smile, and a sharp, clean-shaven jaw that fit his status as clerk and judge.

Carey glanced down at the golden pancake beneath his chin and said simply, somewhat meekly, "Yes, please."

Mrs. Reinalz set the plate down on the table behind him and placed a worn blanket on the floor beside as a resting spot for the old hound in Carey's arms. Treu was glad to reside here and was even gifted a taste of bacon and grease from the pan.

Husband and wife joined him shortly, after Mr. Reinalz placed a second, even larger pancake atop Carey's unfinished first. He liberally applied honey and set a hot mug of coffee at Carey's right.

Silence was a comfortable conversation for the married couple, and an even more comforting one for Carey, whose only regular conversationalist was his hound. Treu whined until his master rested a hand on his head, gently massaging his soft ears with keen affection.

Midway through the meal, the first child entered.

"Mutti," a soft voice said. "Breakfast?"

"Yes, dear," said Isola. "Come into the kitchen, and your father'll help you."

The second youngest Reinalz was a small girl of nearly three, who had dark, tangled hair. She cast a quizzical eye over the newcomer in her kitchen. All suspicions were forgotten upon noticing the great, soft hound with a graying muzzle in the corner. Anneliese Reinalz leapt onto the beast with a great hug and buried her face in the rolls of fur near his neck.

She was delighted to learn that the hound's name was Treu, "on account of hisself being all loyal-like," as his master whispered.

"Anneliese," Mr. Reinalz said, sweeping his daughter into his arms and prying a pancake from the large stack with the finesse that only comes through parenthood. "Will you greet our guest, Mr. Alsch?"

"Hello," Anneliese said, suddenly shy and burying her face in her father's shoulder.

Carey nodded, tugging his hat low over his ears, and murmured some gruff reply. "Sorry I traipsed mud in the house, Mrs. Reinalz." He coughed, then pulled his hat from his head and twisted the edge beneath his hands.

Mrs. Reinalz's eyes widened upon the revelation of Carey Alsch's wild, untamed head of straw-like hair, which was so routinely covered with a tight cap. She pressed her lips to a line, glancing at her husband with a look intended to share her mirth while also keeping it silent. Mr. Reinalz raised his eyebrows, which were rather loud and voiced his opinions so forcefully that his wife often had to remind him to refrain from raising them altogether when the situation required.

"No mind." Isola smiled, leaning back in her chair. "It'll mend."

"I had planned to wait on the steps for 'ee, Holt," Carey said, producing the name of his new friend after a bit of throat clearing.

"To say the most unpleasant thing," Holt said, feeding his small daughter a bit of honey-soaked flapjack.

"Oh?" Isola looked back at her husband, one eyebrow askew.

"I had—" Carey paused, glancing between husband and wife. "I had thought to, well, see, I had come to tell yer husband—I had the idea that I …" He could go no further and leaned back in his chair, resigned to his fate. "I had meant to say that I'd be glad to see 'ee come Christmas, Mrs. Reinalz. And thankee for the invitation."

"Perfect!" said Isola, although clearly suspicious that some change had just overcome the man, and he had not spoken as he had originally intended. "Then, will you also join us today on our excursion? We're off to Lautersee, as soon as all the children wake. It's to be a great surprise, and I hope you join us!"

6
Lautersee

Two wagons trundled down the lane, laden with many children, a mother, a father, a quiet man, and a hound. There was squabbling, jeering, and many a laugh that echoed over snowy-white hills. Noses were red, and breaths streamed into the wind in billowing clouds.

Two rabbits bounded across the pasture on one side, leaving behind the trail of their passing. They were brown spots against a greater blanket of white.

Overhead was a fair blue sky, with a sun that had reasoned to shine brightly. Its shining was rewarded with a crystalline sparkle from the undisturbed snow.

Each cart was pulled by a sturdy horse meant for heavy work. These were not swift racehorses, nor feisty mustangs like they had in the Americas. These were thick-necked, stout horses with long tresses of mane and fur gathered around their feet.

Mr. Reinalz guided one wagon; Mrs. Reinalz the second. They were moving at an even pace, periodically calling to one another. Joy abounded richly in a way that Carey Alsch was wholly unfamiliar with.

He sat at the back with his legs hanging over the edge, one arm wrapped around Treu, the other steadying himself to keep strange children at a reasonable distance.

Lautersee lake was a good two-hour drive southwest from Mittenwald. The road they followed closely matched the curve of the Lainbach, which flowed from the lake into the city. Bavarian alps rose like guardians on all sides, swathed in robes of cobalt, violet, and sapphire against a cornflower sky. It was a day of days, one that was thoroughly enjoyed by all but one man.

Whilst the Reinalz family sang joyous hymns of the season with a harmony and musical quality that only some can hope to attain, Carey watched the muddying of the road. He was silent and scarcely listening, thinking deeply of how he regretted being swayed by pancakes and honey, and how sorely he wished he were back home. The wagon kicked rocks up behind the wheels of the wagon, knocking against his shoes, which dragged slightly in the tracks of sludge.

Clouds hung above the peaks, lifted off the surface of the earth as if they held some trepidation in sweeping too close. The Reinalz children named them, laughing at the various forms they took.

One immense joy the Reinalz children found was in persuading Treu to bray his mightiest bray into the sky. They would whisper among themselves, and then Inge and Wolfgang (the fourth and fifth-born, respectively) would set to howling, lifting their faces upwards and forcing out a fearsome sound. The younger children would follow suit, and Treu would take up the call. Before long there were two wagons of howling children and one old hound giving his best performance.

Carey did not utter one word during the two-hour ride to Lautersee. Upon setting down a good distance from the lake itself, he continued his habit of silence even while they trudged along the path through the woods.

The family formed a long line in the snow, laden like a cargo train extending on into the distance. Mr. Reinalz carried Anneliese on his back, and the newest born, baby Isolde, in a pouch on his chest. Both were covered with woolen blankets and knit caps pulled so low over their round heads that their features were completely hidden. Holt hiked at the front of the line, calling out encouragements to his many children, some of whom called back equally cheerful, whilst others made known their displeasure at both the cold and the difficult work it was to hike in the snow.

There were many tears fallen between the wagons and the lake.

Carey walked at the back of the line, hands shoved deep into his pockets, gaze fixated on the brown contrast of his boots in the white snow. He was a curious form amidst the bright, ruddy-nosed children, who were dressed in an array of blues, greens, and Christmas reds. His coat was nearing a black color after many layers of mink oil rubbed into the surface, and the fur fixed to the hood was that of a black rabbit. His trousers were equally dark, burnished with ash and chestnut from the fire the day before. He was not well-dressed, as he had not expected to make it past the porch on his errand.

He had indeed made it very far past the porch and was now trudging through deep snow in the woods past the bridge spanning the Isar. The wind pushed him back towards Mittenwald, rather against his will.

"What a curse it is for God to have made man so susceptible to the whims of woman's convincing by food," Carey whispered to Treu when he bounded past. "I should be home peeling potatoes for sup' now; 'ere I am forced to go a-walkin'."

Treu barked with the deep, scruffy voice belonging to the canines of the larger variety. He turned and faced his master, haunches lifted, front limbs splayed out, inviting Carey to play.

"I'll not romp in the snow wit' 'ee," Carey hissed. "Get thee gone. There's plently'll play wit' 'ee ahead."

Treu howled at his master, then tore off up the final slope. Puffs of snow flared beneath his heels. The children laughed as the old hound flew past them, covering them in a layer of fine snow. Oscar and Corinna took tight hold of their packs and raced after him, pushing past their younger siblings. Utter chaos ensued, as was the nature of eleven children, two parents, one hound, and one quiet man.

Mr. Reinalz stood on the crest of a hill, shaded by oak and cedar still clinging to their evergreen leaves and mounds of snow. He held one of the branches in a gentle clasp. When his eldest children ran beneath, he shook it, dumping heaps of snow on their heads. The children took great delight in this and were sent tumbling down the hill towards the frozen shore of Lautersee, resting in the great basin of Hoher Kranzberg.

The scenery was just so: a rising mountain, on which a settling of midday sun just barely touched the eastern faces, dipping down to a ridge of jagged teeth on one side. A saddle col branched between the rest of the Garmisch range. Below the range grew a thick, pointed forest of a variety of fir, which grew together so closely that little had been done to ascend those peaks.

The moraine through which ancient glaciers had crawled now boasted of many green-blue crystalline lakes in summer, and perfect, smoothly frozen lakes in winter. The latter was the reason for the Reinalzes' excursion today. Having reached the bottom of the hill, the children now tore open their bags, each pulling out a fine pair of skates with long ties and a knit sleeve covering the razor edge upon which one glided.

There was much chatter among the children as skates were fitted and tied. Some of the chatter was in despair, as one sister tied her skates faster than the other, or one had bluer laces, the other sleeker skates. Mr. and Mrs. Reinalz were coming and going amongst their brood, mending shattered hopes and tying many laces.

The children were required to wait while Mr. Reinalz tested the ice. Layers of snow were piled on the surface of the lake, and there was no sure way to test the thickness until it had been shoved aside and then skated upon.

Snow ramped up around Holt's ankles, creating trenches marking his path from the shore to the middle of the lake. Treu followed close behind, leaping through the snow toward the far shore. His brass-tone brays echoed throughout the valley, bouncing off the steep angle of Hoher Kranzberg and the adjacent peaks.

Two mountain jays, with gray backs and blue-white patterned wings, alighted on branches nearby. They were joined by a tufted titmouse and one crimson-breasted robin. The robin hopped along the surface of a fallen log, leaving tiny imprints in the thin layer of snow. Carey watched these small creatures, focusing his full attention on the hopping robin in hopes that the family might forget his presence entirely.

Mr. Reinalz's strong voice carried swiftly from the center of the lake. His voice was met with many exultant waving fists.

The ice was safe for skating.

European Robin
Erithacus rubecula

7
The Robin and I

Brooms and shovels were carried over shoulders and beneath little arms. Miff Reinalz nearly tumbled sideways, off-balanced by the weight of the shovel that probably weighed more than he. The wool-wrapped boy seemed to find great delight in struggling through deeper snow and was resolute on doing it all himself. His brother Wolfgang, who was nearing three-and-ten, found little difficulty, being far taller and longer-limbed than his brother.

Snow was shoved aside, mounded up on the nearest edges, leaving some thirty meters in either direction free for skating. Coats were doffed, piled atop one another on a blanket laid across a good portion of the frozen shoreline. Mrs. Reinalz sat on the shore, wrapped in a similar blanket, and nursed her baby beneath the warm cocoon.

Soon, ten children, one father, and one hound were skating to and fro on the lake. Joyful shouts echoed throughout the basin, joined by laughter and some cries of alarm as the younger children learned the dangers of too much speed.

Miff and Oscar, the other brother, who was nearing eight-and-ten, would gently glide to one end of the cleared area, then turn and gather up tremendous speed and intentionally collide with the snow banks on the far side. Many imprints of their bodies were left behind, taking on different shapes depending on how high the boys lifted their arms.

Mechthild held hands with little Anneliese and guided her through a series of calm, slow spins. The second eldest, Corinna, was equally involved in Anneliese's lessons. Anneliese oft threw her head back and laughed with so bright a sound that the sun overhead seemed to shine a little more for each joyful outburst.

Carey sat on the robin-log, hands still buried in his pockets. He was studying the shape of his shoes. These were his own craft, so it was vain to study them. He took a deep breath and watched it stream out in a cloud that temporarily shrouded his downward gaze.

Mrs. Reinalz sang a song, some kind of hymn. The melody was sweet, but to Carey, the words seemed rather harsh. He listened closely, inclining his head towards the woman, but not shifting his seat or his gaze.

Isola Reinalz knew Carey Alsch listened to her song and so sang brighter and richer, hoping a song of mercies would reach his heart and perhaps do something to thaw that frozen thing in his chest.

The same robin lighted on a twig above Carey's head. It twittered a small verse, shaking clumps of snow onto his hat. He lifted his head, dusting his cap.

He imitated the robin to near-perfection, causing the bird to sweep down and rest next to him on the log, regarding him with a curious twisting of its head. Carey continued his verse, catching every small twitter and chirp of a robin's voice.

Isola's song faded to stillness, and she very quietly listened to Carey sing to the birds. She did not stir, nor speak, nor look his way, for fear he might fall silent again.

The robin eventually tired of the human who sounded like a bird and was replaced by two angry jays, who fought from tree to tree amidst a flapping of wings and stirring of snow from branches. Carey switched to this song, imitating the angry braw-braw of the jay, and, much to Isola's astonishment, quite convinced the birds to give up their disagreement entirely.

His natural conversation trailed off into silence, stirred only by the wind and the joyful cries of the children on the lake.

The robin returned after a short while and took up another conversation with Carey. The bird seemingly longed for company and had got over its previous mistrust of the human who sounded like kin. Eventually the bird left, having become distracted by an enemy in the form of a black squirrel creeping towards its nest.

"Mr. Alsch!" said Isola, wrapping baby Isolde in a woolen swaddle and tucking her into a swathe tied behind her shoulders, "I did not know you possessed a talent like that! I am thoroughly impressed."

The straw-colored head of Carey Alsch snapped up, eyes wide with embarrassment. He was unused to an audience and had not thought of the consequences of so loudly imitating bird calls. Now, his own precocious twittering had led to a conversation he wanted no part in.

"No talent, ma'am," Carey said, fixing his eyes on the distant shape of Treu skidding across the ice towards three Reinalz children who laughed in uncontrolled hysterics when he collided with them. "Merely the robin and I."

"Well," Isola said, "most of us cannot talk back. They seem great conversationalists."

"Far cry better 'n the jib most of the village can work up." Carey ducked his head, rather chagrined for having spoken negatively of the town to one who lived in it.

"I'm sure." Isola laughed. She worked at tugging the woolen blanket over the edge of her baby's face, shielding little Isolde from the brisk wind that had picked up. She could not fend off the wind and the flurries of snow it kicked over the bank.

A shadow fell over Isola. The shadow acted as a bulwark, so all the wind was swept aside. Carey Alsch held a blanket from the pile. It was stretched out, one end draped over a crooked branch from the fallen log, the other held in a tight grip.

"It's for the little one," he muttered, staring intently at the ground. Isola coughed, covering her mouth with a hand to hide her smile. Carey stood silently, holding the blanket up to protect mother and baby from the cold wind. He did not offer any conversation, nor give any indication that he wished to speak. The tall man moved so seldom, Isola wondered if he were man or tree.

Mr. Reinalz skated towards his wife, coming to a halt along the edge of the shore. "Is everything well, my love?" He cocked his head, breathing out puffs of cold air.

"Mr. Alsch is helping Isolde stay out of the wind. She was cold," said his wife.

"Would you like to trade places, Mr. Alsch?" Holt asked. "You may borrow my skates, I think we are roughly the same size?"

"I don't skate," said Carey.

"Shame." Mr. Reinalz frowned. "Would you like to learn?"

"I shouldn't." Carey looked away. He replaced his cap and tugged it low over his ears.

One of the children cried out, drawing the attention of the three adults. Miff careened straight towards Lieselotte, who screamed for him to stop. Wolfgang and Oscar tore after him, making the unwise decision to garner more speed as they chased their brother. The end result was a great pile-up of Reinalz children, who yelled and cried with varying degrees of amplitude.

"Well," said Mr. Reinalz, "I suppose I'll return in a moment." He turned on his heel and was quickly gone to the pile of children slowly drifting across the ice. They were sorted and set right, dispersing across the plowed portion of the lake. Miff was gathered up in his father's arms and carried towards his mother. The boy was deposited near Isola, and Mr. Reinalz was once again summoned by cries of moderate distress—Amalie was stuck on her back and greatly displeased with any help Lieselotte was giving in attempting to right her.

Isola did not speak to Carey, and Carey did not speak to Isola. They watched the scenery, observed Treu dive into the heaps of snow, and listened to the sounds of jubilation. Isola knew peace whilst watching her large brood enjoy themselves despite the cold of winter. She felt love watching her tall husband guide her children with kindness and gentleness. She felt warmth, hugging Miff and Isolde close beneath the warm blanket. The lady spoke softly to Miff, comforting him and nursing his red, scraped palms.

Carey Alsch was silent and still, becoming more like a tree with each moment. There was within him a loud discontent. It had always been decided in his life that he would be alone. It had always been so, but for Treu and the bugs and things. It had been decided that he was unwanted. His mother had settled such a thing when she had sunk herself in the pond. And it was decided by his father when he had left down the lane and never came home.

This was a different feeling entirely. He held the corner of the blanket, bare hand clenching tighter and tighter, until the knuckles grew white. Something was rearing up within him.

For the first time in his life, he considered the fact that he might have a friend that was not a bird or a hound. He was quite discomforted by the idea.

Eastern Meadowlark
Sturnella magna

8

Of Mountains and Wind

All things considered, Carey enjoyed his time visiting Lautersee, in that he was a quiet observer of other people's fun. He expressed this with a simple, gruff nod of his head and tugged his cap over his ears.

After a lunch of sandwiches and fermented cabbage, Mr. Reinalz declared it was time to pack up and leave. There was raucous protest almost immediately, eventually quieted by both parents and tucked away to be dealt with later. Coats were fought over, and there was much debate over which child had the reddest jacket, and which had an unpleasantly muddied red that nobody wanted.

That particular jacket belonged to Ada Reinalz, who had dirtied it upon finding an old set of her mother's oil paints, and the color was never lifted from the leather. There was no arguing the point for Ada, who was often messing about in other people's affairs and was always the likely culprit when it came to paint spills and messy clothing. She donned the coat and, much to her chagrin, found it fitted perfectly.

The wagons were loaded and set to rolling towards Mittenwald. There was little complaint to be had on the return hike, as it was mostly downhill and there is little anger felt for a downward slope, where nature itself lends one swifter and lighter steps.

Carey Alsch had found his place at the back of the wagon and set a weary Treu across his lap, gently petting down his soft fur. Warm winds ruffled his hair, threatening to toss his cap up between the trees. Carey tugged it down, lowering the ear flaps and tying it beneath his chin with a leather cord.

Miff Reinalz sat beside him, the youth was fixated on the variation of tree overhead. Spruce, silver fir, maple, and beech were the signifiers of high altitude. Gradually the odd oak and pinion were added when the mountains became rolling hills. The hills dipped into valleys that were quite livable, though not yet settled, like Mittenwald.

The wagon ride did not carry the same thrall of excitement to the Reinalz children on the return home as it had on the way up into the mountains. There was a contented silence, mixed with weariness, the hopeful thought of a warm dinner next to a blazing hearth.

Miff was attentive to the changing pattern of the woods; that is, until he collapsed entirely against Carey's arm in the full, deep slumber that overcomes children who have romped out-of-doors for most of the day.

The motion threw Carey's body and soul into a stiff rigidity not befitting one who had become a resting place for boy and dog. He sat stock-still and staring off the end of the wagon, frozen in quiet consideration. The decision with which he wrestled was this: remain still and let the boy sleep—which was most distressing for Carey, who did not like to be close to any other person—or shake the boy off, which would be most distressing to the boy, who had found comfort in the angle of Carey's coat and the strong scent of mink oil pressed into the leather.

He (much to his regret) chose the former and was an unmoving statue for the remainder of the ride. Miff slept soundly, one hand buried in his pocket, the other resting on the curve of Treu's hide, where it had remained since the boy fell asleep while petting the hound.

The sun began to descend toward the western horizon. Mittenwald had not yet appeared to the weary waggoneers. Carey regarded the alacrity with which the red sun dipped towards the earth, cloaking the tops of distant mountains with yellow-orange hues. Abandoning the daylight colors which varied in shades of blue, the peaks took on a sunlit warmth that lingered on into the evening. Though the mountains were warm and illuminated, the disappearing sun left a lingering chill. A mix of pinks, reds, and oranges now hugged the snow banks built up on either side of the road, coating them in color like spun sugar. A flurry swept over the road, the leading edge of a stronger wind that was likely to blow down from the mountains before night fully fell.

Carey watched these natural happenings with a critical eye and was leery of continuing on in such a slow manner. Though the descent was faster than the ascent, there was a lackadaisical sense of movement with both the wagons. Weather was fickle in the Garmisch mountains, and he would rather be home before night fell.

With half an hour left of daylight, the steeples of the bright church appeared over the curve of the last hill. He did not like to be far from home, and even more so detested the thought of being away from home after nightfall.

The Reinalz wagons bumped and trundled into town just before sunset. By this time, the wind had risen and flurries of snow were whipping to and fro in a delirious torment of nature. The once rosy-hued sky now carried a roaring winter storm. In the bitter cold, snowflakes stung against skin as if sharpened into minuscule knives.

The children were rushed inside, shielded from the wind by protective arms, older children carrying younger siblings inside. Miff was ushered up the steps and into the hall by Carey and was laid on a soft couch and covered with a thick woolen blanket. Carey lingered by the door, observing the mad scramble of homemaking with an unfamiliar eye, all the while listening to the roar of the wind.

Mrs. Reinalz drew a single burning log from the embers in the stove and transferred it to the fireplace in the Blue-Rue. She was a lady familiar with the nature of fire and coaxed crackling, roaring tongues of flame from the logs and stove with the ease of one much practiced in the art.

Mr. Reinalz was directing and giving out tasks to his elder children, some for hauling extra wood in from the porch, some for finding extra woolen blankets from the closet, and others for setting wine in a kettle on the stove with a few select spices added to make glühwein for warming the heart in the midst of the blizzard.

Without speaking further to the family so obviously distracted by life, Carey Alsch slipped through the front door with Treu and was gone through the tumbling snow and terrible winds.

9
Winter Winds

Howling, mournful calls do not merely belong to wolves of the woods. The wind may howl if possessed with enough violence to sink and rise between trees and thus produce aeolian tones. Such an eerie call from a non-living thing would strike fear into most foresters, but there are some practiced enough with nightmare sounds to strive onwards despite winter's warnings.

The wind was one of these other-than-wolves when Carey Alsch plunged into the depths and was wholly surrounded. The breath of icy giants wrenched him this way and that, sending his feet stumbling through deep snow. He was possessed with a deliriousness of mind that urged him onward rather than bid him return whence he had come. That place was perhaps more likely to inspire fear in him than the force of wind accosting him. Though a friendly home in all senses of the word, Carey perceived it as a dangerous, unfamiliar place, far too full of life for one who had decided by the age of two-and-ten just how unwanted he was.

There is little room for change in the heart of a man who has been twice abandoned in his youth. A mother's disgrace and a father's shadow had lingered over him for the entirety of his life, and he was not inclined to remove either without a great deal of struggle. Struggle was something Carey would not willingly bring into his life, unless it was in the form of pressing on through a bitter winter storm in hopes of separating himself from the Reinalzes.

His hat was tied with a leather cord beneath his bearded chin, fur-lined muffs pulled tight over his ears. There was a sureness in his visage, a mask of resolution set towards home, unshakable in its lonely determination. Despair was so well known in him that it did nothing to hinder or eschew the surrounding darkness. He pressed on.

Mittenwald was at his back, a regular monolith in the settling night overtaken by an even more monolithic storm. He was up to his knees in snow at the bridge, and to his hips on the lane between the hill and the steep edge of the river. Treu followed directly in the carved-out trail, making a wake to each side of Carey's legs.

A chill struck the man with violent shivers. Wind took hold of his coat, threatening to rip it from his body. He made to tighten the toggles with shaking, gloved fingers but was shoved to his knees by the wind. With effort and a cry into the darkness, Carey made fast the clasps and climbed to his feet despite the raw strength of the tempest gripping him like the hand of an icy giant.

His small house beside the Isar River rose in the distance, a dark stanchion against the torrid mood of the woods. To Carey, the woods seemed to be shifting and rippling with the movement of Waldleute, the forest-folk, who claimed the woods as their own. They seldom came out unless to bring upon mankind nature's most violent destructions: that is, blizzards in winter and rains in summer.

"My home is overtaken, Treu," Carey whispered, finding his voice rather drowned out by the fury of the wind. "Can'st we make it to the door?"

Treu took up a howling of his own, urging his master onward. Carey was again forced to his feet, finding strength in his furry companion. At last he was at the door, grasping with unfeeling hands and aching bones. In a half-delirium, he hauled wood from the porch to build up a fire in the hearth.

Though flame devoured the oak and beech logs, it did little to warm his soul. He was crouched before the fire, peering into its depths in hopes that the heat would burn him from the inside out. The fire swelled, leaving behind glowing embers upon which greater logs of deeper grain were tossed. Licking tongues of flame sought to consume these and produced a heat so comforting that soon it had warmed the whole house, which consisted of one room: bed and desk on one side, stove, hearth, and sitting-chair on the other. A basin left in the corner for bathing held no water but instead was filled with a considerable amount of potatoes and bags of seed for spring. Carey shed his layers of wool, drawing so close to the fire that the hairs on his arm began to singe and there was no going closer. Treu was no wiser for sprawling near the flames. Master and hound were as near to being burned as two wild things could be.

"I think we shall soon be warm, Treu," said Carey through chattering teeth. Bare-chested, he rose and moved around in the small space with vigor, walking round in circles till his blood was flowing close to his skin and he had regained that warm-pink color.

Having found a reasonable temperature, Carey set a kettle over the flames and took bread and cheese from the cupboard on the wall by the door and settled into his chair. Overtaking him was the familiar numbness of staring listlessly into the fire—although, on this night, objections rose within him, crying out that not every night was meant to be spent in emptiness, filled with a hollow gaze. Carey promptly ignored this voice that cried out from within. He ate cheese and did not taste it, ate bread and thought it had no flavor.

Having regarded the bountiful state of good feeling found within the Reinalz home, Carey decided fully that it was not for him. Such a decision returned him to the despondence into which he fell on most nights. He found favor in the position of his chair and felt no disturbing of his spirit by the crackle of the fire. Anything found not disturbing, nor instigating a change of character, he held closely. He had fully decided he would not change and that he was quite thoroughly satisfied with remaining an observer of joy, and not a feeler of his own.

The Weeping House

He had not known goodness and was not seeking it out, for when a soldier lifts his shield to look beyond its protection, he is pierced by a multitude of arrows and surely dies. Carey had decided not to look beyond his shield.

10
The Craftsman

There was a buildup of snow in Mittenwald. So high were the banks and levees filled with ice and hummocks of white that no wagon could roll, nor any traveler travel. The air was still, frozen in cold stagnation. In the eerie quiet, trees groaned. Their branches held tightly to the snow laden upon them. Green needles peeked out from beneath the white, bowed by icicles, giving each branch an unusual arc that is not the normal mode of tree behavior.

A red fox moved silently over the white meadows. His ears twitched and flicked, searching out mice hidden beneath the snow. He was such a bright creature framed by light; a lone forager in a monochrome world of white.

The sunlight drifting over the lanes, meadows, and deep woods had no covering cloud or shadowing storm. The sun shone freely. It was the kind of weather trees wished for, to melt snow and ease them of their burdens. Trees and sunshine share an eternal bond, undisturbed by winter storm, summer rain, or darkened night.

Carey Alsch stayed in his house, having dug a small path from door to outhouse. He traveled this distance alone, comfortable in the space of the one-room house, in which his only companion was Treu, who was equally pleased to spend his days in a leisurely manner.

The house smelled of leather, mink oil, and sharp pine smoke. Discarded scraps of sheepskin, rabbit pelt (both the fur and inner lining, which is a fine, delicate leather), and deer hide were draped over furniture. There was a distracted order to the clutter, when regarded with a closer eye. Deer and sheep were hung from the bed and never touched the floor; rabbit, mink, and martin rested on wooden pegs on the wall. The cut pieces were tossed into a chest beside the desk, to later be reclaimed in a project that had no name and was not yet a concept, although they were saved as if there was a plan for each piece.

Carey bent over his desk, holding a pricking iron in one hand and a saddle gullet in the other. He pressed a design into the gullet with the iron, wholly focused on his task. The design on the gullet was not dissimilar to the design on his forehead, which was created in concentration, although that was not the craftsman's intention. It is merely the way of the world that men look like the things they make, and the things they make look like them. In the way that leather is rich in color, worn by rugged use, and shaped by all the things it has endured, Carey could certainly be described as leathery in appearance.

Two weeks had passed since the storm, and not a soul had ventured beyond Mittenwald. Wisdom advised the Reinalzes to stay home, though they fretted for Carey, whom they had not seen leave and had no way of knowing that he had safely found his way home.

Mr. Reinalz felt sure that capable Carey Alsch had not got stranded between Mittenwald and the Isar River, and told his wife so on many occasions, but she held it upon her shoulders that she had forced him to come on their excursion and forgotten him upon returning, what with so many distractions, and so it was her fault that he had not stayed the night as intended. She also keenly felt that if he had died in the storm, it would be her fault, and therefore she would be one who had killed a friend.

Her husband, being the village judge, assured her this was not the case, but it was not to be borne. She resolved to seek him out before the week was finished, though the thought of finding his frozen body on the road wracked her with a terrible nervousness.

There was little to be done, however, with snow falling most evenings, piling up in greater drifts than were left by the initial blizzard. Husband and wife considered the possibility of snowshoes, skis, plows, and even shovels, to reach Mr. Alsch, but each attempt to venture outside was met with difficulty. Some of that difficulty was the frequent snowfall and some was daily life, food-preparing and fire-stoking. Some was Mrs. Reinalz's very real fear of finding Mr. Alsch's body on the road.

Mr. Alsch was of course unaware of this overwhelming worry hanging over the heads of Mr. and Mrs. Reinalz and continued his work with his usual despondence and tolerance for mundanity.

His mind, when occupied by a prosaic task, found a quiet sense of peace in the small house on the Isar River. He did not mind the snow piled heavy at the door and saw little to affect his daily life. Potatoes were plenty in his basin, and the entrance to his larder was at the foot of his bed, so he had no difficulty in feeding himself.

Months spent salting various meats, drying venison, and stocking constitutional plants in spring, summer, and even into fall left him with ample supply for one man and one dog. He was thusly unbothered, pleased to find himself lost in the mindlessness of handcraft.

Treu slept soundly by the fire. His place there was marked by repetition, scuffed where he often turned and scratched at the same piece of deer pelt that was his bed. His graying muzzle twitched. The only sound disturbing the piece of the little home was the thump of Carey's pricking iron and Treu's snuffling, so deep in slumber that his simple houndmind was alight with a dream.

And so, minutes turned to hours, hours to days, days to weeks. Carey was not seen nor heard in Mittenwald for the whole of November, which in usual winter season was no strange happening. But now that he had been chosen by the Reinalzes as a particular person, he was missed.

He did not know he was missed and therefore was unmissed in his heart, carrying a weight in his chest and a shroud over his head. The weight in his chest kept him bent over his worktable; the shroud over his head kept him from looking up.

That is, until he realized he had run out of mink oil and was therefore inclined to go down into the village.

11
Mink Oil

Treu was left behind on this excursion, simply due to the fact that Carey had yet to construct a set of hound snowshoes. It was likely that these would never be constructed, as dogs of natural constitution are not fond of shoes.

The hound's loud complaint was heard down the lane, even to the crossing of the Isar Bridge. Once beyond the reach of Treu's loud brays, Carey put his head down and made his way through the edge of the forest. He did not regard the splendor of the silver fir laden with snow, nor the holly bearing full-bright berries. The scuffling martin leaping between pines was unknown to him, and the ever-alert deer, shadowed by a tall evergreen, was overcome by tergiversation, leaping away before any man could meet its steady eye.

Carey shuffled along, bearing upon his feet a large set of snowshoes, leaving behind him a trail of overturned powder. His cap was pulled low over his ears, the collar of his coat upturned against the wind, hands shoved into the bottoms of his pockets. He was often making repairs to these, as he pressed so stiffly into the fabric that it was constantly in a state of disrepair.

The sun settled in the sky just before its pinnacle and was rather bright. The crisp, dry air seemed haunted by emptiness. Carey attributed the odd feeling to Waldleute and then ignored it wholly, feeling it was owed to the wood-folk to leave them be. Waldleute fared best when perceived as unknown by the greater part of the world, and Carey fared best leaving them unperceived.

The Weeping House

Cornflower skies backed the yellow sun, like petals framing an amber pistil. There were no clouds, and the only adornment high above was a black raven circling, finding a warm thermal column of air upon which to rise.

Mittenwald peeked over the crest of the next hill, ringed by dark forest behind, and the sweeping edges of the hill that sloped up from the nearest house. Smoke curled from every chimney, giving a clue to travelers that there was life still present in the town. Snow banked against the sturdy walls, and icicles hung from the struts.

Carey was a lone figure approaching the village. No outsider had come by that way for nearly a month and were not expected to do so until some thaw overcame the ridges of snow and ice. He found the road—or at least, where it should lie beneath packs of snow—and was a lonely wanderer through empty streets.

He came by the post office, which was set back from the road, and knocked on the door. No sound returned, and so he pressed it open, finding dark shadows within.

"Hello?" his voice echoed in the musty place. "Mr. Reimenschnell? I have come for mink oil. I sent for it several weeks ago." He waited, peering through the unlit recesses of the empty shop. Footsteps thumped heavily from above, sending clouds of dust and debris down from the ceiling. Footsteps rattled in the walls, then behind a door at the back of the shop, which was thrown open suddenly.

"Mr. Alsch?" a loud voice exclaimed. Two round faces came into view, one with wild hair of a burnished bronze color tumbling over narrow shoulders; the other, framed by black hair standing stock-straight from the crown of his head. His hair was like a hat, in that the start of it so contrasted with the end that it appeared to be removable, though it was fixed to his scalp.

Carey dipped his head, surprised by the disheveled state of Mrs. Reimenschnell, who was usually seen with neat and tidy updos of a modest nature. Every other aspect of her was still of the most rigid, upright manner, with a frock and collar fastened tightly around her neck.

She ducked back for a moment, leaving her husband stuttering at the sight of a customer arriving in the midst of the heaviest snows Mittenwald had seen in years. The lady reappeared with tight braids wrapped over the crown of her head with pins.

"Close the door, Mr. Alsch," Mrs. Reimenschnell said stiffly, "you'll let the cold in."

Carey closed the door softly, stepping just outside its frame in hopes that he could linger longer in the shadows. Mrs. Reimenschnell made quick work of the oil lamps, and soon there were no shadows left in the place.

"What d'ye need, Carey?" said Mr. Reimenschnell, who lounged by the counter, consumed by an attitude so opposite his wife's that it was a wonder they continued so cordially in companionship. They were the best of friends.

"Mink oil," Carey muttered, his voice so low it required husband and wife to lean forward to catch the words.

"I think it has come in!" said the husband. He quickly disappeared behind the counter, leaving Carey alone with the rigid woman, who regarded him as a teacher regards a misbehaving student.

"Couldn't remove the snowshoes before coming inside?" said Mrs. Reimenschnell with a critical eye.

"I—" Carey hesitated. His gaze dropped to the shoes in question, which held a compacted pack of snow and had tracked in a mix of mud and debris. "Sorry," he muttered, then set about removing them, which only kicked off more mess and drew a great sigh from the woman.

"Leave them," she snapped, waving her hand dismissively. Her husband returned a moment later, carrying a glass jar filled with a dark oil, emblazoned with large, disordered letters: MINK.

The price was arranged between the two men, under the direct supervision of Mrs. Reimenschnell, of course, who was quite knowledgeable in all things economical. Carey withdrew the agreed-upon gulden, placing the coins upon the counter, along with a small file and a round rock (things always being collected in his pockets). Flushed with embarrassment, he shoved the file and rock away and collected his mink oil.

The door closed behind him with such a violent swing that both Reimenschnells were unable to speak for a long moment.

"What a peculiar man," said Mr. Reimenschnell, pocketing the gulden. His wife said nothing. She regarded the door—and the mess left behind—with a stern eye.

12
Nonny

Carey fixed his snowshoes to his feet and was away down the middle road of Mittenwald before any could catch sight of him and hinder his return home. Beneath his arm he held the jar of mink oil, protecting it as if were a great treasure and he its dragon guardian. He passed the Kinderkopfs' house without turning aside and sidled alongside the curtained windows of the Hauskrafts' gothic home to avoid being seen by that family.

Adornments and embellishments were the hallmark of the Hauskrafts, who had seven children and were often seen walking in a line with them through town, not dissimilar to a mother goose and her line of goslings. Mrs. Hauskraft's husband was also one of these goslings, for he loved to follow his wife. His only usefulness lay in crafting gothic homes, and not in knowing anything beyond the end of his nose or the curl of his mustache. His usefulness was certainly not found in the rearing of his children.

Carey made his way quickly through town, coming to the lane that angled up one of the more reasonable hills of town, into the upper reaches of the woods where his home rested along the Isar River. Rising over the edge of the hill, Carey set his mind wholly on reaching his home within an appropriate hour. He was so steadfastly attentive to this task that he did not hear the soft singing meeting him in the lane, nor see the woman coming around the corkscrew curve of the slope.

He was quite alarmed upon colliding with said woman and found himself laid out in the snow in a state of complete disarray.

"Oh my!" she said, sitting bolt-upright in the snow. "I'm so sorry!" She crawled toward him, sinking deeper in the snow.

"Stop!" Carey held up his hands and frowned. The left was soaked with a mixture of blood and oil. He cried out, attempting to scoop handfuls of mink oil that had spilled onto the snow into the broken halves of his jar.

"I've just gone and made a mess of everything!" the woman said. "Look at you—you are bleeding, sir! Let me help you."

"No, no," Carey said without looking up. "No! I am fine. Quite fine, thank you."

"But it's all my fault!" She was in despair.

"I still have some left," Carey whispered. "I shoulda put it in the bag." He shook his head, muttering under his cold, streaming breath.

"Let me help!" She took hold of his hand and pulled it close, causing Carey to slump back in the drift they were caught up in. He grimaced, finding it a great struggle to right himself while she clung to his hand, and so he resigned himself to this torment.

The woman pulled his glove free, laying it in the snow beside her, then took out a white handkerchief from her pocket.

"This is freshly washed," she noted, "and I have not used it." Ignoring his protestations, she wrapped it firmly around his hand, which was cut across the side between thumb and forefinger. She tied it off with a neat bow and held his fingertips in what Carey would have described as "very lovely hands."

They were captured in gloves, but ever so slender and tapering near the nail. Her gloves were of a soft blue, embroidered with edelweiss and holly. The gloves were met near her wrist by a similar blue cuff, folded and buttoned with a pretty gold button. Covering the cuff was a thick woolen coat of blue tweed. The woman was obviously fond of the color.

"I am so sorry to cause you trouble," she said, squeezing his fingertips. "I was going down the hill and had rather got too much speed. There's such a sharp turn here—with the twists and turns--and before I knew it, I crashed into you! Are you quite all right?" She sat back, adjusting the laces on her snowshoes, which were caked with snow.

It was at this moment that Carey chose to look up and was rendered quite speechless by the face looming before him—in full, unconscious ignorance of the beauty held therein.

In a man, there are several simple truths. The first is this: a woman possessing lovely eyes is a terrifying creature capable of much destruction. The second: a total annihilation of the spirit is required to continually gaze into such eyes. And thirdly: a man must continually protect against these spiritual capitulations if he is to remain unhindered in his conquest of the world.

Carey Alsch had no aim to conquer the world but found great difficulty in meeting the eyes of the woman in the lane. The man was suddenly laid bare, forgetting completely of mink oil and stinging cuts. He was reminded instead of a woman traipsing through the woods on a warm winter day, before the heavy snowfall, stripping bark from willow trees and speaking to them as if they were quite alive. She was the same, the woman in the woods, who had explained her need for willow-bark and its medicinal qualities to the trees themselves.

She was near his age, with a face holding all the loveliest signs of life. Her eyes spoke of frequent smiles, and her red lips were as shapely as her cheeks. There was an enviable spark of life in her eyes, one that drew him like a moth to the flame.

"Hello," she said. Her mannerisms were in all things sweet, to the point that her words were soft and her bearing still. In her face was no unsightly shape, blemish, or unseemly feature. She was wholly a woman, and wholly bright. Upon finally seeing Carey's eyes lifted towards hers, she smiled in a soft way. "Who are you?"

Carey said nothing. He blinked twice, finding himself unable to speak, though he tried more than once.

The Weeping House

"I am Nadia Von Stein." She smiled again, and his soul nearly separated and fled his body. "Please just call me Nonny."

"Hello." Carey ducked his head, as if to avoid the full impact of her radiant smile, which was accompanied by two dimples and framed by dark tresses falling wildly about her shoulders. "Carey Alsch," he whispered.

"Alz?" She leaned forward, a motion that caused the man to flinch and retreat into deeper snow.

"Alsch," he corrected.

"Pleasure to meet you, Mr. Alsch." Nonny was still quiet, feeling the stark awkwardness that Carey typically exuded. She offered a hand to him, which he promptly stared at as if it were some foreign object that could harm him. "I am so sorry to have knocked you over, and now we are quite stuck, aren't we?" She looked around, regarding the snowbank surrounding them. Carey shifted his gaze and, without speaking, lay on his back and rolled out of the drift. He carefully set his feet beneath him, steadying the large snowshoes one beside the other, and was righted in two quick motions.

"Oh." Nonny looked curiously at him. "You've done this before."

Carey nodded and tugged his cap low over his ears. He turned and looked up the lane, thinking of his home and Treu, wishing to not be slowed on his return.

"Will you help me out?" she asked, holding her hands out in a fashion that reminded him of Anneliese Reinalz commanding her father to lift her into his arms.

Carey's eyes widened in a small recognition of what to him was a frightening scene. This was unfamiliar territory, and he was no adventurer. Women were over-theres and not-heres in his mind. Now, one was directly before him and spoke to him as if they were old friends. He sniffed, pulling at the edge of his mittens.

"It is quite cold, Mr. Alsch," Nonny whispered. One of her perfectly formed eyebrows quirked.

Carey grunted, striding forward on ungainly, snowshoed feet. He took hold of her gloved hands and pulled, stretching her out on the lane in the most ignoble of attitudes. She lay face down on the road and sighed deeply. After a moment, Nonny climbed to her feet and ducked her head in embarrassment. Ice clung to her wild hair, framing her face as a little wilderness, with pinion needles mixed in among bark and other remnants of her adventures in the deep snow.

With a powerful feeling in his chest, Carey quickly collected the remnants of mink oil from the snow and bid the lady good day, turning on a sharp heel toward home, his gaze once again fixated on the trudging pattern of his boots. He was quite overcome, spirit greatly affected as it had not been affected before. Warm, brown eyes danced through his mind, shining like amber and iridescent suns.

When he had returned home and settled in his chair by the fire, he saw, upon looking into the flames, reflected light similar to the color of that woman's eyes.

He was quite overcome indeed.

Barn Swallow
Hirundo Rustica

13
Rectification

November delivered its full complement of snow. Familiar winter winds invaded just before December. Certainly, the season had no shortage of days that imprisoned most people in their homes. A typical Mittenwald home boasted a full, green Christmas tree, decorated with ribbons and glass balls. Ornaments were hung from the lowest branches, bending the boughs with festive tidings.

Carey had no such tree in his home, and no ornament in the windows. No wreaths were draped from his lintel, no Advent creche upon his mantel. Despite this lack of festive embellishment, he still hummed a carol, bringing a taste of gladness into his small house. This was the first Christmas season in which yuletide feelings were invited in. All others had been spent in the abject recognition of his own emptiness.

Treu sat beside Carey's worktable, chocolate eyes tracking each of his master's movements. The hound was an attentive apprentice, though he was unable to ply the trade himself. If the merit of Treu's knowledge could be tested, he would have been marked as an excellent craftsman. It was a shame he did not possess opposable thumbs.

Carey bent over his table, fashioning a leather sheep. His hand was fully healed from his misadventures in the snow with Nonny, though he still found himself touching the scars more than once a day.

He pressed one end of the leather down with an awl, pinned between metal and wood. It was scraped until it held shape, then threaded with a heavy needle until perfect loops were fixed in the place of ears. He set it aside, placing the sheep beside a similarly fashioned cat, hound, bear, and fox.

The Weeping House

These were the last of many renditions of leather animals he had attempted to make over the past two weeks. He considered the figures revolutionary, regarding them with quiet attention, assuring himself they were constructed with utter perfection.

Gathering the animals into a sack, he pulled on his thick winter coat, cap, and scarf. He whistled sharply, calling Treu to the door. Together, they set off toward Mittenwald.

The master carried the sack over one shoulder and his dog over the other, until he reached the end of the lane, where the snow was less deep and Treu could run feely without becoming entrenched in a drift.

Mittenwald appeared in the distance, painting a perfect picture against the rural landscape. The streets had been plowed and sowed with hay to prevent icing. Lanterns glowed full-bright in the early dusk shadows, and every window was draped with laurels and holly. A tall tree rose in the center of the town. It was decorated with all manner of delights, from red-gold glass balls to strung wooden beads and pearlescent ribbons strung between layers of needled boughs.

The center square was illuminated in perfect holiday bliss. It was crowded with townspeople, who wandered and intermingled in their Sunday best. Children ran in and amongst the adults, calling to one another raucously. The evening chill smelled of spiced wine and fresh bread.

Carey entered the square, lingering on the edge. Treu raced past him, loudly announcing his presence to the fold. He was received with great amusement and soon found himself engaged in a game of chase with a large swarm of children.

Not fully emerging from shadow, Carey observed the crowds, which were quite voracious in their festivities. Special chocolates were passed from hand to hand—most seriously coveted, as if some wealthy stranger brought them as a gift. Warm mugs of glühwein were clutched close in hopes they would be a warming spell against the cold.

"Mr. Alsch!" cried Holt Reinalz. He crossed the square with a quick stride, Anneliese propped on his hip, her hair tied in bright ribbons that peeked beneath her fur-lined hood. She lifted a red mitten and waved.

Carey flushed, embarrassed to have been found avoiding the festivities. He shifted from foot to foot, unsure of how he would fit into this place of full joy. While he possessed unmatched skill with leather and awl, Carey did not possess any skill in the realm of friendship or conversation. His only friend was a dog. He inhaled deeply of cinnamon and studied the top button of Mr. Reinalz's coat.

"Come," Holt said, gesturing for Carey to follow him. "I have stollen for you. It is freshly made by Isola. She is inarguably the best bread-maker in town. You must try it."

"I've not brought any treats," Carey said, grimacing. "I don't eat 'em, see. I wouldn't know how."

"That is all right, Mr. Alsch." Holt smiled. "We'll share all that we have. It's not a requirement for visiting, I hope you know. Our house is always open to you and Treu."

"Thankee," Carey said. Joining the crowd, he was welcomed by a swarm of Reinalz children. They were full of questions about Treu, who was already their dear friend. They were adamant that it was rude of Carey to keep him away for so long. He was most certainly required to bring him round at least once per week, so he might play chase and fetch. Carey found himself agreeing to this arrangement, though it seemed contrary to his usual way. He considered the notion, finding nothing truly errant in visiting Mittenwald more regularly. His status was elevated to favorite grown-up among the children.

Treu was given a bright red ribbon, tied round his neck in a bow. The hound pranced through the snow, seeming rather proud of his new adornment.

"Mr. Alsch," Isola Reinalz said, placing a plate with a large piece of stollen into his mittened hands. "I saved you a piece! And we have pfeffernusse over by the tree. Do you like pfeffernusse?"

Carey did not know. It had never been offered to him before.

"You have to try it, Mr. Alsch," said Miff Reinalz, who appeared beneath his mother's arm in search of Christmas bread. Miff had grown at least two inches in the time between the ice-skating excursion and Christmas. He seemed proud of the fact and swelled his chest out beneath his thick coat and woolen layers.

"Just might." Carey grimaced in a half-hearted attempt at a smile.

"Are you cold, Mr. Alsch?" Miff cocked his head beneath its warm fur cap.

"No, no." Carey waved a mittened hand. "I am fine."

"You made a face like you were cold," Miff said. "I do that when I am cold." He proceeded to show the exact face he often made whilst cold.

"Enough, Michael," Isola said, tugging at the boy's coat from behind. "Leave Mr. Alsch alone." She looked at Carey. "Please, do try the pfeffernusse. Michael'll show you where to find it."

Miff took hold of Carey's gloved hand and tugged him through the crowd, not waiting for a reply or giving heed to the older man's polite reasons for not needing cookies. To Miff, the idea of not liking, or even never tasting pfeffernusse, was odd, clearly something that must immediately be rectified.

14
The Fear of Dinner

After carols had been sung and candles lighted for service, the folk of Mittenwald returned to their homes. The resurgence of merriment was not lost on this exodus, however, as home meant gifts, and in most homes, a feast. In dispersing, each family took up their own carol, singing brightly through the snow-ridden lanes. Most carried candles to mark their yuletide bliss. Cold winds pushed and drove the little flames, making them flicker in the night.

Mr. Reinalz shielded his sacred flame from the wind with a mittened hand. His wife and children trailed behind him, moving together in small groups. The children whispered amongst themselves, feeling the effervescent emotion of Christmas. Mrs. Reinalz walked with one arm tucked in her husband's arm, the other holding Isolde on her hip. Mechthild hugged Anneliese tightly, protecting her from the cold.

Carey followed at a reasonable distance, a rather skulking pace. He did little to hide his expression of wishing to not be included, and how he would prefer to be at home, filling out his Christmas tradition in the same manner as every year prior. His only grace at this moment was Treu, who pressed against his leg in familiar comfort. They were two, and always two, unless weather or other disaster arose.

The Reinalzes' house was decorated for Christmas. Some arrangements—seemingly done by elder children, mother, and father—were elegant in design and shape: boughs of holly tied up with red ribbon, strung beads, candles lighted in nooks and crannies, and a roaring fire in the hearth. Others were obviously fashioned with love and ungainly hands—

half-formed snowflakes and stars of starched paper, misshapen branches with few berries hanging onto bent and broken twigs, and a nativity made of collected sticks of varying proportion. These decorations were given places of honor in the household and were praised by all.

Carey lingered in the vestibule, resting one hand on Treu's round head, the other clinging to the gift-filled sack slung over his shoulder. The vestibule where the Reinalzes removed their coats and shoes was half in shadow, half open to the light of the fireplace. Carey pressed himself further into the shadows, not feeling unwelcome because of anything the generous family had done or said, but because he had unwelcomed himself. He considered the fact that if he was not present, the Reinalzes would have a far merrier time, and so, he should get himself gone. He had turned to lay hold of the doorknob when the swinging door between the hall and the kitchen swung open and a very merry figure appeared there.

"Oh," said a quiet voice, "I had not realized you would be home so soon. Dinner is almost ready!"

Carey was frozen in recognition of an ailment that had twice before consumed him. He feared for a progression of the malady that was settling over his chest and wondered if the quickening of his pulse and the warmth in his face were just that. It was a strange contraction, one that struck deeply with a protracted effect. His last affliction still lingered within him. Some symptoms of this disease were bright dimples, lovely eyes, and rosy-red lips. The same features which welcomed the Reinalz family into their own home.

"Sorry, Nonny," said Isola, and hung up her coat. "Isolde was growing cold. Most of the others are in their homes now as well."

"Well," Nonny said with a smile, "I have lit the fire. Please sit, Isola. All of you Reinalzes. Do no work." She leaned forward, peering around Oscar and Lieselotte. "Besides, Mr. Alsch can help me."

Carey Alsch needed a doctor.

"Oh"—Mr. Reinalz's eyebrows rose—"you already know Mr. Alsch? Carey, this is my cousin from München, Nonny Von Stein." His children dispersed beneath him, swarming the hearth and the various sweets Nonny and Mrs. Reinalz had baked earlier that day. Stollen and lebkuchen were the most fought-over delights.

"We met about a fortnight ago," said Nonny, ducking her head sweetly. "I had fallen into the snow in the woods past the bridge outside of town. He pulled me out."

"How very kind of him!" Mrs. Reinalz met her husband's eyes and communicated a thing that could only be communicated between husband and wife.

"'Twas nothin'," Carey said without looking up. He was bent, fixated upon massaging Treu's cold ears in an effort to bring some warmth back to them.

"Well," said Mr. Reinalz, "I shall sit by the fire with my wife and children. And, Nonny"—he inclined his head toward their guest—"I will keep Isola there, do not worry."

"Perfect," said Nonny, returning to the kitchen, but not before requesting that Carey follow her there.

The man gulped, then hung his coat on the rack and left his boots by the door. He was wary of the melting snow on the floorboards, bent on keeping his socks dry, and left Treu in the hall with some of the children. His gift-bag sat in the farthest corner, where he hoped it could be forgotten.

Bearing his affliction with shrewd fearfulness, Carey pushed into the kitchen. The stove was hot. A little flame flickered in the wood compartment. On the smoking griddle was a pan of sausages and vegetables of varying green color. Potatoes were roasting on a separate pan, cut into medallions and sprinkled with dried dill. The outer skins of these were scorched to a perfect color. Chunks of butter were melting over the po-

… tatoes, sweating in the pan with a delightful crackling and popping sound.

"Will you cut the roast?" said Nonny softly but clearly, gesturing to the large roast of pork sitting on the wooden counter. Mr. Reinalz had cooked it to perfection earlier in the day, when the sun still warmed the air. The pig had been a prize of Farmer Welch, who lived just south of the woods Carey oft walked in.

"How do 'ee want it cut?" Carey muttered without looking up.

"However you feel is best, Mr. Alsch. Chopped and sliced would be perfect." She nodded as she set about moving pans and pots from places on the woodstove.

Carey took up the large boning knife on the countertop and set about shearing large pieces of pork from the roast. Terribly hungry, he made quick work of the large roast and soon had it piled on a platter provided by Nonny. She worked diligently in silence with a rather serious expression, organizing food onto silver and tin serving dishes, arranging them by order eaten and size.

Upon finishing his task, Carey stood in the corner, hoping he could remain unseen. To his relief, the woman rarely spared any glances in his direction.

"Do you often stand like that?" she said quietly, placing potatoes on a silver tray with ornate handles. "I think you mean to hide from us."

"Not hiding," he said. "Trying to stay out of the way."

"You are not in the way, Mr. Alsch." She looked at him for a moment with a surprisingly steadfast gaze; there was something unfamiliar in her expression that quelled Carey's spirit even more than it was usually quelled.

"I'll do fine right here." He nodded.

"It would be finer if you would carry things to the dining room for me. The cloth is set. All that remains is bringing in the feast."

"There seems to be a fancy sort of order to it. I'm not familiarized wit' the ways of fancy order."

"Those go out first." She pointed to the salads, carrots, beets, mushrooms, and other greens. "And those second,"—the potatoes—"and third," the pork roast. "There is wine in a carafe in the dining room, and the children's cordial is beside it."

She left him alone to call the family to dine. Carey stood still, staring at the array of fine foods, being the first man to truly fear Christmas dinner.

Alpine Ibex
Capra Ibex

15
Filial Unfamiliarity

There was no shortage of joy found at the table of the Reinalz home. Though the feast was much thought about and impatiently waited for, it was not the centerpiece of the celebration. There was a closeness found there, in the bosom of a family who enjoyed one another's company, that was unlike anything Carey had seen in his life. While time usually seemed to drag on in emptiness when he ate dinner in his home and stared into his fire, here, each minute ticking by was precious. He consumed each of them like a starving man receiving food, holding them close to his chest.

When Oscar teased Inge about her eccentric mannerisms, she was wholly amused, seeing that her brother spoke not in disparagement, but in the most filial of loves. When Anneliese ventured to speak, the whole family fell silent, allowing her time to work out her words. She was praised for her contributions and was a pretty, smiling thing. Every word spoken was found to be affectionate, humorous, and wholly unlike any family Carey had known.

Nonny was a listening ear to any and all of the Reinalz children. She nodded, frowned, and laughed when they spoke. There was in her a glow of goodness, like a candle bearing flame, or woods dappled with sunlight.

She was somewhat aware of the hesitant gaze of Carey Alsch, who was often found to be looking at her. This was the first Christmas he had looked up, and he found it rather lovely.

Mr. and Mrs. Reinalz held hands beneath the table, gazing fondly at their world. Both were gratefully aware of the wonderful life spread before them. Eleven children and two guests held a merry party in their home.

The Weeping House

Isola and Holt Reinalz found it wholly remarkable to have such wonderful warmth spread in their home. Such goodness as was before them was certainly divine and no ordinary occurrence. It was the result of the heart and any gentleness it possesses, allowing a work in them to flow outward, illuminate darkness, and attend the lonely.

Carey Alsch was recognizing such a feeling in himself. One that was shaming all the emptiness and desolation he felt. It seemed cruel to have—in the middle of his life—just learned of filial goodness. He did not attribute this to anyone other than himself, as he had long ago decided that the abandonment of his family had been owing to some issue within him. Because of this self-reflection, where he should have felt keen wonder, he felt instead that if he had been someone else, someone like any of the Reinalzes, he would have been loved.

He watched with some rapture how even Nonny had a place in this family. It was a strange thing to him, whose only companion was a hound. This woman had lively companionship at a table where he was a mere observer.

These were the two spirits battling within Carey Alsch while he ate Christmas dinner. One of shame and inner bereavement, the other, a mounting desire to feel what these people felt.

"—do you think so, Mr. Alsch?" Mr. Reinalz's voice cut through his quiet musings.

"Huh?" Carey moved so sharply that one would think he had injured his neck. "Sorry," he dropped his hands beneath the edge of the table, balling up his fists there.

"Do you think we should finish up and open gifts? I think Saint Nicolaus has come to visit." His eye held a glimmer of amusement. A ripple of similar excitement passed through his children, and an exultant cry rose up among them all. Everyone was in agreement; Christmas dinner was ended.

The Reinalz children were quick to clear the table and clean up all remnants of the feast. Only the adults—or those near enough—were allowed to handle the expensive dishes reserved for special occasions. The silver was cleaned and organized, and the kitchen thoroughly scoured.

Carey stood to the side, wishing in vain that he had been given a task. Treu joined loyally where his master pressed his back into the wall decorated with wainscoting of a deep green. Mrs. Reinalz made a pallet of wool near the hearth in the Blue-Rue for Treu. Furniture was rearranged, and soon the whole family were gathered in the little parlor, changed from their going-out clothes into comfortable pajamas and shawls.

Mr. Reinalz led the family in hymns and prayer, starting off with a strong tone. His wife joined, daughters harmonizing with their mother, sons with their father. The result was a lovely, layered song that filled the whole Blue-Rue.

"Shall we?" said Mr. Reinalz when he had finished. He gestured to the tree decorating the room. Beneath it were myriad gifts of varying size and shape.

Mr. and Mrs. Reinalz handed gifts out one by one, kissing the head of each child as they did so. There was one present from the parents to each child, and something handmade from the children to their parents.

Anneliese had collected sticks enough to construct a small figure, tied neatly with cord by her sister Mechthild. Mrs. Reinalz accepted this gift with grace, tactfully asking her youngest child to explain the practicality of such a design. It was apparently a sheep, meant for decorating the mantel.

Mrs. Reinalz presented Nonny with a set of lace handkerchiefs and a necklace strung with a topaz, a shade of blue that perfectly matched the periwinkle dress she now wore.

When all the gifts were given out, Mr. Reinalz turned to Carey and pulled a well-made hat from beneath the tree. It was crafted of fine leather, with thick mink fur muffs and a sturdy brim.

"I know you make hats for all of us, Mr. Alsch," said Mr. Reinalz, "but

I think this would look rather smart on you." He presented the hat to the quiet man and rejoined his wife on the blue settee.

Carey took the hat in silence, turning it over in his hands. He inspected it in its entirety, following each seam with a practiced finger.

"Thankee." He coughed. "It's a fine hand that's made this. Better'n my own."

"Oh, come now," said Mr. Reinalz, "nothing compares to your handiwork, Mr. Alsch. I've looked in the shops in town, trust me. I only thought of giving you this because I thought how nice it would be for you to not have to make all of your own clothes and hats. This one is from München. I picked it up on my last trip there several months back. Please, only wear it if you wish to, Mr. Alsch."

"It's Carey," their guest said low, scarcely able to speak. "Call me Carey." He held the gift in a tight grip, nearly turning his knuckles white.

Holt Reinalz looked at his wife, then back at Carey Alsch. "Only wear it if you wish to, Carey," he said, smiling broadly.

Carey wished to. He did not remove the hat for the rest of the evening, though they were indoors and there was neither sun nor wind or rain to require such a hat. He did, however, sit a little straighter, look a little higher, and smile the faintest smile in his new hat. He had never been given a hat before. He had never been given anything as a gift. Though a hat seemed a reasonable gift to any Reinalz, it was quite unreasonable to Carey—an almost unfathomable gift to be given. The mere fact he had been thought of was remarkable to him, and it needed considerable pondering to ascertain how such a thing had happened.

In the corner of the room was a little chair of dark wood with an embroidered pillow and cushion. There was nothing notable in the chair's situation, so it was usually left empty, not taken regularly by any of the family. It was in this chair that Carey remained quiet and unobtrusive throughout the remainder of gift-giving and celebration. He was not entirely content in the way others might be—typically wishing to be spoken to, of, and included in general conversation. But, in the ways that mattered personally to him, he was content. Nonny was present, and very lovely. Treu was comfortable and cared for, even adored.

Overhanging all this—certainly mixed in with his other myriad, unusual feelings was a creeping feeling that was disheartening. He knew in his heart that this was not his family, that he had no kin and no kin had him. There was no family set aside for loving and loving him. He wondered why such a thing had transpired as being born unloved, but he did not think anything else could have befallen him. Fate was a sure thing in his mind. Life did not seem to vary.

Everyone left. No one stayed. And that was the life of Carey Alsch.

Red-Breasted Nuthatch
Sitta canadensis

16

Edelweiss and Holly

There was general discussion about dessert, what it entailed, and when it would be had. Carey sat very quiet and still in the unremarkable chair in the corner, thinking fiercely of his bag stuffed in the corner.

He had not considered the possibility of receiving anything other than food and an overabundance of company from the Reinalzes. The man had gladly partaken of the former and was no longer as reluctant to experience the latter. Only now, he considered how to discreetly retrieve his bag, so as to not make it look like he had hidden it in the first place.

Rising from his seat, he quietly stole into the hallway. Upon taking his burlap sack into his hand, he was overcome with embarrassment by the homeliness of its appearance. It was ragged and fraying, patched multiple times, and not bound nearly as neatly as any of the other gifts given by the Reinalzes. He stood quietly in the hall, considering the effect such an ugly bag would have on the family just beyond.

"What do you have there, Mr. Alsch?" came Nonny's quiet, gentle voice. Carey started, meeting her eyes with not a little alarm.

"Gifts for the children, and the like." Carey tugged at his collar.

"How lovely!" Nonny said. "Shall we bring them in?" She looked closely at him, thinking thoughts he wished to know. He pulled the bag away from her, fearing that its uncomely appearance might be to her a plague. "May I?" she whispered, reaching further still. She gently took the bag from him and nodded toward the parlor. "They'll love it, regardless of presentation."

"I had not—" Carey hesitated. "Nothing I make is near nice enough for them."

"I think the quality of the creator matters more than the creation," Nonny said. She spoke in complete gentleness of spirit. There was nothing of belittling or commanding in her tone, nor any of overt righteousness or humor. "It'll be well received, I promise." She paused, eyeing him critically. "I thought you had slunk off—I was come to drag you back."

"What if I didn't want to be dragged back?"

"Then you would have forgotten your loyal hound, who sleeps by the fire," she mused. "I think that is not your way. Though slinking off is certainly your way."

He flushed, eyeing his burlap sack of gifts. "I make my own by my own. No need for over-conversing."

"I used to be shy, Mr. Alsch," she said. "It was not in my indwelt nature to speak to strangers. I thought that I should practice to do what I do not naturally do. And here I am now. There's no harm."

"D'ye think to know me?" He was taken aback. "Deciding what's harm and what's not." He frowned at her. "Harm is harm."

"Will you come back?" She cocked her head. "I think dessert is waiting. Have you had cake?"

"I've not." He shook his head, confused by her kind redirection of his complaint.

"Then I think we had better go in." And with that, she turned in, taking his gifts with her. Carey sucked in a deep breath, thinking in his mind that she was not a shy person, though she claimed to be so. Perhaps she was reformed in her timidity, or braver than he, for she spoke like one well practiced in social interaction. Steeling himself, he followed her into the Blue-Rue. Once there, Nonny handed him the burlap sack and seated herself by the fire. The whole thing was done discreetly.

"What have you got there, Carey?" said Mr. Alsch, gesturing to the sack.

"Gifts." Carey dipped his head so that his face disappeared beneath a mound of brown curls.

"Oh my! Isola," Holt called, "come to the Blue-Rue. We'll have dessert in here. Carey has a surprise!"

The Reinalz children flooded into the room, returning to their spots. The idea of eating dessert in the Blue-Rue was as exciting as the prospect of a Carey Alsch surprise.

Carey inhaled deeply, thinking of his little home by the river and its quiet aloneness. No, he thought to himself, this was no scary thing. There were ordinary people around him, who did ordinary things, and spoke ordinary words. He glanced at Nonny. She smiled.

"I'd put together some things." Carey scratched his head and reached into his bag. The children held their breath. "I'd not seen the likeness of these," he continued, "my own creation. I didn't know what the children favored, but I had got up enough for 'em all." A tremor of excitement passed through the room when he drew out a small leather bear and handed it to Lieselotte Reinalz, who was sitting closest to him.

"Oh, Carey," said Isola, "it's beautiful!"

He sheepishly handed out the animals one by one, retrieving from the bag a cat, a dog, a horse with a curling, leather mane; a martin, mink, ferret, a cow, and several other creatures, enough for the children to each have one. The gifts were met with squeals of excitement and not a little coveting. Carey smiled, observing the work of his hands and the joy it created. A warmth rushed over him, and any desire for his lonely cottage and his routine hermitic life was forgotten.

Next, he produced a pair of fine shoes for Isola, which fit with an accuracy that astounded the receiver. Holt received a sturdy, wide-brimmed hat for keeping the sun from burning neck and shoulders. A braided cord wrapped around the crown.

Carey was still for a moment, accepting compliments with not a little struggle and awkwardness. Steeling his nerves yet again, he drew forth an ornate satchel and strap, worked all over with an edelweiss and holly design. He held it in a tight grip, finding himself unable to move further.

"Who's that for?" Miff asked, hugging his leather lion tightly. Everyone waited for the announcement, hearing instead the crackle of the fire.

"Carey?" asked Mr. Reinalz.

"Miss Nonny," Carey finally got the words out, holding the bag towards the lady in blue.

"Oh my," said she, putting a hand to her chest. "Mr. Alsch, it's lovely." She willingly accepted the gift, laying it on her lap and inspecting the remarkable craft. The Reinalz girls crowded around, asking a multitude of questions and hanging onto the trim of Nonny's dress for a glimpse of the pretty bag.

"'Tis possessed with a place for your gatherings inside," said Carey, "so 'ee don't lose 'em."

"Thank you, Mr. Alsch." Nonny smiled.

Looking fully into her face, Carey Alsch smiled back.

For a brief moment, he was possessed with all the good feelings of Christmas, and none of the lonely. But upon returning to the chair in the corner, he was reminded of his own place in the world. It seemed ill-born in him to try to shirk the former bonds of apathy. Lots were cast and decided early in life, and not typically changed. He recognized that momentary feelings such as these were a mere stupor with the alcohol of happiness. An intoxication, certainly, but simply passing, not lingering.

Thinking these thoughts, he sank deeper into his chair, considering the long, cold months coming towards him rapidly. Christmas was a brief respite from the despair of winter; cold, quiet, and dark, wherein he would gloom and be cast back into apathy and despondence. There would be no alteration from this scene; it was how he had spent the last thirteen winters, ever since his mother drowned in the pond.

17
All Natural

December being over, the rest of the winter season passed quickly. Soon, buds sprouted from the trees, and a sense of greenness settled over the woods. The Isar River first set to trickling, and then to rippling, and then to fully flowing, carrying glacial flour from the upper mountains. Gentian, edelweiss, and trollius sprouted up from the ground, staunchly growing despite remnants of melting snow.

Carey oft went walking among the woods near his home, collecting arnica, masterwort, sanicula, and elderflowers for drying and steeping to make spring salves. These were saved for the duration of the warm season and stored throughout the cold for use on days when one could not leave one's house for fear of being trapped in the deep snow.

Rain had come earlier in the day, leaving the meadow damp. Drops clung to curling ferns and vines that hung from overhead. Larks fluttered from tree to tree, searching for swarming gnats to feast on.

Carey walked beneath the arch of a cedar's great arm, disturbing a flutter of moths. One, a great Viennese emperor, passed overhead with a wingspan matching that of a small bird. It lighted on a nearby tree, blending into the mottled bark, appearing to have eyes on the back of its delicate wings.

Treu kept close to his master, moving at a slower pace than in previous springs. He sniffed out a badger, giving wide berth to the shadowed den, previous experience being his precedent for doing so. Previous experience being the scar on the tip of his left ear.

Sunlight filtered through the trees, painting designs over the earth. Fern, sapling, and nettle pushed through every undergrowth, establishing domain.

The Weeping House

There was always a conquest in deep woods, wherein each tree, bush, and vine battled for the choicest bathing of sunlight. Some trees were kind neighbors, establishing what some called crown shyness, or the separation of leafy treetops to allow undergrowth a reasonable attempt at reaching sunlight. Carey looked at all of this with a brighter eye. His study, apart from leatherwork, had always been books on nature, concerning the identification of trees, bugs, birds, mosses, and the like. Despite this knowledge, he rarely spent time studying them for beauty and natural adornment. Previously, they had only been set into categories, this one to that section, that one to another. Today, he looked most seriously for anything blue, finding now that it was the loveliest of colors. Cloudless skies were now sapphire, blue campanula now the most elegant, and gentian flowers now seemed like the gems of a crown.

He whistled a tune while he walked, thinking of flowers and cornflower skies. Branches hung overhead, laden with early blooms and spun cocoons. A crisp pine scent filled the air, carried by a warm spring breeze. Leaves ruffled in the wind, waving with more cheer than nobility on parade.

An old logging trail ran through the western portion of the woods, where two small springs flowed into the Isar. Ruts from wagons cut through the moss and grass cover, winding deeper into the forest in a maze. Carey approached this trail, settling his hands on his hips. Two trees had fallen over the path, both of considerable circumference.

"Should I harness ye up like a loggin' horse, Treu?" Carey asked the hound, who pressed his nose into one of the ruts and puffed air out through his nostrils, stirring up a cloud of scents. "I s'pose the snow was too much for them," he mused, looking up into the treetops. There was a large opening where the sky could be seen clearer. Beneath the gap were two overturned stumps, laid aside and exposing their complex network of roots. They looked sad.

Carey took a hatchet from his pack and set about segmenting the branches. He set the quarters aside, thinking he would take the choicest pieces home and add them to his pile for winter.

Warm spring breezes are no wonder to an unacclimatized body, and Carey, having spent a very cold winter wrapped up in wool, was drenched in sweat after a bit of work. Figuring that he was very alone, he removed his coat and threw off the straps of his trousers. Even the thin white shirt he wore was too much for the heavy work, so he threw that one off too.

Now, being a man who works out of doors, who does plenty of lifting, hoeing, chopping, and other types of manual labor, Carey Alsch did not possess a sickly figure. He was braw, well-formed, and healthy, though still pale from the long winter months.

Setting his mind to his task, he soon forgot about the day and its plans. The two branches had many dissecting limbs, making the work difficult. Well into the morning he regarded his progress, noting the size of the pile of kindling on one side and sap-rich heartwood logs on the other. He stepped back, wiping sweat from his brow, then continued his labor.

He was so engrossed in his work that he did not hear the crunch of leaves, nor the surprised gasp from behind him. It was only his need for a sip of water from his waterskin that persuaded him to turn away from the road. In turning, he spied Nonny, dressed in a light pink working-dress and apron. Her face was flushed with a bright color. A hand hovered over her mouth, attempting to hide her embarrassment. The two of them stared at each other in surprise for a rather lengthy time, neither able to work up the courage to explain their situation to the other.

"Mr. Alsch," Nonny eventually said, looking off into the trees as a means of distraction. "I had not expected to meet you out here in—" Her eyes were wide, and she suddenly found the ground at her feet to be very interesting. "I am only out to gather gentian and nettle. Lieselotte and Anneliese are in a bad way. They have great difficulty in swallowing and their eyes are quite full of tears. I was thinking to make a tea." She continued rambling on in a nervous manner, looking at him only occasionally. Carey said nothing. He stood still, hatchet clutched in one hand, his gaze uncharacteristically steady.

She still spoke rapidly. "Only, I do not know where the largest meadows of nettle are, so I thought to take the old logging road and see if I might find them that way. And that was how I found you here, in a state of—well, all-natural. Oh my, I am quite a disaster, am I not? I did not mean to startle you. I'll be on my way."

"Don't go," Carey said quickly, taking a step toward her. He flushed the color of a holly berry, then snatched his shirt from the ground and held it against his chest. He struck the axe against the fallen tree, leaving it embedded in the wood.

When he moved to pull his shirt over his head, Nonny turned away, blushing as red as he. She waited while he fastened his suspenders and placed his wide-brimmed sun hat over his straw-like mop of hair. He took his foraging sack and hung it across his chest.

"I'll show 'ee where the nettle is," he said quietly. "Gentian, too. If it's an itching throat and tearing eyes, I'll give 'ee some fresh honey. I have it at home and all whipped up."

Nonny frowned. "Thank you, Mr. Alsch." He left the axe behind, gathering up his coat over one arm, and gestured for her to follow him into the woods and away from the logging road.

18

Brighter Woods

If the woods had seemed bright on his first walk through them earlier that morning, it had become a truly shining day to Carey now, as if it were the center of all sunbeams. The vines arching overhead guided his steps; leaves crunched underfoot. Fallen branches, stones, and other things that littered the ground seemed as treasures to him.

Nonny stayed a shy distance behind Carey, the leather bag detailed with holly and edelweiss strung over her shoulder. She did not notice the music of the leaves, and only knew the crunch of leaves beneath the foot of a quiet man with heavy boots. Carey's foraging boots were made of thick, hard leather for traipsing in bogs, crossing streams, and climbing up crags to reach any and every treasure hidden in the mountains.

He cast a glance over his shoulder. Nonny was the only place his eyes ventured besides the roots and trail before him. During these glances, his expression sometimes revealed the gentle meeting of his brows over the eyes, or a curious flutter of his long lashes. A branch of the Isar curved lazily toward them, thick with the silt dumped here by glacial melt. Nonny wished to stop here a moment and watch the movement of the water over the polished stones on the river bed.

Carey stood apart, pulling at the green portion of a leaf so only the veins remained intact. His eyes were steadfastly focused on the far shore. There was nothing to distract him there, only gentian and sapling firs waving in a gentle breeze. When Nonny's desire for looking at river stones had been sated, they continued on.

"Do you live near here, Mr. Alsch?" asked Nonny after they had been walking a few minutes. Suddenly her dress caught on a buckthorn bush, its tangled branches like reaching arms, grabbing at the layers of light pink. She exclaimed softly, noticing that Carey was unaware of her predicament. "Oh, it is going to tear my dress!"

Carey quickly came to her side and pulled at the branch. "'Twill be all right, miss," he said stiffly. The dress came free with little marring to the material. Nonny thanked him profusely, flattening out the many folds of her skirts. She watched Carey harvest several handfuls of yellow-orange berries from the bush, adding them to the foraging sack hung around his chest.

"What are those for?" she asked.

"The berries make an oil," he said. "Good for the constitution."

"If I help you collect more," she said, facing him, "will you give me some of the oil?"

"Do 'ee need constitution?" He frowned.

"Who does not take in health what is needed when sick? I shouldn't think to only constitute myself when I am near to die."

"I live down that way," Carey said suddenly, which had the effect of making Nonny close her mouth and open it twice as she tried to work out a response.

"Oh?" was the only reply she could muster.

"Ye wondered where I lived." There was a shyness in the fully grown man that rivalled the coyest of characters.

"Do you live there with your family?"

"Have no family," said Carey, tucking another handful of berries into his sash. Treu pranced around Carey's feet, requesting a sturdy ruffling of his ears.

"Me neither!" Nonny exclaimed with an unusual degree of congeniality. She covered her face with a hand. "I didn't mean to—I only meant that I came here to Mittenwald alone. Goodness, I am a bungler. There is no mending such an outburst. And you spoke so solemnly and I so glib!" Her words were sweet, though the energy of their oration was not so.

"No harm," said Carey. "Nettle's over here." He pointed through a line of elder trees where a meadow basking in afternoon sun glowed brightly. Nettle grew thick along the edges of the meadow, climbing around the trunks of the encircling trees. He cleared a path for her, holding back a branch laden with elderflower. "These are good for all manner a' mending," he said, pointing to the white flowers creating an arbor overhead.

"I would love them too!" The face of the lady brightened so miraculously, with such a cheerfulness of spirit, that Carey forbade himself from speaking for fear of dampening her mood. He only nodded in a rather stout manner. "How do you know all these things, Mr. Alsch? I thought you plied leatherworking for trade?" She lifted her leather bag, showing him evidence of his own handiwork.

"Books." Carey shrugged his shoulders, picking elderflowers from the branches and placing them in his sash. "'Tis good to know of the woods."

"Will you teach me?" said the lady.

"Teach 'ee? I am not a teacher, miss. Not good for speaking."

"It'll just be us," she said, looking closely at him. A breeze struck the branches overhead, ruffling leaves and shifting patterns of light across her face. "And Treu. I'll bring you jams and cakes—I'm very good at making sweets, you know—and I'll even pay you!"

"No." Carey shook his head. "Can't ask for money of 'ee."

A loud, pleasant twitter of a songbird rang through the meadow, joined by two other similar calls. The birds sang in lovely harmony. Nonny held still, lifting her chin to gaze into the trees, searching for the source of the nature song.

"It's a bee-eater singing to his mate," Carey said, "and there's a lonely one trying to join in." He imitated the bird with perfect intonation. His sharp whistle echoed through the forest and was returned by the bird after a moment.

"He's lonely?" she asked, tilting her head to look at him. Dappling light drifted over her skin, turning her eyes a golden shade of amber.

"He is." Carey nodded.

"Can we remedy that?"

"I think he has made hisself out to be a lonely bird," said Carey. There was a strange tone to his words, as if they were spun in a mixture of uncertainty and hope.

"Teach me?" Nonny asked, shading her eyes with a soft hand.

19
I Will Love All That I Can Think Of

Nettle hung from Carey's sash, overflowing at his hip, so that he resembled a Greek victor enshrouded in laurels. Small red bumps covered his hands and forearms, the expected result of harvesting the stinging plant. The man did not mind; his attention was elsewhere, and itching hands were of little consequence.

Treu circled the husk of an old oak. Gnarled, twisting branches sprawled overhead. Though it was spring, the branches bore no green buds and only rattled against one another in the wind. There was no shade beneath the dead tree, but in a crook high above nestled an old owl. He crouched there like some Machiavellian lord of the woods. Though small and unassuming, he was perhaps the most cunning of creatures, more like Waldleute than any natural animal. As to guile and deviousness, he was perhaps only rivaled by the fox, who is known as thief and forest schemer. The white-mottled bird watched Treu intently. Each time he circled around the tree, the bird turned its oddly mobile head, following every movement, then whipping around to catch sight of Treu reappearing on the other side of the tree.

"How lovely!" Nonny covered her mouth with her hands, craning her head back to study the small owl.

"'Ee's Tengmalm's," said Carey.

"I'm sorry?"

"'Tis the owl's name." He coughed. "Tengmalm's the naturalist who found him."

"Are you a naturalist?"

"I?" Carey laughed softly. "No, miss. I don't have feelin' for trees 'n' things like, I just know 'em."

"I think that's not true," said the lady, shielding her eyes to watch the owl perched in the crook of a dead branch.

"Mine's a practical knowin', see. Tis how I know 'ee mostly hunts at night, wonder what's woken the beast?" Carey cleared his throat. "I'd only know him practically, 'ee's just an owl. No need for getting all lovin' for things that die."

"Surely there is," Nonny said. "All things die. How does that make them less worthy of love?"

"It's just the way. No feeling 'bout it."

"If one wishes to move through life without living," said Nonny, with much feeling. "But Mr. Alsch, why does the owl have such large eyes? He looks like a toy!"

"For seein' better," said Carey. "At night they look like black marbles. Hunting at night, the little varmints are hard to see. Large eyes makes 'em more clear."

The owl unfurled his wings and leapt from the branch. He swooped low without a sound, gathering spring breezes beneath his wings. No creature living could move with such silence, not rustling or disturbing a feather. His shadow traced the ground, and for a moment the shape of his wings was silhouetted by a bright afternoon sun. Nonny followed the bird with her eyes until he blended into the scene of the forest, enveloped by shadow and leaf.

"Do you know I never set foot in a wood before I came to Mittenwald." Nonny was quiet, still studying the ranging depth of the forest. A woodpecker alighted on the dead tree behind her, taking flight after finding the tree had no substance.

Carey said nothing. He shoved his hands in his pockets and studied the lady studying the trees. In his eyes there was a constant war, one contender being hesitation and natural shyness, (this the less noble of the two, and something he rather despised), the other being the full attention of an affected soul.

For the first time in his life, Carey was deeply affected. There was a blooming feeling in his chest that struck like a burning arrow whenever the lady was near. He was suddenly a soldier ready to die, not because he had given up all hope of victory, but because the offensive line had far greater weapons than he. Weapons that were lovely eyes and even lovelier smiles.

"In the city, there are muddy lanes, and all the houses are similar," Nonny said. "Trees are placed as sporadic ornaments, there are few colorful birds to occupy them, excepting doves and fat birds that fill the streets. Carriages are so fast, I thought I would be killed if I stumbled in the road. No one smiles. I hated it there. The very air is sick."

"I've never been," Carey said. "Never left Mittenwald."

"How lucky!"

"I don't know if I am lucky," said Carey. "There is little worth constitutin' a life here. Trees are not so special. I should like to see 'em as ornaments."

"But they are ornaments here," said Nonny. "And so many of them. Arrayed in so many colors. I did not know there were so many greens, Mr. Alsch. Green is like the loveliest color to me now."

"I thought ye liked blue," said Carey, tugging his broad-brimmed hat a little lower over his face.

"I do." She turned to look at him with a peculiar narrowing of her eye. "But can a woman not love two things?"

"As many things as ye can think of," said Carey.

"What?" Nonny turned toward him.

"Love as many things as ye can think of." His head was so angled, he could barely meet her eye beneath the edge of his hat.

"I'll do that." Nonny smiled. "I really will, Mr. Alsch."

"Call me Carey." He coughed as he said it, forcing the words to be expelled from his chest.

"I will love all that I can think of, Carey." She was a woman made of sunshine dressed in blue. "And I am Nonny. No more of that 'miss' formality. If you are to be my teacher of the woods, we shall be friends."

"Ye really want to know?" said he with quiet effort.

"I want to know trees, plants, birds, and things." Nonny's eyes brightened considerably. "I want to know where to find them, what they do. I want to know the woods like you know them."

"Very well," said Carey. "Once a week until summer I'll teach ye what I know of the woods. Ye must do reading. I'll give ye my books."

"Perfect!" Nonny clapped loudly. "Can we fetch them?"

"I've to bring home the wood," Carey said, "what I left on the logging lane. 'Tis getting late in the day. I'll bring 'ee the books on the morrow."

"I'll go with you at least to the logs. I can find my way home from there." Nonny took a large handkerchief from her pocket and tied it round her head, tucking loose strands of raven hair behind her ears. "Perhaps I can help. I am needing to do work, Carey. You have no idea the amount of sitting we ladies do. I think if I should sit any more I will turn to stone."

"Stone?" said he, wondering at her lament.

"I would soon become unmovable, like carven marble. That is what ladies in the city are. To be paraded around like jewels. Not that I minded all the loveliness of it, but it wore away and, well, I thought, 'Life ends, what's the use of all this?' and I wanted to feel more. I think there are so many stone figures in high society, and none of them know how to feel. It's more like a museum."

"And we folk know of feeling?"

"The Reinalzes are like a spark of life! And the Albrights, I never saw such laughter. Have you tried their beer? It runs so freely from the barrel, I thought there was more on the floor than in our bellies last time."

He listened to her stories, describing the people of his town with more color than he thought reasonable. But what he knew of them was from those brief moments on the back porches of their homes when making deliveries. He smiled at her animation, walking through the nettle meadow until they found the bend of the Isar once again. Following along the shore, they wandered at a steady pace through a grove of evergreens, remarking upon the deciduous kinds that grew between the needled trees. Treu splashed in the shallow river's edge, spying out minnows in the reeds. Here began the first lesson, and after a brief lecture, Nonny was required to give a description of the marked difference between conifer and deciduous. She was a quick study, and soon could order the genus Taxus, Alnus, and Acer.

Black alder was in white bloom with spring flowers that would bear scarlet berries when summer came. Underfoot grew in burgeoning patterns a variety of Poaceae, sprouting small buds that resembled wheat on the end of their stalks.

In the village, Carey Alsch was considered a quiet man of few words. He kept to himself and was known to be hermitic. He worked leather, plied his wares each season in the small market of Mittenwald, or made deliveries to families throughout the year. He was paid for his work and spent no time in idle chatter.

Here in the woods with Nonny, he was a wealth of conversation. His knowledge of flora and fauna rivaled that of any professor. He quoted passages of books written by dead naturalists as if he had written them himself. He espied the movements of minute harvest mice shivering beneath the arch of a fern, and turned over several logs, allowing the lady to marvel at the rippling movements of bugs and worms hiding in the humus.

She watched and listened with close attention, wondering at how the man could say he did not love the forest and only found practical interest in the matter, when his great affection for decomposing earth was so evident. She learned the crucial role of worms and figured no person alive could have such keen interest in vermicompostion as he.

Arriving at his pile of newly chopped lumber, she waited while he loaded the wood onto a large, leather tarp. After a short discussion and much pleading on her part, he allowed her to assist him in carrying choice logs to the pile. When he was satisfied with the load, he cinched the straps tight over the lumber and fastened it to his shoulders, making a sort of sled-and-horse arrangement, wherein he was the horse.

Nonny by his side, he dragged the pile through the woods by way of the logging road. The route was longer, which bothered him little, and only meant the lady would not leave so soon. Treu danced around her, finding ample affection in her hands. She tossed sticks into the woods for him, which he returned quickly. He found youthful cheer in the play and forgot that he was old and worn out.

Reaching the end of the logging road, Carey turned toward his way home, watching Nonny follow the steep decline down to Mittenwald, which peeked over the rise of the next hill. He stood still on the branching path, not moving until she passed out of view; not moving even as the sun began to set behind the range of mountains in the distance; not moving until night fully fell. When he finally turned towards his cottage by the Isar, he did not realize how long he had been looking up, how lovely the sky was, and how light his heart felt.

20
Graves

When Carey sat by the hearth in his house that evening, his regular gloom overtook him. His house was poorly lit, casting long shadows over his desk and bed. The garden was barren, potatoes and turnips long since abandoned. Weeds grew thick among the dried-out braid of grapevines. His apple tree bore no fruit—it was planted by his father and had not been grafted—and the walnut was split and withered. Lightning had stuck that tree many years prior. It leaned over the house in an ominous threat to soon fall if too much life stirred in that house.

Carey stared into the fire. Despondence crept over him like a devilish snare, binding his woefulness in tight knots of apathy. Here, he was on a knife's edge, balancing between familiarity and the world beyond the abject life he had lived so far. His was the sort of despondence found in returning to where ghosts live in the attic, fear binds the beams, and curses hold fast the hinges of the door.

Though his mother no longer drifted in the pond behind the house, she lingered in each ripple of the water. Each disturbed motion of the pond was caused by some memory of her hateful spirit.

Though his father did not remain by the gate and eternally reenact the moment he abandoned his son, there was a shadow of reproach hanging over the rotted fence. In the garden there was the sound of a child begging his father to stay. There echoed in that place the cries of a child pulling his mother's body from the pond he had once played in.

Behind the house there was a painted memory of a boy digging an early grave. A child laying his mother to eternal rest. There was a child learning he had no right to love, nor any knowledge that he could be loved.

There was Carey Alsch.

It seemed that no matter the spirit in which he returned home, it was overtaken by the shadows lingering there. And so, he stared into the fire and did not move for many hours. Treu curled in his place, resting his head on his master's foot. This sense of normalcy was pleasant to the hound, who did not know of his master's sorrows.

When morning came, Carey collected five of his most thoroughly read almanacs and natural field guides, binding them up with a belt and clasp. He left before the sun rose, Treu close at his heels. Songbirds twittered, flitting over the path the man had worn between his cottage and Mittenwald. On his way, he found a small glen of blue cornflowers. He collected a bundle of these, removing excess leaves and a small black beetle. Each step away from his home brought him further from shadow, and he felt almost new by the time he reached the Isar bridge.

A nervous energy overtook him, secondary to the image of swishing blue skirts and rose-red lips passing through his mind. He released a breath, lifting his head to espy the Reinalz home. Treu crossed the bridge, braying loudly to announce his presence to the village.

Smoke curled from the chimney, and a new bundle of flowers rested in each window basket. They were arrayed in such fine colors that Carey felt keenly the uniform nature of his own nosegay. Treu tucked against his leg, waiting patiently for his master to proceed. Setting his resolve, Carey set his foot on the porch, raising a hand to knock and announce his presence.

The door was flung open, and a terrified white face appeared there.

"Carey!" Nonny exclaimed, grabbing him by his sleeve and pulling him into the house. Treu swept in behind him, practically falling into the arms of Michael and Wolfgang. The boys buried their gloomy faces in

Treu's remaining winter coat.

Several Reinalz children swarmed close, tears brimming in their eyes. Nonny took a breath, her eyes glistening with the weight of unrealized grief. "Lieselotte and Ada are sick, so very sick." She took Carey by the hand and led him up the narrow set of stairs to the second floor. He crouched at the top, unable to stand to his full height on the landing. "Holt has gone to town to fetch the doctor. He says we haven't had a doctor in town for years—I don't believe it! How can such a thing be? Oh, Carey." She turned to look at him, brown eyes welling up with tears. Her voice dropped to a whisper. "The girls are like to die before their father returns."

Carey pushed gently past her, leaving her standing in the hallway. She clutched Amalie and Anneliese Reinalz close. Oscar, Michael, and Inge lingered on the stairs. Corinna paced in the kitchen below, singing a song to Isolde, who cried with a powerful voice for having been separated from her mother.

In the upstairs room, Carey found Isola Reinalz seated on the edge of a large bed. Her face was puffy and red. A sweet song escaped her lips but had that tone which strikes a perfect note asunder. That sound of a song sung by one who grieves.

Carey set his stack of books on the bed and came close to the girls. Isola regarded him quietly. Her eyes betrayed how close to hopelessness her entire being had come.

Two sickly and wan children lay beside her, hovering somewhere between the land of somnolence and wakeful delirium. Lieselotte, the elder, had a pallor of death hanging over her eyes. Jaundice colored her skin, and her lips were ashen. The girl's chest moved so seldom she appeared dead. Soft, blond curls clung to her forehead, soaked with sweat. Ada held the same cast of death, though less hallow and gaunt. Her eyes opened when Carey approached, and she smiled ever so softly. The girl's gums were pale, nearly gray in color, and her eyes had a haunting pallor.

"Carey," Isola whispered, "don't. You'll get sick."

"Won't." Carey shook his head, speaking softly. "When'll Holt return?"

"He left two days ago. I think something has gone wrong, or—I don't know—how far is München?"

"It'd be a day more afore he is returned," he said with gentleness. "How long have they been so?"

"It started four days ago with dear Lieselotte," said Isola. "She was very tired and vomited through the first night. I gave her ginger and dandelion tea, and she felt better. But then her skin began to blister, like an angry rash—like this—and she complained of aching bones. Carey," her voice wavered, "I think it is scarlet fever. We have no doctor."

"May I?" Carey asked, stepping beside the bed. Isola rose, moving to stand in the corner beside the window. She seated herself on the small seat built into the frame, dropping her head into her hands. Carey leaned over the children, touching their heads with the back of his hands. "I bain't a doctor, and have no practical knowledge of sickness, nor precedent in dealing with scarlet fever," said he. "But I've books, and I've in my home a collection of tinctures for remedy. The rest of the children are in danger here, Isola. Would ye let me take 'em to my home and care for 'em until the doctor comes? I think Lieselotte'll not survive the night unless something's done."

"I can care for them—" Something in the woman broke and she sobbed into her hands. Nonny quietly entered the room and, taking her friend's hands, gently led the woman away.

"Take them, Carey," said Nonny upon returning without Isola. "I'll help you."

Carey took Lieselotte into his arms with the utmost tenderness, resting her head on his shoulder. She could do little to hold her head up and released a soft groan. Her sweat-soaked curls clung to Carey's shirt.

Nonny gently lifted Ada, holding her steady as they left the room and descended the stairs. The Reinalz children had been ushered into the kitchen by Nonny, and while the elder children now comforted their mother there, the younger ones peeked through the swinging door in the hall.

21

The House

The woods were not so quiet, not so somber, not so hushed when the two figures carrying little bodies came up the path. A dove cooed overhead, perched on the slender branch of a silver fir. It fluttered to a higher branch when Carey passed beneath. His hurried footsteps thumped loudly against the earth. The burden in his arms groaned in the weakest of voices, whispering her mother's name. A tear traced down Lieselotte's cheek, making trails towards the tip of her little chin. Carey looked over his shoulder, counting the paces between him and Nonny, who struggled under the weight of the seven-year-old girl in her arms. The woman's face was resolute. Her lips moved, whispering words of life over Ada. Though sturdy in character, Nonny had little substance to her body, and was unused to labor. Sweat beaded on her forehead despite the cool midday breeze.

"We're almost there, Nonny," said Carey. His voice carried a sternness and sense of urgency in their journey that Nonny struggled to achieve.

"I'll make it," she said, her voice wavering. Her dark brows angled upwards at the center, creasing her forehead. She breathed deeply, a ragged sound in her chest building with each step, but she pressed on.

At the top of the hill, Carey split from the popular trail onto the one worn by his own steps and sled. Treu raced on ahead. The trail was cut up the mountainside with switchbacks. Deep ruts from Carey's sled divided the path. It was cleared of debris, overhung with vine and fern and grown over with yellow arnica.

The Isar flowed past, rushing down heavy stones with the full force of snowmelt. The spray that gathered at the foot of a small waterfall drifted across Carey's path. He shielded Liselotte from the damp. Nonny did the same for Ada, and soon they were within sight of the little cottage on the upper reaches of the river.

A woodpile was built up on one side and the little shingled roof reached out to form a canopy over the lumber. Behind the house was a small shed with a thatched roof and open hayloft scattered with drying hides. Chickens clucked in the yard, half-wild with neglect. They scattered when Carey crossed the yard, hiding in their overgrown garden.

Treu pushed the oak door open with his nose, disappearing into gloom. Carey ducked through the low entrance, laying Lieselotte upon the bed and searching for a lantern. Nonny placed Ada beside her sister.

"Their fever is worsening," said Nonny, touching Lieselotte's damp head.

"Circulation," Carey said, descending into his shadowed larder. "Blood-fever, purpura, swelling and vomit," he muttered loudly over the tinkling of bottles. He soon reappeared, burdened with an array of tinctures. "Remove as much clothes as is respectable," he said, opening the windows that had not been opened for half his life. Light streamed in and a breeze flowed through the dead space of the house.

Nonny undid the buttons of the girls' nightgowns, exposing much of their fevered skin to the cooling air now flowing through the house. She covered them with a thin blanket, muttering a prayer over their small, sickly bodies, chests flush with angry red rashes.

"Feverfew! Hyssop, angelica, thistle." He listed off the tinctures as he set them on the desk near the bed. Measuring a dose of each, he dripped small amounts into the girls' parted lips. Going back outside, he built a fire in the yard. When the fire was caught, he set his kettle over it to boil water. The first kettle was poured into a basin in the house kept for clean water. In the second, dried snakeroot and dandelions were steeped to make a warm tea. He set these aside, letting them cool on the windowsill.

He soaked rags in water, chilling them by waving them through the air, then wrapped one around Lieselotte's neck, the second beneath her arms. Ada was given the third and fourth in the same manner.

"Ephedra!" said Carey suddenly, quickly returning to his larder. He emerged a moment later, carrying a small bottle. He dripped this slowly into Lieselotte's mouth, then leaned against the desk to watch her closely.

Nonny sat on the edge of the bed, holding Ada's small, pale hand in her left, and Lieselotte's in her right. Her lips moved but she made no sound.

Treu paced in and out of the house, periodically scaring the wild chickens hiding in the garden. He felt his master's solemn mood. Though solemnity was nothing unfamiliar to Treu, it was out of place, as his master was not in his chair by the fire, and there was not a foot to rest his muzzle on.

"Is there anything else to do?" Nonny asked, feeling Lieselotte's forehead.

"Wait," said Carey. He passed a hand through his hair, then sat on the floor beside the bed, leaning against the humble frame. There was a curve in his back that bespoke a very heavy weight. His head hung from his shoulders, similarly weighted.

A hand lighted on his upper arm, gentle in pressure but momentarily lifting some of his burden. The man who hated to look up looked up and regarded Nonny for a long while. Neither spoke, but continually looked at each other.

Lieselotte sighed deeply, striking the two from their silence. Carey leapt to his feet, replacing the cold rag at her neck. An hour passed, then two, and still the girls retained their sickly pallor. Ada cried out in her sleep, her words a jumbled mix expressing her want of mother and father, being unable to find them in the muddle of fever-induced dreams.

Every hour, Carey would measure out a dose from each of his chosen tinctures. He took a nameless paste from a bottle and rubbed it on the inside of Ada's cheeks with a wooden spoon, doing the same for her sister.

Darkness fell and still Nonny remained in the house. She had not moved from her vigil, protectively watching over her charges while Carey prepared his herbal mending. Stars peered through the trees, and a chill breeze now blew through the house. Lieselotte moved anxiously, whimpering in her sleep. She whispered of fire and burning. Her skin glistened in the pale light. Ada was still, excepting her slowly moving chest.

"Will 'ee sleep on a pallet I set up on the floor?" said Carey, handing Nonny a plate of boiled potatoes. A small piece of roasted venison touched the potatoes, steaming in the cold, spring night.

"I won't sleep." Nonny accepted the plate.

"How can 'ee not sleep? Sickness'll overtake 'ee."

"I'll stay here," she said.

"It's not noble victuals." Carey dipped his head. "But the taste is natural and the substance sturdying to the body. I'll make coffee." He disappeared through the low door again, not returning until he had two mugs of black coffee in his hands. Nonny's eyes widened upon sipping the dark drink.

"'Tis foul?" he asked, brow setting in worry.

"It's … good," said she. "Only, I've not had coffee in my life."

"Would ye prefer tea?" Carey asked.

"If this will keep me awake, I'll drink it," Nonny said, drinking deeply from her mug.

22
The Importance of Having Many Books

The singular rooster, patriarch of the wild chickens at the little cottage on the river, crowed with a powerful voice. Red wattle and comb bright against the morning dawn, he clung to the gatepost, brow turned to the sky. It was unkown whether the sky moved at his beckoning, or he was beckoned to crow by the lightening of the horizon. Regardless of who beckoned whom, it was dawn, and crowing was required.

Carey sat in his chair by the hearth, though not settled in despondence. Instead, he rolled a thread of dried verbena between his fingers, turning the leaves to a powder. Aged vinegar rested in a pot at his feet. He poured a measure of the liquid into a bottle, dropping leaves in, one by one. His eyes were heavy with fatigue and a bit of the vinegar spilled over his fingertips, dripping to the floor beside his socks.

Cold shadows lingered in the corners of the room. No fire burned in the hearth, purposely left unkindled to keep the house in a chill. The bed was mussed, sheets torn off the end, cast in a pile on the stone floor.

Nonny sat against the bed, arms limp by her sides. Her booted feet were tucked beneath her, peeking out from beneath folds of blue fabric. Thick locks of dark hair hung over her face, fallen from their careful braids. Her head rested against the frame of the bed. Thick, black lashes touched her cheeks, not moving even when the rooster crowed.

Carey set the bottle on the mantel, pushing aside a charred pipe and two little picture frames. A drawing of his mother was encapsulated in one, his father in the other. Though they were small, the images dominated the mantel. The house seemed colder on that side.

As quietly as possible, Carey stood. His chair creaked and he froze. Nonny stirred but did not wake. Taking out a loaf of dark rye from the cupboard, he sliced it and spread thick white cheese made from the milk bought in town earlier that week. His mother had called it quark. Currant compote was spread over the top, so it appeared bright and cheery.

"Is it morning?" Nonny's voice was quiet and heavy with sleep. Then came the sound of stirring and a little gasp. "Oh, Carey, they are still so deathly pale."

He cleared his throat before he spoke. "But they have made it through the night, and Liselotte has no fever." He stepped forward, offering her the plate with its single slice of dense rye bread.

"What is the white bit?" Nonny whispered.

"Quark." He drew over his face an embarrassed grimace and moved to take the plate back. ater She refused, holding it protectively against her chest.

"I'll eat it." And eat it she did. The first taste was tentative and unsure, but upon discovering the sharp tang of red currant jam and mellow cheese, she ate the rest with great delight. "Did you make this?"

He nodded, moving back to the kitchen area to eat whilst leaning against the wooden countertop. "It's not like Christmas dinner, but Treu and I make do."

"Make do? Carey, this jam is the best I have ever had."

He smiled.

Setting her plate on the desk pushed up against the wall, she sat on the edge of the bed and took Ada's hand.

"Ada still feels warm," said Nonny, pressing the back of the girl's hand against her cheek. "She has a fever still, Carey—can you give her more? Where is the bottle with the strong-smelling herb?" She made to rise but he shook his head, setting his own plate aside.

"I put up some more just now. The verbena is run out. Haven't much left," he sighed, running a hand through unkempt hair.

"Verbena is for …?"

"The fever 'n' other things."

"How long till the tincture is ready?"

"Half a day? Even so, it won't have the same potency as the first I administered. The longer it sits, the more potent."

"I wish Holt would return!" Nonny said, squeezing Ada's hand.

"Nonny?" Lieselotte stirred, her pale lips barely moving.

"Yes, dearest?" the lady gasped. She flew to the girl's side, stroking her face with a gentle hand. Lieselotte blinked slowly in the morning light streaming through the window. The rooster had ceased his crowing. He now paced in the yard like a noble guardian.

"Where am I? It smells of leather and cedar." She wrinkled her nose. Her voice was weak, barely above a whisper, and she spoke through cracked lips. "I'm aching in my bones."

"You've been sick, Lotte," said Nonny, "and your father went for the doctor because you were like to die. Mr. Alsch and I took you here to his cottage so your siblings would not catch the fever. Mr. Alsch has natural medicine, and it has probably saved your life!"

"Oh," Lieselotte said in a small voice, "will you thank Mr. Alsch? I'm so tired."

"He's here," Nonny said, taking a step away from the bed, gesturing for Carey to approach. His eyes widened and he gripped the countertop, feeling that the shadows in his little house had grown darker for a moment. Nonny insisted and he eventually obliged.

"Thank you, Mr. Alsch," Lieselotte whispered, pale lips lifting in a soft smile.

"Think none of it." Carey's voice was no louder than the child's.

Lieselotte shifted, feeling the other body in bed beside her. Her face worked into a frown and she looked steadily at Nonny.

"Ada," said Nonny, brushing past Carey to come close to the girl. "She's still with fever. We must pray, Lotte."

"I will," said Lieselotte. "Where's Mutti? I want to see Mutti."

"She is home. You'll see her soon, dearest."

"Need to move Lieselotte; her body'll warm Ada, it'll not do," said Carey, clearing his throat. "I'll make up a cot." He went to the shed, returning with an array of supple hide and furs. Moving the potato-holding basin that was soon to be converted back to a washing basin, he laid the furs on the ground, creating a comfortable pallet for sleeping. Treu immediately thought this bed was made for him and curled up in the center, finding comfort for his aching bones. Carey shooed him away, speaking pleasantries to the hound as he did so.

He carefully lifted Lieselotte from the bed and laid her on the pallet, covering her with a blanket. Treu returned to the pallet against his master's wishes, finding a place there in Lieselotte's arms. She said she did not mind. The hound was not bothered again about the matter.

"Carey!" said Nonny, "Ada is so hot. And now she is shivering."

He came close, leaning over the small girl and feeling her cheeks with his palm. She began to shake violently, retracting all the skin around her neck. Her eyes stared towards the far wall, rolling upward so intensely that nearly all of her iris was hidden beneath her eyelids.

"Hold her down!" said Carey as he descended into his larder. Nonny threw herself over Ada, attempting to still her violent convulsions. The rooster crowed outside. Clattering and soft curses echoed from the larder, until Carey returned clutching an armful of dried leaves and bottles. He threw these on the bed beside the girl, who was wracked with shaking so intense she seemed possessed by some dark spirit. Lieselotte wailed, hugging Treu and crying into this fur. The hound's tail thumped rhythmically.

Carey took a bottle and forced Ada's mouth open, dripping some of the liquid between her tightly clenched teeth. Next, he dumped his potatoes basin over on the floor, scattering spuds across the room. Some rolled beneath the bed, where they would be eternally forgotten. He gently moved Nonny aside and took Ada into his arms. "Draw up water from the pump outside!" he commanded, then placed Ada in the basin, where she continued to convulse, though less violently than before.

Nonny came running in with a tin pail of water, emptied it into the basin and fled out the door almost immediately to fetch more. Carey took another pail and ran to the river, pulling water from the icy depths. He poured it in the basin, filling it to Ada's ankles.

She ceased convulsing when the water reached her hips, and Carey leaned over the edge, holding her face away from the hard edge of the basin. Nonny knelt beside him, gripping the rim with white knuckles. With her other hand, she gently splashed water over the girl.

"What in God's name was that, Carey?" she whispered. "A demon? I felt darkness here, but not such violent, convulsive spirits. Why does she not stir? Is she alive? What did you give her?"

"Skullcap," he said, quietly observing the girl lying in the water, her round cheek resting against his hand. Nonny continued to speak rapidly, softly, almost under her breath. She whispered prayers.

"Is Ada alive?" came Lieselotte's quiet voice when Nonny finished speaking. She was crying softly. Still weak with sickness, she came to the side of the basin and stroked her sister's hair with a gentle touch. Tears stained her cheeks.

"She is," said Carey without turning. "She's returning to us."

"Carey," Nonny whispered, "how did you know what to do? You are not a doctor, are you?"

"I am not," he said. "I have books."

"Those were not the actions of someone who merely reads." She touched his arm and he flinched. A breeze entered the still open window, ruffling Nonny's loose strands of hair.

Carey dropped his head several inches, resting his chin on the edge of the basin. "I have many books."

Fallow Deer
Dama dama

23

Mother's Rose

When Ada began to complain of the cold, Nonny dried her and changed her into a dry garment, then placed her back in the bed with the sheets drawn down. Treu rose from Lieselotte's side and gently licked Ada's hand where it hung over edge of the bed.

Her fever remained throughout the day, intermittently rising and falling. She tossed and turned in the bed, crying out for her parents. Nonny sat beside the bed, holding Ada's hand. Her head rested against a leg of the desk and her feet were curled beneath her, still shod with brown boots, though the laces were undone. Lieselotte slept on the pallet, her head and arm resting on Nonny's lap. Treu added himself to this comfortable position, lying on his back in the crook of Lieselotte's body.

Carey sighed and sat himself down in his chair at the little worktable beside the bed. His elbows rested on the desk in a pile of leather scraps, head pressed against his palms. There was no place to hide himself in his little house now full of people. He had no respite from community and was bearing up in full resignation that he might never return to the life he had carved for himself. That ignoble life of solitude and craft.

There are three paths a man can take in life, the first—oft praised as the ultimate success—money, notoriety, and family. It usually leads to a sort of well-lived life, if done in a respectable manner and with genteel character. Another being that torrid life of being given over wholly to the vices of the spirit and flesh and succumbing to the whispers of the dark corners of the world. Residing in that realm has little to do with goodness and should generally be avoided. The third is perhaps most lamented and desired by unhappily married men. This path, more easily obtained by young, unattached men, is that of solitude, a cabin, and a craft, preferably in the woods. Solitude is best met when fully separating from society and returning to man's true form, wild and unkempt in the mountains.

Carey sighed again, sinking lower into his chair. Taking a deep breath of cool spring air lilting over the edge of the open window, he righted himself and went outside. Standing in the yard, he pulled the dead tomatoes, uprooting them and tossing them into a pile. When they were cleared away, he cut the dried-out braids of grapevine, then the rotted squash, and finally the husk of a rose. Setting these all in the center of his yard, he lit them on fire with a single match.

The flames devoured the dead branches, and with them, memories of a green garden started by his irate father years ago. The rose was swallowed by fire, and so was the vision of his mother trimming back the leaves. In those days, Carey had heard more from his mother of care and worry over the rose than for her child. When she cut away unwanted stems and leaves, he had wished he were that rose, and that she would cut away the bloom, so he might watch himself wither. In seeing the rose wither, he might have felt some resolution in his soul, believing that whatever happened to the plant was what he deserved, being so unlovable that even his mother loved a plant more than she loved him.

So, he burned the rose. It succumbed with terrifying ease, becoming ash in seconds. Hours passed and the fire settled down to glowing embers in the afternoon sun. The women slept in the house, so he busied himself in other areas.

His chickens were delighted to find that he still had some corn sealed tightly in a barrel in the haybarn and became a little less wild when Carey cast it in the yard. He watched them—and their patriarch—scuttle in the dirt to find every last kernel.

Every hour, he ventured into the little house and assessed his patients.

When Ada's fever broke and she slept in a gentle sleep, he lifted Nonny into the bed. She moved beside Ada, pulling the girl into her arms so they slept comfortably beside one another.

Carey sat at his desk and fashioned a leather barrette with a whittled pin of ashwood. He embossed the barrette with gentian flowers, sweeping the curling scraps onto the floor with the rough hand of a craftsman.

When night fell, he walked along the edge of the river, crouching near the icy rush. He took out several smooth stones from the river bed and threw them, skipping them across the surface of the water. Going back inside, he lit a candle, set it in the window, and took out one of his books to read in its dim light. He would not spark a fire in the hearth, for fear of spiking temperature in the girls, and—though the thought did not form consciously in his mind—for fear that he might be found in his despondence, that Nonny might find him there, gazing into the fire, appearing dead for how little he stirred.

"Carey?" Nonny's quiet voice pulled him from a long paragraph on the difference between the common eider and king eider—there was not much difference, only the size and color of the crest about the bird's head—and he looked at her. She lay on her arm, the other being claimed by Ada's head as a pillow, and had her knees drawn up to her chest. Blue skirts hung over the edge of the bed, revealing her brown boots and the white of her stockings at the trim of the shoe.

He looked at her, resting his chin on his hand where he was hunched over his desk, the book spread open before him.

"What is the smell of smoke lingering in the air?" Her brows sank in the middle, and her brown eyes peered at him so intently that his heart forgot its next two beats. "It does not smell like a single candle. Did something burn?"

"I burned my mother's rose," he said.

"Oh."

The Weeping House

Silence lingered between them, interrupted only by Treu shuffling in Lieselotte's arms.

"Why did you burn the rose, Carey?"

"'Twas an ugly rose," Carey said, "and I hated to look at it."

"Then why do you look so sad?" she whispered.

"I'm not sad."

"I think you are always sad. It makes me wonder what makes a man so forlorn. Do you cry?"

"There's no need for cryin'. No help it does, no help it'll be."

"Why are you sad?"

"Where's it been said that I'm sad?"

"This whole house is sad, Carey. I think it holds more grief than any heart I have encountered. From where does it come?"

"It's not sad," said he, "just needs to be cleaned, is all."

"If you are not sad," said she, "then why did you burn your mother's rose?"

"It needed burnin'. Lots of things in need of burnin' this season. That's what spring is for."

"Spring is for flowers." She watched him and the light flickering about his face. When he would not speak further, she watched him read, imagining that the reflected light from the candle was mirrored in his mind, a gentle dance half between life and death. Nonny looked and saw in him a great sadness, far greater than her own, and she resolved to find out its source, though the man seldom spoke but to describe plants and trees.

Carey did not know this stalwart resolution was being formed in the lady but felt her eyes lingering on his face while he attempted to continue his nightly reading. His endeavors were ill-met, and he read the same paragraph three times over without making sense of it, then abruptly closed the book and went outside to look at the stars and feel cold.

24
Dismissal

Booming thuds sounded in the night. Carey was ripped from a deep sleep, disoriented for a moment in that space between wakefulness and slumber. He rolled over in the hayloft, spitting out a few pieces of hay. The thuds continued, followed by chatter in the yard. The wild chickens squawked and Treu took up a loud howl, sounding the alarm for his master from within the house.

Carey leapt from the hayloft and nearly flew across the yard. He tore the low door open and ducked beneath the lintel. Breathless, he stumbled in the darkness, finding his house far more crowded than usual.

Holt Reinalz and a little man with a dark beard stood near the bed. Nonny sat on the end, blanket drawn around her shoulders. She held a candle in one hand and clutched the blanket against her chest in the other. Light flickered over her face, casting it in a warm kind of gloom. She looked at Carey when he entered.

"The doctor is here," she said. Carey nodded, lingering near the mantel, his hand resting on the unfinished wooden edge.

Ada Reinalz clung to her father, her little head tucked in the nape of his neck. Lieselotte sat on the edge of the bed with her feet hanging a few centimeters off the floor. She smiled at Carey, still appearing pale and wan.

"You have done well, sir," said the bearded man, turning to Carey. He dipped his eyebrows and peered around the house, looking like a magistrate searching out a crime. "What did you give the girls?"

"Plants," said Carey without looking at the man.

"What kind of plants?"

Forgoing an answer, Carey crossed the room and descended into his larder, coming out with an armful of small black bottles. Passing the physician and Holt, he laid them on the desk and jerked his head toward them, then returned to his place by the mantel. There, he studied his feet.

"Ephedra and verbena. Skullcap—for what?" the doctor muttered under his breath, sorting the bottles with a rather delicate white hand.

"Convulsions," said the quiet man by the hearth.

"Who seized?"

Nonny pointed to Ada, held in her father's comforting embrace. She slept soundly in his arms.

"What else was given?" asked the doctor.

"Angelica," Carey said.

"And thistle," Nonny added in a small voice, "and hyssop."

"Where did you learn these remedies?" the doctor pressed, holding a tincture of hyssop to the weak glow of the candle on the window sill, lighted by Nonny.

"Books," said Carey without looking up.

"No, you misunderstand me," the doctor interrupted, "who did you study under? What school did you attend?"

"None," said Carey. "Taught myself. Learnt by readin' here." He pointed to the chair by the hearth.

"I don't believe you," the doctor said, laughing. It was a harsh sound, not pleasant or congenial.

"Thank you, Carey," said Holt, placing a hand on the doctor's shoulder. "It appears you have saved my family. The doctor has prescribed rest for full recovery. He said there is no reason to not allow them to come home. I can never thank you enough, my friend."

"'Tis nothin'." Carey shook his head. "Needed to be done, so 'twas done."

"Don't think to give advice and play doctor, young man," said the doctor, stepping close. He was made diminutive by Carey, even though the quiet man stood with a hunch by the hearth, clearly weighed down by some unreasonable guilt impressed upon him by the vain little doctor. "You are not a doctor. These bottles worked,"—he clinked the hyssop and verbena together—"and this was an emergency. But the people in this town will suffer if you play doctor, being as uneducated as you are. My association will be sending a physician for residency soon. Be civil, mind you. And clean this place up." He turned sharply, black physician's coat swishing against the worn doorpost.

"Carey," Holt said, "I'm sorry. I'll send the doctor away immediately. He's a fool. Please, he is no friend of mine. You are. You've done a great thing today. You have done the best. We're forever grateful. Come and visit before the week is over. We require your presence in our family." He clapped Carey on the shoulder, still holding Ada with his other arm. "Nonny," he said as he turned to her, "we are leaving now. You should come with us; it would not be proper to stay alone."

"I'll be along in a moment, Holt," she said, clasping her hands in her lap.

"Very well," said the father, coming by the bed to lift Lieselotte into his other arm. His load was heavy, bearing a daughter in each arm, but he was not weighed down when he ducked through the low door.

Carey did not lift his head. His hand rested on the back of his chair by the hearth and a forgotten potato touched his foot. Nonny came to stand before him, illuminated by a candle resting on the hearth. Her face was a painting of warm hues of ochre, sienna, and gold, shining in the darkness.

"You did something magnificent, Carey." Her voice was quiet in the candlelit house.

"'Twas nothing," he repeated in the same hushed manner, looking steadily down at her face. There passed a shade of light across her face that matched the amber in her eyes. Carey thought it was the same shade revealed when sunlight pooled in their depths. He studied the colors playing about her lips and the shadows cast by the well-shaped curve of her cheeks and neck.

She placed her hand on his where his knuckles grew white against the edge of the chair. Never was so brief a touch and so gentle a motion able to convey without words as much as Nonny's did in that tiny house of gloom on the river. She smiled, then followed Holt Reinalz into the yard.

Treu bayed at the wagon disappearing down the first angle of the lane. He returned to his master's side, proud of his defense of their cottage. Carey ruffled his ears, then lay down to rest in his bed.

The hound padded to the bed and set his large head on the soft covers. His eyes were pleading, dark pools conveying the feelings of a mind consumed by little other than companionship. Carey propped himself up on an elbow and gently pulled the old hound onto the bed. Treu circled on the bed for a moment, pawing the blankets until he found a comfortable position.

When he finally lay down beside Carey, man and hound were soundly asleep before a minute was counted.

25

The Matter of Warmth

Carey did not stir for two days. To an observer, he might have appeared as one taken by death's quiet embrace, though his chest moved with even, deep breaths and his skin was not sallow. His loyal hound followed his regular routines while his master slept, going out into the yard to chase chickens and drinking water at the river's edge, though he always returned near nightfall.

The second night of Carey's prolonged rest arrived with one of spring's thunderstorms. Rivers formed in the yard, pooling in the newly cleared garden. The edges of the Isar swelled, sweeping away new sprouts and piling them up further down the river. Rain pounded against the peat-moss roof, and traces of ice-cold water dripped through the cracks in the rafters.

Though the sky rumbled, and lightning cracked, Carey Alsch did not wake. He wandered through dreams of dark spaces and unfamiliar rooms. Stone walls encircled him, and the voice of his mother echoed through the halls. Father was coming home. Father was returning and would deliver to Carey what was owed and deserved.

The shadow of that cruel man appeared at the end of the hall, more real and dominating than any darkness and terror of actual life. Carey cried out in his sleep and was awakened suddenly by a crack of thunder.

Bright lights shone through his window. Red, orange, and yellow waves danced across the ceiling. Treu began to howl, his voice rising with the wind. Dazed by heavy sleep, Carey sat up in the bed, unaware of who he was, where he was, and what was happening. Treu howled. The wind howled. In a frame of torrential rain, orange flames devoured a tree in the yard.

Coming to his senses, Carey leapt to his feet, taking up the two pails still set by the basin in the middle of the house, and ran into the yard. The fire hissed in the rain, struggling to climb into the upper branches. Wreaths of flame wrapped around the trunk, originating from a blackened scar splitting the tree in two.

Carey filled the buckets at the swollen edge of the river and flung their contents on the fire. It shrunk away, sputtering yellow beneath the deluge. Treu raced around the yard, howling and barking in a flurry of excitement. Splashing through the flooded garden, Carey refilled the pails and doused the fire until all that remained was a thin tendril of smoke soon to be eliminated by large raindrops.

When all the fire was reduced to ash, he stood in the yard and did not move. Rain fell, but Carey did not stir. Rivulets traced down his cheeks, soaking his beard. His clothes were sodden and his feet bare. Mud squelched between his toes and splattered his trousers, but still he did not move. His chest heaved from exertion. Dropping the pails, Carey let his hands fall to his sides. Rain dripped from his fingertips, mixing with the flooding patterns in the mud.

A chill crept over him. Starting at the base of his neck, it traced down each vertebra. There, in the middle of his yard at the little cottage beside the Isar River, Carey Alsch became completely numb. He did not cry, he did not scream, he did not move. His feet were soon covered with a slurry of mud and water, and he still did not move.

The sound of his mother's voice seemed to fill the void of emptiness left behind by the cracks of lightning flashing overhead. In each lull between rolling thunder, he heard the whispers of a hateful mother. When each bolt of electricity tore open the sky, Carey felt the looming shadow-presence of his father.

His bones began to ache with cold, tormenting him like his memories.

He cursed the feeling, but it would not leave. There was lingering darkness in the yard, similar to the gloom settling in the corners of the house. Roused from apathy at last, he was keenly aware of how far he had sunk into the mire of indifference.

Calling Treu sharply, he went inside and lit a fire in the hearth. When the fire had taken form, he took candles from the cupboard on the wall and set them on the cabinet, windowsills, desk, across the mantel, and in every alcove, until the last shadow fled.

One by one, he stripped off each article of soaked clothing and set them to dry on hooks over the fire. Then, shivering with cold, he dressed and warmed himself by the flames. He did not sit in his chair by the hearth, feeling that the piece of furniture was solely responsible for the despair that appeared when he rested there. Instead, he found a woolen blanket and a book and took up Treu's place in front of the hearth.

The hound joined him there, still soaked through. Carey reclined his head against Treu's hide, angling the pages of his book towards the fire to illuminate the scribbled notes along the border. He tilted the book, reading every annotation. These were a collection of his myriad observances of local flora and fauna. The manner in which the notes were written was intelligible to Carey alone, who never had a proper education to learn his letters and therefore made do with a variant form of script of his own invention.

Warmth spread through Carey, and he sighed deeply in his chest. The warmth overcame the cold gloom persistently clinging to his life. Each candle was placed strategically to combat the enshrouding darkness. It was to him a brief respite from the abysmal familiarity of his life. He knew the familiarity; the kind that drives us to ignore the bitter parts of daily living. That corner of the house not swept which always grows cobwebs; that edge of the counter where a crust might cling if not frequently scrubbed; that ring left on the stovetop when a pot is forgotten and boils over.

To Carey, that familiarity allowed him to ignore the desiccation of life in his home. It was the emptiness of his chair by the hearth, and how it held him captive for hours. It was the cold austerity of his desk, bed, and counter, which had not changed since his mother was drowned and his father run afield. The gloom in his house was a mirror of the gloom within, and if he lingered in familiarity, he would never notice how his house gave that despondency life and added favor to the haunting presence of those no longer living.

Having enjoyed Christmas in a home as warm and bright as the Reinalzes'—and with people as full of life as that family—he felt even more keenly the divide between himself and those who were forcing their way into his life. It was not that all of his love had been used up or wasted; it was that he never had any to begin with. He was not cold because of the season, or rain, or because the fire sometimes went out. He was cold because there was no warmth within. There never had been.

So, Carey crept closer to the fire, desperate for some deep warming of his soul. Any heat from the flames only penetrated his skin, leaving all else cold and worn out. Lying there, he found slumber with a cold heart and hot skin and did not stir until half a day had come and gone.

26

As a Brother

When several days had passed, Carey found himself venturing down into Mittenwald. He brought with him honeycomb, gathered from a wild hive filling the husk of a fallen tree. Treu pressed at his heel, tail beating against the back of Carey's legs.

Bright sunlight struck the shingles atop the steeply angled rooftops clustered together at the base of the first hill. Rain dripped there, fresh from a mid-afternoon shower. Some rainwater was collecting in barrels positioned at the edge of the eaves.

Barn swallows swooped from these crevices, building nests in the rafters. They were excellent architects, collecting a variety of mud, twigs, and snarls of miscellaneous textured grasses. Two reed warblers flitted from fence post to fence post, chattering to each other in happy sing-song tones. Their array of beige and tan feathers allowed them to blend nearly completely into the pale grass beyond the fence, where Farmer Knappen was leaving his field fallow for the season. Unbeknownst to Carey—albeit very beknownst to Treu—two field mice were burrowing beneath the fence post in question, beginning to build a nest of grass and winter fur sheddings.

The dark trim of the Reinalz house appeared, settled just behind the pristine steeple of Saint Peter and Paul Kirche. Michael and Wolfgang Reinalz played in the yard, actively engaged in war strategy and hitting each other with sticks. Inge sat by, throwing mud into a form and packing it down. Beside her rested ten other such cakes, stabbed with an assortment of sticks and leaves.

She looked up when Carey approached, smiling brightly upon recognizing him.

"Mr. Alsch, sir!" She leapt to her feet, mud coating her hands and bare feet, spread across the front of her dress, and smudging her chin. "Would you like a cake?"

Wolfgang halted mid-swing, looking towards Carey. His ceasefire was not recognized by his opponent, and Miff slammed his stick into his elder brother's thigh. Wolfgang howled, then tackled his brother. They rolled in the grass and soon settled the disagreement, one enduring a bloody nose, the other, a smarting leg.

"Cake, Mr. Alsch?" said Inge again, picking up a half-formed mudpie.

"Don't eat it, Mr. Alsch!" cried Miff, "'Tis poisoned!" He wiped away a trickle of blood. Carey's eyes widened and he glanced back and forth between the children.

"Poison?" His eyebrows rose even higher, nearly hiding beneath his hat.

"How can you tell him that, Miff?" Inge cried. "The whole point of poison is secret. How am I supposed to destroy enemy forces if they know my secrets?"

"Mr. Alsch is not an enemy," argued Miff.

"He approaches our defenses." Inge crossed her muddy hands over her chest. "And the commander has not allowed such advances."

"Commander went inside," said Wolfie, frowning deeply. "Mutti has real cake."

"This is real cake." Inge, instantly offended, took hold of her crumbling mudpie. She threw it at her brother. He dodged and made great insult to her aim and the strength of her arm. She threw a second cake at him, which found its target in the small of his back. Claiming her victory, she declared him poisoned, and consequently dead, then went into the house.

"What do you have, Mr. Alsch?" asked Wolfie Reinalz, noting the package tucked beneath the man's arm.

"Honeycomb," said Carey. "Would ye like some?"

"Yes, please!" both the boys said loudly, crowding close to him. Squatting in the yard, Carey placed his case of honeycomb on his knee and withdrew a small pocketknife. He cut each boy a sliver of decadent comb.

"Careful," Carey whispered, "it may be poisoned."

"I can sense poison." Miff lifted his chin with pride.

"Cannot!" said Wolfie.

"Can!"

"Cannot. Prove it!" Wolfgang's argument was enough to inspire Miff's competitive spirit, and they argued about the nature of poison recognition all the way up the porch, into the house, and into the kitchen, towing Carey along behind them. Treu was left on the porch, now actively engaged in a game of tag round the outside of the house with several boisterous Reinalz children. His loud barking echoed throughout the neighborhood.

"Carey!" said Holt, rising from his seat in the kitchen. He approached the taller man, appearing rather jolly. Carey stood in the doorway, his entire person consumed in awkwardness and the feeling of unwelcome he always carried with him when going out into community. "Come in, come in, please. You are a hero in this house!"

Isola came rushing into the kitchen, baby Isolde held in a fabric swathe on her chest. She welcomed Carey into the home with even more enthusiasm and zeal than her husband, inviting him to sit and serving him cake before he could speak. Ada and Lieselotte entered the kitchen shortly after, their faces full of color and bearing soft smiles. Relief swept over Carey, seeing the girls in nearly robust health. They thanked him for his care and were each given a slice of cake and told to eat it on the porch with their other siblings, who had all been banished outside.

"I brought honeycomb for 'ee," said Carey between mouthfuls of plum cake. He set his gift on the table and pushed it towards Holt, who sat opposite him.

"Thank you, Carey," Holt said, shaking his head, "but we should be showering you with gifts, not the other way around. You saved our girls. Our family is whole because of you."

"'Twas nothin'." Carey dipped his head.

"'Twas everything!" Isola said loudly, with an emphatic declaration of her feelings.

"Carey." Holt leaned forward, resting his elbows on his knees, looking very serious and full of remorse. Anneliese pushed into the kitchen and demanded to be lifted to her father's knee, where she played with his beard and pulled his glasses from his face. "I have been wretched and dreadfully obtuse."

"No such—"

Holt raised an interrupting hand, requesting a full hearing of a speech that had been practiced before his wife the night before and found to just meet the full measure of his intention.

"That fool of a doctor has been sent away, and if another comes, I'll send him away, too. I should have rejected him the moment he spoke to you in such a way. He treated a friend and savior with the most vain and selfish behavior. You saved my daughters' lives." He took a deep breath. "Your actions were nothing short of miraculous, and my family is whole because of you. I'll never—never, I say—let anyone speak to you in such a way again."

"Speakin' is no matter," Carey said, pushing his plate away from the edge of the table and leaning his elbow against the smooth wood grain. Anneliese grew tired of the serious conversation and slid to the floor, wandering off to find an interesting sibling.

"It is a matter!" said Holt, leaning stoutly against the back of his chair. "It is a matter how people speak to you, Carey. You aren't deserving of diminishing words or hateful candor, and I stood by and let it happen. You, who are a part of this family, should be bulwarked by all that we are and believe in."

"I'm no Reinalz," Carey replied, looking at his friend, "but an Alsch."

Though he denied the invitation to familial belonging, some kind of mixture of hope and hopelessness swept over him. His chest threatened to cave in, and his arms became lifeless and limp, and he worried that he could not lift them from their resting place on the table.

"You are as much a Reinalz as I, as any living in this house!" Holt said, almost sternly and with a fatherly tone. "You've made our family whole, Carey. Please, allow me to apologize for not immediately defending you, and let me promise that you'll always be welcome here as a friend and as a brother."

"I've not—" Carey paused, hoping the brief interlude between his words might allow some feeling to return to his fingertips. "I've not had a brother."

"You have one," Holt said. "You're our family, Carey."

For the briefest, smallest moment, Carey was warmed internally and had no need for his hearth, nor of candle and flame.

Barn Swallow
Hirundo Rustica

27
The Albrights

A knock sounded on the kitchen door and a well-dressed figure pushed through without waiting for a response. Standing there in the doorway was a large man accompanied by a diminutive woman with spindly arms and ankles that looked like they might snap if she took another step. The man wore a round, brimmed cap of a more modern, city style. He grew his mustache thick and brushed downward like a comb. His brow was so heavy, and face so cushioned by a decadent way of living, that one could more imagine he had eyes than see them clearly.

"I say, Holt, what a fine day this is," the man said, his countenance jolly. "Mr. Alsch, too, the hero of the hour! What a man you are!" He came forward and clapped Carey on the shoulder rather firmly. Carey wanted nothing more than to diminish and be unseen in that moment.

"I'd not say this to just anyone, for I'm not a woman much for talking," the woman beside him said, speaking with a voice nearly as spindly and light as her frame. "But, Mr. Alsch, that was very well done. Very well done indeed. What a thing. To cure the Reinalz girls with nothing more than the plants of our very mountain forests. Why, I should write that in my memoirs. They shall want to read it one day, don't you think, dearest?"

"Of course!" said the husband, with full heart.

"Thank you for your kind words, Mr. and Mrs. Albright," Holt said, standing and dipping his head toward them. Carey arose with ungainly abruptness, turning his chair over backwards. He went about righting it, muttering under his breath all the while. The degree of his discomfort was evident, at finding himself seemingly cornered in a house that was not his own.

"I must say," said Mr. Albright, leaning against the doorframe, "I should like to purchase some of the tinctures I have heard so much of. It's the talk of the town. Mr. Alsch, you are a wonderman."

"Shan't be for purchase," said Carey in a hushed tone. "'Tis not right, being uneducated. Can't be claimin' to know things."

"Uneducated! By all God's graces and designs," said Mr. Albright, "you are rightly a genius, man! A genius! Why, they should know of your genius in München. The physicians' guild would be lucky to have you. Will you write to them, dearest?" the large man asked his small wife.

The man was rather loud. Isolde Reinalz began to cry, so her mother carried her swiftly from the room to find quieter company. Mrs. Albright hushed her husband with a kind demeanor. Mr. Reinalz cleared plates from the table, setting them on the wooden countertop, then served two pieces of cake to the new visitors. Mr. Albright accepted his readily, although his wife was more hesitant. She picked the plums out of the crust and only ate them, albeit with much relish.

"Please don't write." Carey raised both hands towards the couple, then immediately dropped them by his sides.

"Have pride, Mr. Alsch! It's not every day we have a miracle worked in our small town. Why, I think there's not been something of this miraculous nature since Dean Jhules married Anita Kabath."

"That was miraculous indeed, dearest," his wife agreed. "Two obstinate, hardheaded, stalwart-type people. Now, look, there are seven Jhules. Five healthy children of strong stock. What good that was."

"Well," Holt broke into the bright chatter of the jovial couple, "I think Mr. Alsch has to decide for himself what he'll do with his miraculous wonders. I am eternally grateful to the man and was just calling him my brother before you entered. I hope you'll treat him as my family."

"Mr. Reinalz, you never had to speak it, friend! Carey Alsch is a man among men! I never knew it before but for seeing him so briefly, with deliveries and the like. Never knew you had a fondness for knowing natural things, Mr. Alsch."

"Not a fondness, sir." Carey dipped his head. "Just a knowin'."

"Well, knowing is sometimes from fondness and sometimes a natural inclination," said Mr. Albright, "sometimes for vengeance and sometimes for practicality. I suppose you may choose which is your inclination, Mr. Alsch."

"Where is Miss Von Stein?" asked Mrs. Albright, peeking through the door into the hallway. "I'd not seen her these last two days."

Carey was suddenly attentive, listening for an answer to the question that had been on his own heart, although he had not been able to speak it. Her absence was chiefly known to him, and rather disappointing.

"She has returned to München for a few days," said Mr. Reinalz. "My uncle wrote to her, and she was needed home."

"Does she leave often?" Mrs. Albright leaned forward, though with her slight frame, she seemed like to tip over and fall.

"Perhaps once a month? For a few days," Holt said. "She comes back with gifts every time. Why, half the Christmas decorations we had in the square were from her!"

"Why does she go?"

"We're not entirely sure," Holt said, glancing at his wife. "She's very attached to her grandfather—my uncle—and I think his health is declining. She never stays long, though. Only a week, sometimes two."

"When will she return?" asked Mrs. Albright, with a pouting lip. "I miss her pretty face. What lovely eyes she has. I was just saying to Mr. Albright, how peculiar it is for her to be unmarried and nearing thirty. Why, not that I think she is any kind of old maid, mind you. But I should like to see her in the delightful throes of marital bliss."

"It's meant to only be a brief trip," Holt said. "Although, including travel days, I think it might be a bit longer than she intends."

Carey sat down.

"Are you all right, Mr. Alsch?" asked Mrs. Albright.

Isola returned at that moment, bearing with her a tearful child. "She will not relax, Holt," said his wife, handing him the wailing infant. He took Isolde against his chest, cooing to her in gentle tones.

"Mr. Alsch," said Mr. Albright with a shining eye, "one would think you are taking strongly the news of Miss Von Stein's absence. Has a pretty eye caught your attention?"

Isola shot the man a warning glance as she cleared the table. Mr. Albright saw the expression but did not interpret its exact meaning and so plunged onward. His wife, being of keener eye than her husband, tugged on the trim of his neat jacket.

"Why, she is your age, perhaps younger. Full of bright youth," Mr. Albright said, listing the absent woman's finer qualities. "Does she have a fondness for plants?"

"She does," Carey said quietly. Both pairs of married couples looked at each other over Carey's head, eyes wide with surprise and equal amounts of hope.

"How delightful," said Mrs. Albright, her intonation careful.

Another knock sounded at the door and a tall, stern man pushed through. At his side was a narrow woman with severe eyes. Her hair was pulled back so tightly that it permanently lifted her eyebrows, so she appeared to be in a continual state of surprise.

"Ah," said Holt, "Mr. and Mrs. Tilfen …"

"The children let us in," said Mrs. Tilfen in an abrupt way.

"Isola," Holt said, holding a sleeping baby against his chest. "Do we have any more cake?"

"I think so," Isola said, taking out more plates from the cupboard. She cut a piece of cake for each of the Tilfens, realizing there was a third person hidden behind the man. The son, Tobin Tilfen, appeared just as severe as his mother, although not nearly as rigidly styled. A starched collar encircling his neck required him to keep his chin lifted in an attitude of obligatory condescension.

"We have not come for cake," said Mr. Tilfen. "We came to inquire after your daughters' health. I see we were not alone in our cordiality."

Mr. and Mrs. Albright dipped their heads accordingly, giving one another the kind of glance a husband and wife who like one another very much share when they know they will have much to discuss as soon as guests are no longer within earshot.

"I must say," said Mr. Tilfen, "since we are all here, I have something to say." He looked at each person in the room, then finally at Carey, who still sat in his chair, looking rather like a sad dog. "My wife and I were discussing, prior to our visit, how deeply inappropriate this whole incident has been. Indecent, I daresay."

Barn Owl
Tyto alba

28

The Indecency of Man

"What?" said Holt, rather abruptly.

"Indecent, to be sure." Mr. Tilfen nodded curtly. "To have your own cousin stay in the house of an unmarried man for two days, with no chaperone, and there has been no discussion—as far as I am aware—as to how deeply improper the situation is."

"Improper—sir!" Mr. Albright sputtered, setting down his fork.

"I knew you would disagree, Jonas," said Mr. Tilfen, not looking at his portly neighbor. "I'd not asked for your opinion. It is between my family, Carey Alsch, and the Reinalzes, who hold a little bit of pride in this town. Have we all forgotten that Mr. Reinalz is practically the town judge and magistrate."

"I must disagree …" muttered Jonas Albright, somewhat calmed by a strategic placement of his wife's hand on his arm.

Mr. Tilfen turned to Holt Reinalz, his face a stone cast of disapproval. "It is most indecent to consider that any cousin of yours, being unmarried and raised as properly as Miss Von Stein, was allowed to behave in such a way. And the disreputable man himself is here, and with nothing to say. I consider the whole thing indecent, irreparably indecent."

"Indecent?" It was Isola Reinalz's turn to speak. She had been quietly cutting cake in the corner, and with each word said by the newcomer, her grip on the handle of the knife grew firmer, and each slice more deliberate. She turned slowly and repeated scornfully: "Indecent?"

"I say." Mrs. Tilfen nodded, defending her husband's words in a room filled with silent tension.

"How dare you come into my home and speak in such a way," said Isola. "How dare you speak to a member of my family thusly? A man who has saved the lives of two of my children—I am beyond words, Hilde." The room temperature seemed to drop a degree or two colder from the mere impact of her tone.

"He is only speaking what's right, Isola, and you know it." Hilde Tilfen lifted her stiff chin. "You, a respectable, married woman, should know. And with your husband bearing the position he does! It is most imperative that your entire family behave above reproach. In fact, I am appalled you allowed him to take your daughters to his home."

"Get out," said Isola, wielding her knife without realizing how threatening the posture appeared. She had entirely forgotten she still held it in a white-knuckled grip.

"Dearest," said Holt, taking the knife from her and laying it on the counter. She blushed but continued her advance, stopping before the Tilfens with all the bearing of a warrior of old, lacking only shining armor and sword.

"I can't bear to think you are allowing your name to be so defiled by bringing that man into your house," said Mr. Tilfen, pointing to Carey as if he were not in the room. Carey Alsch did not look up. Instead, he studied the shape of his shoes. "You know what happened to his mother. His father? You know of the sins borne in that house."

"I only know of a defiled name coming from an ugly heart and unforgiving nature," said Isola. "Your collar is starched, and your dress ironed, Hilde, but your soul has wrinkles."

"Carey Alsch is a disreputable man! and Nonny Von Stein is defiled by association. Who knows what transpired in that place? And to allow your sick children to be thrown into the midst of this unsavory situation? Why, Isola, I would think you had fallen too."

"This man is my friend and like a brother to my husband," said Isola.

"He is my family. If you speak against him, you speak against me. If he is disreputable, then my family is as well, and I would more gladly be known as fallen from your favor than fallen from his."

"Do not insult my wife!" interjected Mr. Tilfen.

"Don't insult mine, then," said Holt, placing a hand on Isola's shoulder. "Anything my wife has said should be considered as repeated by me with full heart."

"That man is poison to this community!" Mrs. Tilfen nearly shook with rage. "His family is the name of doom, and his medicine is more than a curse. Be wary, and do not expect to be invited to my home, any of you," said the woman, with venom heavy on her tongue. "It is not a place where fallen people may gather. Isola, consider your invitation to my weekly luncheon revoked!"

"I never liked your cooking anyway, Hilde," Isola retorted. "Too much salt."

Hilde took great offense to this and stalked from the room. Her husband was shortly to follow, equally stiff and vehement as his wife. Tobin glanced around the room, unable to turn his head due to the rigidity of his collar. He grimaced once, then joined his parents.

A long silence filled the kitchen, interrupted by the slamming front door.

Carey put his hand on the table and slowly rose. "I'll be going then," he said quietly.

"Sit back down!" said Isola, taking a deep breath. He sat twice as quickly.

"Don't take to heart what those creatures said," Mrs. Albright crooned, looking steadily at Carey. "They are not kin of mine in blood or affection. Any of us here know how good you are. And how you are most noble. That 'respectability' nonsense is not any kind of belief my husband and I adhere to."

"Nonsense, nonsense is all that couple had to say," Jonas said. "I am ashamed to call Mr. Tilfen my neighbor, Carey Alsch. There's nothing in his head but vile self-righteousness impressed upon him by that woman. Practically a pharisee, I say."

"There's no reason to pay heed to anything they have to say, Carey," Holt added. "Their sentiments are not shared by any in this town. We only hope you can forgive us for having to endure hearing such words."

"What's been said that's not true?" said Carey glumly. "'Tis not a thing that's unknown, how my family was. Testament to how things are not forgot, though time passes. I'd not thought to be familiar with ye; sorry for any trouble I caused."

"Carey Alsch," said Mr. Albright with a firmness of spirit that filled the room, "you have nothing to apologize for. Hold your head up high and be made of sterner stuff!"

"I'm not filled with the same spirit as ye, Mr. Albright," Carey would not lift his gaze from the worn edge of his boots. "I hear and take account of what that man said, and I hear ye. I'd not want to do any like thing to hurt Miss Nonny's reputation. Even if ye say to continue my way, I can't for her sake."

"If Nonny were here," said Isola, posting her fists on her hips, "she would find keen fault with your words. Stop that, and listen well. You will not listen to the Tilfens, and you will hold your head up high in this town. You have worked wonders, and we are indebted to you."

"I'll stand by you, miracle-man," said Mr. Albright. "An' if anyone thinks less of you, then I will think nothing of them."

29

Spring's Full Measure

Nonny was gone longer than anticipated, and by the end of the third week, those not related to Holt Reinalz and company began to say she might not return. Birdsong carried through the hills, and Carey suspected that the returning boreal owl had made her roost nearby, noted by the echoing of her calls throughout the twilight hours.

In daylight, Carey collected specimens of angelica, thistle buds and stalks of varying size, and had uncovered, beneath the foot of the old owl-roost, a collection of dead mouse bones. He organized all his findings in wooden trays constructed from the logs harvested on the logging road. By the end of the third week, the shelves were stacked high by the door. Treu inspected them routinely, drawn by the lingering scent of owl pellets.

These three weeks, Carey oft walked to the end of his road, standing on the high point that overlooked Mittenwald. Townsfolk were very active these days. All indoor mending had been done during cold winter days and needed little attention throughout summer and spring, so most people were out of doors, doing out-of-door mending. Fenceposts were festooned with nails and binding, rugs were beaten in the yards, horses shod, cattle whacked along the little roads, trimming field after field to bare roots. April showers lingered in the skies, painting a renaissance scene of overwhelming thunderheads looming over little people afield. Eastward, a bright spring sun pierced the clouds, barely touching the full green show in the land below.

"Well," said Carey, dropping beside his hound, "seems like she won't return. Seems like 'tis just you an' me. Seems like 'nother season, 'nother day, 'nother year. Times for tradin' leather draw near; Holt said Knappen will go to slaughter soon. Tomorrow, most like. We need tenfold hide."

Treu made a gruff response.

"I hadn't thought she'd stay forever," he mused, ruffling his dog's soft ears. "But she'd 'spected to come see the critters and learn ere names of the woods 'n' like. Shame, ye find it?"

The hound looked at his master with eyes of melting sunlight. He whimpered.

"'Tis not for grand things I'd planned." Carey shook his head. "Not that I 'spected any other thing to happen. 'Tis the way with us, Treu. None stay for long. They like to be going from our lives. I should n'er have even thought it'd be different." He sighed. "But I knew she liked quark 'n' compote. Wholly gathered to only teach her how to tell the difference between the lace and the lark. One's deadly, like poison, see."

Treu stretched out, settling his head on his master's thigh, looking up at him with great big eyes.

"I'd not make a poison, Treu," said Carey. "I'd not do that. There's plenty afield to make such a thing, but it's not in my heart." (This was the first time he had spoken of things in his heart, and the hound was quite taken aback.) Carey was quiet a while, watching the busy happenings in the fields and yards below. A bright serin flitted to a branch nearby. It turned its eye towards him, inspecting him thoroughly. The yellow finch seemed to find nothing offensive in his person and remained on his perch until he spotted a large grasshopper farther down the meadow.

"'Tis not that I feel she has any holdin' her 'ere." Carey's head hung heavy from his shoulders. "Only, I had liked to show her the owl's new roost. She's taken up in the dead pine near that place I always say the Waldleute hide. I saw 'er when you slept last mornin', when yer hip was botherin' ye."

Carey had not fully considered how keenly he would feel Nonny Von

Stein's absence. He attributed her disappearance to this being the mode of all people in his life and did not expect anything more. He had already numbered the days Holt Reinalz and his clan would continue to find him in their favor, and the Albrights were a simple matter to dismiss. Clearly, that man had little discernment for good goings-on and bad, though his wife was certainly shrewder. No, he thought, it would not be long until he was fully alone again.

Nonny was no different, though she spoke kindly, and with bright smiles. There was certainly something cursing the word friend in life. He knew not to hold anything tightly. It was as Mr. Tilfen said; the nature of his mother's unseemly death and his father's infamy were full enough reason for any member of good society to stay away.

There was not, however, a dark shadow enshrouding Carey's person at this moment. That gloomy spirit that usually clung to his shoulders and pulled his eyes to the ground had been flung off, and though he felt his usual sadness, it was not that weighty grief. He was sad to think how things would end; he was sad at the absence of Nonny; he was sad to think he had almost found even a taste of goodness.

Though his friends had spoken in his favor, he did not like to make himself known in a town where some did not wish him to be known. Holt had come by the little cottage every few days, inquiring after Carey's health and offering him the weekly schedule of Mittenwald happenings. They smoked cigars on the porch and drank schnapps, but Carey would not venture down to Mittenwald. Holt was ever disappointed, telling Carey how his wife would berate him for his continued absence.

"D'ye think we have to go tomorrow?" Carey sighed, petting Treu's velvety head. "I'm sure hide'll be for purchase. Got to deliver bridles and the like." Lying there for some time, he watched the sweeping formations of clouds buckle and break over the distant ridgeline of mountains. Misty lines drifted below the dark line, showing how those slopes were being drenched in rain.

When the clouds finally wandered closer, he took his hat and whistled for Treu to follow him up the trail. Rain fell gently over his shoulder, soaking a dark stain in his shirt. Spotted deer fled from the main path, alerted by his footsteps. Leaves shivered, each touched by a single droplet, as if the sky had organized an orchestra with the land, and the rain played the tune. Carey took up the natural sounds, adding them to his own devised whistling song. It was a far merrier tone than he usually produced and seemed to add color to the darkening woods around.

This color was not borne by him for long. Each step seemed to bear upon his shoulders a heavier weight, so that by the time he arrived at the threshold of his home, his song was gloomy, and his head hung low. He threw his cap aside, finding each corner of his home dark and damp. Lighting a fire, he stared at the chair by the hearth and felt a strange array of feeling, despondence being the chief sentiment.

Bordering the edges of his darker feelings was a lighter and brighter sense of life. There was not enough of such life-feeling, however, to keep him from sinking into the chair by the hearth and lighting up his corn pipe. As was his regular habit, he did not move for several hours, and appeared like one dead asleep, though his eyes were wide and would not be torn away from the dancing flame.

30
Done Waiting

The day for Farmer Knappen's slaughtering came with a heavy rain. Night was booming thunder and torrential deluge, driving all creatures great and small into some form of shelter. Wind tore, ripping limbs from trees. The zephyr battered against sturdy walls and tightly fastened shutters, though it had no power over the deep roots of trees and well-driven nails.

When dawn broke, so broke the inundation. Heavy clouds split and revealed an early-morning sun. The daylight was soft, seeming to dapple the ground and catch like diamonds on the misty droplets clinging to the swathe of green growing along the road to Mittenwald. The grass shone like peridot and tourmaline. A burst of light encapsulated in each droplet the full measure of a radiant gemstone.

Treu kept close to his master's knees, moving with the stiff posture that had settled over him since winter's full departure. His bones were old and his muscles leaden. Carey made slow progress, allowing the hound time to warm his muscles.

Dawn supplied the remedy to the night's driving storm. Birds of meadow, field, and deep wood were out in melodious cacophony. Though their songs followed diverse forms and structures, there was harmony to each note. A lark there sung of the lovely morning, a vireo here searched for a mate; over the hill, a jackdaw was being chased by the little marsh tit, who was full of adamant rage toward the larger bird invading its territory. In the branches overhead, a whitethroat sang lustily his practiced tune, halting only when Carey passed beneath his perch. He took up the song again once the stranger had become a distant outline.

Carey crossed the Isar River bridge while keeping his head down and his hands in his pockets. His wide-brimmed hat was pulled low over his eyes, partially to keep off morning sun, and partially to hide his face from eyes in town.

Mr. and Mrs. Tilfen's words still rang heavy in his mind, playing round the spool of thought like thread on a loom, with more weight and oppression with each repetition. Words spun endlessly in a lonely mind have a tendency to warp and take on an enduring, sepulchral tone that does not match their initial intonation. In Carey's mind, uplifting words did not linger, as he never saw any truth in them to begin with.

"'Tis just for buying cowhide 'n' like," Carey said to Treu. "Not for more, 'specially not for chatter. I'd not run into that man again. You'd not know the power of words, being a dog. Weighs on ye like."

His plans to not remain in town long were easily thwarted, owing to his heart blooming like spring; his heart seemed eager to overcome the unwelcome spirit he always carried. His footsteps carried him to the porch of a pretty house with dark beams and white paneling. Looking up from beneath the wide brim of his hat, he stopped short.

Nonny Von Stein sat in a rocking chair on the porch of the Reinalz home, chin leaned against her palm, elbow resting on the arm of the well-made chair. She stared east, watching the sun break between clouds and slowly warm the sodden earth.

"Miss Nonny?" said Carey slowly, taking off his hat. She turned to look at him, a tired, worn expression painted on her face.

"Carey?" She leaned forward, dropping both hands into her lap. With a pale hand, she pulled her shawl tightly around her shoulders, covering her bare arms. She wore a long nightgown with fluttering sleeves capped around her upper arms, dark hair tumbling over her shoulders in a wild, untamed brace.

"Thought ye'd be gone," he said. Treu raced up the stairs, flopping his great, big head upon her lap. She smiled and ruffled his ears, stroking the velvet fur between them.

"I only returned yesterday," she said, her voice strung with fatigue. "You are here early."

"'Tis an early day." Carey shrugged. "I've got work to do in town that's firstly."

"Oh," she said, settling back against the chair.

"Are ye all right? Ye seem—"

"I'm fine," she said quickly, then sighed. "I am only a little tired from my trip."

"Treu missed ye," Carey said, gesturing to the hound, who was practically melting into a puddle in her lap.

"I missed him," she said, looking so steadily at Carey that he felt he could no longer stand upright. He caught himself on the railing, looking up at her. "I am sorry I was gone so long, I had not—it was a thing—there was more to do than I thought."

"I know," he said. "But ye are back now. 'Tis all still here."

"It is." She smiled. "Carey, I heard about the Tilfens—"

"No matter." He traced a thumb along the edge of his hat.

"It is a matter, Carey." She scooted to the edge of her seat. "It is a matter. I wish you would make it a matter."

"Why should I fuss?" he said. "What good'll it be?"

"Not fuss," she said. "But you are a worthy man, not like some people paint."

"'Tisn't something I press over," Carey lied. She was quiet, watching him with a peculiar expression. He could not place the meaning behind it, but when she looked at him in such a way, it struck through him a weakening feeling, and he needed the rail for support.

"May I still come learn from you?" Her voice was quiet, almost a whisper in the morning sun.

"Ye may come anytime ye like," Carey said. "Treu'd be most happy to see ye come by."

"I shall."

"I've got to get on," said Carey, turning away from the porch.

"Where are you going?"

"Knappen's farm," he said. "Today is slaughterin' and butcherin' for half his herd. I come to help, an' he gives me a discount on hide for my leatherworkin'."

"Oh." She paused, leaning back and looking again at the morning sunlight drifting through the misty yard. "May I come with you?"

"Ye'd not like it," he said. "An' I'd not want to bother ye with all the death."

"I'm not scared of death," she said. "I'd like to come. Will you wait for me?"

"I'd always do that," he said quietly and without thinking.

"What?" She looked at him with a scrunched brow, unable to hear him. His head was hung low, words barely above a whisper.

"I'm good for waiting for 'ee," he said emphatically. "I'll be here." He turned his back to the white trim of the porch and faced the sunrise. The morning lark sang a tumultuous, lovely song, one of mirth. When Nonny's footsteps receded and the door closed softly, Carey released a sharp breath and leaned steadily upon the railing.

31

To Slaughtering

A rooster crowed, alerting any nearby creature that the sun had fully risen. His ki-keri-ki was a fanfare cutting through the loud voices of the cows on the field. Cut-grass fluttered along the edges of the lane, pressed against low stone walls. These walls were among the oldest structures in Mittenwald, being of stouter material than any wooden fence in town. Farmer Knappen's fields were surrounded with long stretches of such a low stone fence, built by his father's father. Many of the stones came from the Isar and were now cracked and worn with time.

"Why is Treu limping?" Nonny asked, wrapping a blue shawl around her shoulders. She had changed into a ruddy-colored dress of sturdy stock, designed for labor and outdoor work. It buttoned at her neck and was cuffed at each wrist, with loose sleeves and a pinafore apron.

"He's old," said Carey. "His bones're stiff."

"How old is he?"

Carey paused, slowing to allow Nonny to catch up with his long strides. "Not sure. I had him before—well," he stopped before answering fully, "I had him a long time."

"Would you ever tell me about your life, Carey?" She tucked her arms across her chest, hiding her hands beneath the cover of the shawl.

"'Tis not much of an interest." He shrugged. "Mother's dead, father's gone."

"How did you learn leatherworking?"

"Father taught me," Carey said, rubbing his forearm. His long shirtsleeve hid an array of crisscrossed scars where his father had struck the lash in an attempt to better teach Carey his trade. Or so was his reasoning for such wrath.

"And when did you begin to study the natural world?"

"Can't recall," he said, tucking his hands into his pockets. "Been a long time since."

"I think you should write a book," said she, "detailing all of your knowledge of the woods."

"I learned it from books," he said with a laugh. "Can't claim it as mine if'n I learned it somewheres from someone."

"But your knowledge is tenfold what is found in books!"

"I can't write for others to read." He looked at her, tugging his hat low over his ears.

"What do you mean?"

"My pen is wild." He grinned. There was a delight in his face and mirth in his words so unlike his usual downtrodden attitude. He did not seem to mind talking to Nonny Von Stein as much as he minded talking to anyone else.

"Wild?"

"I'd not learned any proper form," he said. "My letters is squirreled and backwards. I can read it, but I'd think ye can't."

"I could try and translate," she said, laughing as well. "Let me look at it and decide for myself. May I come for my first lesson this week?"

"'Course," he said. "On a day that has no rain, otherwise we'll be soaked for wanderin'."

"The next morning with no stormclouds." She pulled her shawl tighter around her shoulders against a buffet of blustering wind. "I'll be there."

"I'll make ye cheese and jam," he said.

"A perfect day, then." Their eyes met, then broke apart, for a warm feeling was flushing each face.

The top eave of Knappen's farmhouse peeked over the tall strands

144

of Lolium fluttering in the wind. A sycamore hung over the house. Its white-mottled bark had not yet begun peeling for summer, having only just experienced the first warm gusts of spring.

A broad-winged lammergeier circled overhead, searching for discarded bones in the paddocks below. Coming close to the house, two ridgeback hounds raced from the front door, barking at the visitors. Treu pounced protectively before Carey, hackles raised, until the two approaching dogs announced themselves to be friends. The three dogs quickly disappeared round the back of the house, where Farmer Knappen and his large group of temporary farmhands worked in the mud.

"Ho, Alsch!" yelled Farmer Knappen, standing and waving at the approaching man. Knappen was a tall young man, energetic in manner, with long, blond hair usually tied back with a leather band. He had a wife, Eliza, and three children—two sons and a daughter—who were all afield today, helping with miscellaneous tasks. The sons helped their father, pinning the cattle with large ropes, then exsanguinating them with a deftly placed laceration to the neck. Knappen's daughter, Ulke, collected cuttings of fat in a bucket and helped her mother rinse intestines in a large barrel at the back of the house.

"Ho, Knappen," said Carey, in much softer a tone than the boisterous farmer's.

"We were about to clear this one. I've got quite a store for ye!" Knappen held a large knife, meant for slitting and skinning cowhide away from the skin. The butcher, Fritz Wistom, stood beside the farmer, his leather apron smeared with blood and viscera.

"Miss Von Stein," shouted Wistom, who was young and quite unmarried. He looked long enough at Nonny to rouse some small amount of enmity within Carey. It was well-known that the butcher was in search of a wife. Even one as hermitic as Carey Alsch knew of the butcher's matrimonial ambitions. "You are looking very lovely this morning!" the butcher continued while Carey eyed him not a little suspiciously.

"Thank you," she called back.

"Ye always look lovely," Carey grumbled while they were still out of earshot.

Nonny looked sharply at him, her face abloom with red color. Carey's eyes widened and just barely met hers. He abruptly looked away and stalked to Knappen's side, heavy boots squelching in the mud.

Nonny stared after him until her attention was diverted by the butcher, who approached her, wiping his blood-stained hands on his already stained apron.

"What brings you here, Miss Nonny?" asked Fritz with keen attention. "I'd not seen you in town these few weeks."

"I was required in München by my grandfather," she said quickly, watching Carey strip off his outer coat and toss it over one of the wooden fenceposts. He set his hat atop it and worked his way through the paddock to the main area chosen for the slaughter.

"I should like to go to München," said the butcher, "in fact … there was owed to my father a place in that city, though he was swindled by his business partner. By right, I should have been a wealthy butcher in München. 'Tis sad," he sighed, "I should have loved to give my wife a kingdom, whomever she may be." He looked steadily at her as he said the last line.

"I'm sorry?" Nonny said, dragging her attention back to the butcher.

"It so happened …" the butcher continued his story, paying little heed to Nonny's distraction, thinking her mere presence at the farm was owing to his fine skill with a knife and cleaver.

Over by the cattle-culling, Knappen welcomed the humble leather-worker. "Glad ye came, Carey," he said, forgoing a handshake due to his bloodstained hands. "Yer help is always welcome."

"'Tis a rainy day for slaughter," said Carey.

"'Tis a rainy day every day this month." Farmer Knappen shrugged. "Can't be choosey-like."

Carey nodded, taking measure of what work had been done and what was still needed. He took a skinning knife and began cutting away layers of fat and fascia, releasing the thick hide from the meat of the dead cow.

"How goes the season?" Knappen asked, looping a rope around his forearm. "The woods in full sway? I heard what you did for the Reinalz girls. Always knew that field work ye do would matter for some wonder. I'd not known anyone to understand the bugs, slugs, and trees as ye have a knowledge for 'em."

"Not as grand a wonder as ye think," said Carey. "I'd give credit to the power of my tinctures. Ye know Eliza found use of the raspberry leaf, but I'd not thought there'd be contention."

"Tilfen?" Knappen asked with a deep sigh. "A small-minded man, he is, Carey. Don't mind his words. I heard what he was sayin' to 'ee. It bain't the truth, not for you or for Miss Nonny. Everyone knows the character ye have. I'd not give hem 'n' haw to anything he speaks on. Small-minded man, to be sure."

"I'd not care, but for her," said Carey. "She'd not get drawn into any mess, if not for me."

"There's no mess!" Knappen was adamant. "There is no mess to speak of, Carey. I swear it."

"I can't say I hear truth." Carey did not look up. "But I'll try and believe 'ee."

"'Tis an amiable lady you've brought with ye to a butcher field," Farmer Knappen said, changing the subject and hiding a grin beneath his full beard.

"She'd not hear my swayings," said Carey, glad to move on to brighter topics. "I told her 'twas a pretty mess. She'd not listen, said she wanted to."

"Came she for the slaughter? Or for another reason?"

"What other reason'd there be?" Carey looked closely at the farmer, who was another of the few people whose conversation he enjoyed, though they seldom were brought together but for trading leather and wheat.

"Certainly not Fritz Wistom," said the farmer, with full mirth. He dipped his head toward the sturdy butcher, who stood with his hands on his hips, engaging Nonny in an evidently one-sided conversation. She leaned past the man, meeting Carey's eyes across the way. There was something of humor in her look, and a plea for rescue from endless self-aggrandization.

"She'd not look at me but for conversation," said Carey.

"She's lookin' at ye right now, friend," the farmer whispered. "Thinks me, ye should rescue her. Be mighty fine, like Siegfried, Fritz bein' the dragon."

Carey stood straight, holding tight to an edge of cowhide to stretch it, allowing one of Farmer Knappen's farmhands to slide a skinning knife along the deep edge. The hide came away neatly. Still watching Nonny, he stacked the hide with the others, organizing them by thickness and quality of skinning.

"Wistom," called Carey, with sharper quality and more emphasis than his words usually possessed. "I'd need your help; this here's got an odd withers, can't skein my knife along its edge."

The butcher was ever happy to see that others required his help and thought it might improve his appearance in Nonny Von Stein's estimation. He excused himself from her presence after much description of his life's dreams and the execution of said dreams.

32

The Butcher

Farmer Knappen's wife—a strong, well-made woman with a straight back and calloused hands—found a means of additional rescue for Nonny. Eliza Knappen dumped a bucket of fat into a pot set over a flame at the side of the house, enough away from the paddock to keep the intermingling smells at bay. The fat boiled in the bottom of the pot, rendering down to oil while occasionally stirred by the farmer's wife.

Nonny helped Ulke gather fat, separating out the layers of fascia with a small knife. Ulke claimed one of the cows' stomachs, setting it aside and commanding her mother to leave it alone. The others were washed and cleaned like the intestines. They were kept for sausage-making.

Five cows had been slaughtered thus far. Only three more were set to be gutted and cleaned by the end of the day, and two for the morrow. The next day was for preparing the meat with salt and making sausage. The sausage would be hung in the curing house behind Wistom's shop in town, and there it would be portioned between Knappen's family and his customers in town.

Carey worked to his elbows in viscera and hide, though he was oft distracted by the pretty lady coming to him periodically with a bucket to collect the scraps of fat cut away from the hide. Her smiles were far richer in sustenance to him than any food, and when they broke from work to sup, he claimed a seat beside her on the log in the yard.

Eliza served potatoes and cabbage, along with several trimmings of beef, drenched with salty fat. The air was filled with the scent of viscera, rendered fat, and succulent steaks.

"D'ye feel all right, Miss Nonny?" Carey asked, offering her a plate of steaming food. "Ye aren't overworked by the labor? Eliza bain't one to ease up on the load."

"I am enjoying myself, Carey," she said, holding the plate on her knees. "I hadn't realized how much work was shared here. It's not like this in the city."

"'Tis only for a season," Carey said, "an' soon this'll be done. Then off to help Farmer Welch with the same. Though he's not near as good a man as Knappen, in my estimation."

"Then I shall think the same," Nonny said. "Your estimation is a good estimation. The best, I think."

"'Tis not so." Carey laughed. "Wonder why ye think highly of me."

"Holt Reinalz calls you a miracle-worker," Nonny said quietly. "Isola calls you an honest man. I respect their opinions, as they are some of the greatest, most loving people I know. I never heard them tell a lie. And … I call you my friend."

"'Tis an honor to be friends with ye, Nonny," he said very seriously.

Fritz Wistom approached, looking for a seat. He placed himself between the two and began to weave a story about how his father sold meat to none other than King Maximilian I, and was thanked in court for such fine slicing and cutting as was found served to the king.

Nonny leaned back, looking at Carey over the butcher's shoulders. Carey followed suit, finding a look of amusement scrawled over her face. He grimaced, biting back any expression of humor. His look drew from her a quiet laugh. He considered that to be the finest sound known to man.

Finishing their meal whilst listening to the orations of the butcher, the entire group quickly returned to the work at hand. Schaften, the cattledriver, loudly announced that he had better things to do than hear 'hark 'n' haw of a small-town butcher,' and set to his work with more vigor than the rest.

Though he sliced evenly with the skinning knife, Carey was not entirely attentive to his work. He oft looked up, seeing how Nonny got along, whether she was overworked, happy, or seemed in need of respite. He was so captivated by this audience that he did not notice how the brisket curved sharply, and so the skinning knife caught deep in his hand.

He stood upright, dropping the knife and grabbing his bleeding hand.

"Ye fare cut yourself, Carey?" Knappen asked, holding tightly to a rope wrapped round the thick neck of a cow not yet slaughtered.

"Not but a scratch." Carey grimaced, staunching the flow of blood against his abdomen. He excused himself to the well and iron pump at the side of the house, where the ladies were washing intestine.

"Oh, Carey!" said Nonny, jumping to her feet. She rushed to his side and demanded to see his hand. He shied away, embarrassment being his penultimate emotion, second only to his annoyance at his carelessness. Nonny was adamant, posting her hands on her hips when he turned away.

Eliza Knappen called Ulke into the house on the notion that they would find bandages for Carey. When they were gone, he turned his back to Nonny, refusing to face her.

"Let me see your hand, Carey Alsch!" she said.

He turned abruptly, looking at his feet and holding his hand out to her. She took it without complaint. Commanding him to crouch beside the well, she pumped it and flushed the wound thoroughly. Her touch was gentle. Between her brows was a scrunched, concerned look that was mirrored in her eyes. She was keenly attentive to his injury and did not notice how he studied her face.

Her hands were soft against his skin, seeming to slowly draw along the portion where he had not been cut. She took extra time to clean his wound, he thought, and he felt strongly that he did not mind. Nonny could take all the time in the world.

Carey Alsch had never looked more intently at anything in his life than he did now. The face he regarded produced in him a strong feeling that he could not name.

He found he liked her a great deal; the mien of her face; every curve and line it possessed; the dimple in each cheek, revealed when she laughed; features arrayed in such a way that he could not draw his gaze to anything else, lest it be found plain and simple by comparison.

The feeling tugging in his chest—he thought it akin to admiration—was a sort of thing he could not comprehend, as love was not a word present in his vernacular. There had been nothing like a pure love showed to him at any point in his life. He had a name for sorrow, a name for gloom, and a name for his own despondence, but did not have a name for love.

33

Lingering

By the end of slaughtering, Farmer Knappen and Farmer Welch declared there was to be a feast to celebrate with those who helped. When all was finished at Farmer Knappen's paddock, everyone moved to Farmer Welch's over-green meadows, where a smaller herd of cows were to be cut and processed. Nonny came to help here as well and was oft followed about by Fritz Wistom. He sought constantly to be by her side, bringing small gifts in the early mornings and offering to walk her home in the evenings, as their paths only diverged at the very end. His suit was well-known and a topic for discussion in Mittenwald.

With a longer walk up the hill and more to his mountain cottage, Carey had no excuse to accompany Nonny home, and no gumption to be so obviously going out of his way for her. There was a chasm to cross to reach her. Carey hated crossing chasms. After two weeks of roping, butchering, and sausage-making, a brief respite from work was welcome to all.

Concerning the feast, there would be brisket, dancing, and the famous raspberry cordial prepared by the petulant Elise Kinderkopf. There would also be mead, of course, but it was less desired than the cordial, due to the hazy nature of the drink resulting from Mr. Basch's poor attempts at sieving. No improvement had been made from year to year, so it was expected to be just as cloudy as the year prior.

Although not everyone in town had provided hands for slaughtering, the feast was to be shared with all regardless—though it was assumed that some would not be in attendance. This was made clear by Mr. and Mrs. Tilfen's statement in seemingly casual conference, that if a certain wild medicine man and an unmarried newcomer were present, they would not make an appearance. This, they claimed, was due to not wanting to appear stained by two people who had so little care for matters of propriety. Nonny Von Stein's three-week absence directly after the incident further supported their decision. According to the Tilfens, as repeated by Eliza Knappen to her husband in avid frustration, being in the presence of such people was directly affecting the reputation and thus the outward look of the town. The result being a town in shambles and the devastation of a community. According to Mr. and Mrs. Tilfen, that is.

There was little to be remarked upon in town other than Nonny's return from München. Mr. Tilfen made known his disapproval, and neither Isola nor Nonny were invited to the Tilfens' house. There were few women in town, however, who had any desire to spend time in Mrs. Tilfen's company in consideration of recent events. The presence of a hypocritically vain tongue seems to divide people into three groups: those who wish to be seen as above reproach; those who tell them they are; and those who do not care.

The first group are those who cannot decide for themselves whether they are good; they must have someone else tell them that they are. The second group does the telling, somehow being imbued with an innate societal righteousness to which all others are subject. The last group has decided that constant vying for the appearance of righteousness is not so real and true as genuine goodness found in the face of humility and gentleness. They typically seem to bleed sweet blood, not bitter poisons like resentment, pride, and vain purity. There is something about not minding the business of others that creates a peaceful, good heart.

Carey minded the stinging words, not because he was vain or imbued with pride, but because he was so internally unstable as to not know when he was good and when he was not. He thought his own goodness was a curse, and his darkness an even darker stain. So, he thought there was not anything good about himself.

He now stood on the cusp of joining the festivities, at a place bordering the road just past the Isar Bridge, hands tucked into his pockets, wide-brimmed hat pulled low to hide his eyes. Treu stood by his side, ears turned keenly toward the sounds coming from up the road.

"But if I go," Carey said with the deepest of sighs, "then the Tilfens, and the Hauscrafts, and mayhaps even the Olstens won't be able to go. But if I don't go, Nonny'll be left alone with the butcher, and 'ee'd make his love known, sure as rain." He slapped his thigh. "But I already am known as a pariah, with mother and father behind me. 'Tis not different. And the Tilfens are so stiff, I'd not think they'd know how to be festive. Her face couldn't smile, Treu." He grimaced. Mrs. Tilfen had entirely forgotten to enjoy her life.

Treu was silent but listened as loyally as any hound devoted to his master.

"I'd not know how to be festive either," Carey mused, "'Tis not for bright colors, nor for sweets, nor for a piece of brisket, but for Nonny. 'Tis all for Nonny." He stepped forward, following the path down to the center of town, where at Christmas the tree had been raised, and now in spring was decorated with a long table and poles set with ribbons and flowers.

"Mr. Alsch!" Miff Reinalz cried out, running towards the man with reckless abandon. "D'ye know how to make a bowstring? The wax on mine's plum run off and I can't fix it."

"I'd give ye beeswax if ye wanted," Carey said. "Got plenty of it."

"Please!" said Miff whilst jumping up and down.

"Next time I come down," Carey said, "I'll be sure to bring it."

"When will that be?"

"'Tisn't something I plan," he said.

"Can you plan it now? I need it before the squirrel hunt tomorrow. Mr. Knappen is takin' us squirreling. We're learning traps and all!"

"Well," Carey said, "I suppose I can come by in the mornin'."

"Mother'll make ye victuals if you come by! We have porridge and strawberries with fresh milk in spring."

"I'll come by," said Carey.

"Can I play with Treu?" Miff asked, resting a hand on the hound's silken back.

"His bones are stiff," said Carey, nodding. "Mind ye play gentle with him, he's not young."

"I will!" Miff called the dog to his side and ran off to find his siblings beneath an old sycamore. The bark had only just begun to differentiate, preparing to peel when summer came.

Bright, cheery music rang out across the park, and a circle of bodies moved in patterns, taking up a dance. Carey stood aside, studying the faces intermixed in the gatherings. He saw one with blond hair and fair skin, another with dark, heavy eyebrows, another with a laughing face, several more with varying shades of honey hair; but did not see the fair face he searched for.

Carefully walking closer, he crossed his arms over his chest, attempting to look relaxed. He did not.

"Do you know dancing, Mr. Alsch?" said a familiar voice. He turned to see Mrs. Reimenschnell approaching to his left. He nodded to her, touching his hat respectfully.

"I'd not try," he said, shaking his head.

"How's it been, up there?" She gestured back the way he'd come, towards the upper reaches of the mountains behind them.

"Fair," he said gruffly.

"You're in town more these days," she said. "I saw you with that girl, not just for slaughtering. 'Tis a shame." She shook her head.

"Shame?" he looked over at her nervously.

"Why, she'd marry that butcher, of course. I thought it'd be you, but he's got to it quicker. Shame, Mr. Alsch, real shame."

"Marry …"

"Aye," she said, nodding. "I'd got it from my husband, who got it from the butcher himself—we are neighbors after all—and he said he'd only just proposed before the fair, to announce it on such a joyous day."

"But she—" He bit his tongue and clamped his mouth shut.

"She's what?" Mrs. Reimenschnell leaned forward. "That business with the Reinalz girls was messy. I think she'd want to clear her name speedy-like, don't you?"

"Business," Carey grumbled, "was no business. 'Twas only for goodness's sake, and I'd not—never mind." He shook his head, claimed again by the unwelcome spirit that followed him. He had almost abandoned it, but at the mention of the butcher's proposal, it swept over him once more.

European Bee-eater
Merops apiaster

34

Education is a Real Thing

Bearing a heavy conscience, Carey wandered along the edge of the gathering, hoping to remain unseen to all, and now wishing to hide from Nonny. Although he had helped with slaughtering nearly every year since his youth, he had always avoided any celebration afterward, fearing that he would ruin the happy mood. He considered himself a bearer of gloomy tidings.

"Carey?"

He turned at the sound of Holt Reinalz, who looked at him curiously. Holt held Isolde in the crook of his arm, swinging her to-and-fro in a rather intense rocking motion. She slept soundly and did not seem bothered by the movement.

"Holt," Carey said, nodding curtly.

"Why are you lurking?" Holt quirked a bold eyebrow, so it lifted above the rim of his glasses.

"Lurking?"

"Lingering near the edge, hoping not to be seen?" Holt explained. "Why are you over here and not over there?" He nodded to the festivities.

"Why are you?" Carey returned.

Holt lifted the sleeping baby, offering that as his explanation. It sufficed.

"I'd not want to be a bother," Carey said.

"Why should you be a bother?"

"I seem to cause a scene wherever I go." Carey hunched his shoulders. "'Tis not for me to even try, only end up bein' misunderstood."

"Who is misunderstanding?"

"Everyone." Carey shrugged.

"Everyone being the Tilfens and like company? We don't share the feeling, Carey. You do good, and it's recognized," Holt spoke firmly. "Man to man, Carey, you have to start believing in yourself a little more."

"Why should I?" Carey grumbled. "'Tis not like I inherited my bones from a saint. I'd not want to cause alarm in anyone."

"That's the very thing," said Holt. "You don't cause alarm, and never have. My children talk of nothing but you. They love you, Carey. You are a good man, and you need to start believing that."

"Good men don't cause talk."

Holt stamped his foot. "The talk is nothing, Carey Alsch. Will you not listen to your friends?"

"I don't know why ye want to be my friend." Carey did not look up.

"Why not? Are you some strange creature of the woods, like Waldleute? Maybe." Holt laughed. "But I think not. To be honest, I am always surrounded by children and people asking for help. Isola provides vibrant, scintillating conversation, of course. But I found myself in need of a friend who was not like me, not like most of Mittenwald. Is that so cross of me?"

"'Tis not something I'm good at, bein' friendly-like. I'll let ye down. Don't count on me, Holt."

"And I'm sure I'll let you down—already have, not defending you to the physician—that's only to be expected."

"I fear ye'd do much better with the butcher, or Knappen. They are of natural trade, and work with the earth. That's not like you."

"The butcher is vain, in case you haven't noticed, and Knappen is a good man whom I respect—he's half my age. I'm an old man, Carey," Holt sighed, "and eleven children have stretched me. Some stretching is good, but if I'm to be elastic, I need a friend who is as intellectually minded as me."

"I'm not intellectually minded," Carey argued.

"Hush." Holt laughed. "I know how many books you order. The postmaster can hardly keep up!"

"'Tis not intellectual books." Carey grimaced. "That's learnin' for the woods."

"Education is education, man."

"Knowin' a few plants is not—"

Holt sighed, throwing his head back. "One of these days I pray I'll get through to you and have you actually appreciate something about yourself."

"I never—" Carey hesitated.

"Never what?"

"I was never told I had anything good in me," Carey said. "How am I supposed to know of it, if alls' been said to me since I was a kid was that I shouldn'ta been born."

"What do you mean?" Holt took a step forward, brow drawing in concern.

"My mother said I was a curse; my father said I was a waste," Carey said without emotion. "Ye have a good life, Holt. Ye are surely a blessed man, and a kind one, but I'd not had anyone for half my life, and the other half was spent bein' told I was worth less than a whip, less than a bushel, less than a dog. Don't tell me I have to believe in myself if there's nothin' left in myself but a dry old man!"

Holt froze with eyes wide, brow lifted fully above his glasses frame.

"I'm sorry, Carey," Holt said. "I didn't know."

"Ye didn't know 'cause I didn't tell ye." Carey sighed.

"Will you let us tell you that you aren't a waste?" Holt asked. "Can my children tell you they admire you and want to be like you? Can Nonny tell you how you've inspired her? Can Isola tell you how great it was that you saved our daughters' lives?"

"Ye aren't beholden to me," Carey said. "And Mr. Tilfen's already made it clear that if ye spend time with me, ye won't be considered in company with him."

"Do you think any of us care?" Holt asked. "You shouldn't care what people think, Carey."

"But I do."

"Why?"

"Because no place I've been has had people that wanted me there."

"That's a lie," Holt said with blunt affect. "And if you keep telling yourself that, you're doing a disservice to all the people who love you and care about you. My family loves when you are around, and it hurts to think you believe we are all lying."

Carey was quiet a long moment, disturbing the grass with a booted foot. "I'll try," he said eventually.

"I didn't mean to be harsh with you, Carey," Holt said. "I speak a little too freely sometimes."

"What ye said is good," Carey said. "Bein' as old an' lived as I am, I should be more like ye said."

"I only think you should hold your head up high and look around," Holt said. "The colors are brighter from here, the words less stinging, the people less staring and harsh."

"I'd think my soul is as hunched as my neck," Carey said, almost laughing, "for how much I look at the ground."

"It'll fix that posture, too." Holt grinned, relieved to see his words finding some small impact within Carey. He was worried he had spoken too harshly; that they would not see Carey for the rest of the summer, per his usual act of disappearing upon the slightest difficulty.

35

Schlachtsefeier

The feast commenced with a crackling fire and spit on which hung a large brisket. The flames sizzled, catching drops of fat on the logs. Miff and Oscar Reinalz helped Knappen turn the spit, building a wall of cinders and burning logs at the back to cook the meat evenly. Potatoes were buried in the ash at the front, slowly cooking in the cooler parts of the fire. Eliza Knappen collected fat drippings in a tin cup from one end of the brisket and poured it over the top, repeating the process to keep the meat from drying out.

On a table away from the heat of the flame, an array of fresh produce was remarked upon, measured, cut, and placed on long platters of silver and tin. Bright red tomatoes bled on the table; carrots were thick and vibrant with color; pickled cabbage was piled on plates; the tail ends of asparagus were cleaved and tossed into a kettle with leeks and various other cuttings. An assortment of mushrooms was balanced beside the tomatoes, carefully stacked with caps downward. Heavy loaves of rye and pumpernickel lined one end. Between the vegetables and bread rested large wheels of cheese and bowls of cream and yogurt.

It was a feast possible due to the combined prowess of Eliza Knappen, Isola Reinalz, and Gerda Welch. The latter two ladies directed chopping, shaping, and stirring. Wolfgang was set to violently stirring a pudding to keep the eggs from curdling. He was superintended by his mother, who cut even slices of rye and arranged them in neat patterns. Lieselotte and Inge decorated the main table—with enough seats for ten families—with an array of ivy and wild grape between the silverware. Music lilted over the gathered families, spreading around a feeling of cheer like spring and rain and good harvest.

Upon entering the general vicinity, Carey was commanded to drag a canvas tarp from the back of the wagon and fasten it to poles set up by Farmer Welch and Mechthild earlier in the day.

Carey tied leather loops through the eyelets and pulled the tarp taut, raising it over the table bursting with food as partial shelter, in case rain decided to crawl over the mountains and deluge.

"Will you be staying for the meal?" Isola asked when Carey passed close to her bountiful table.

"I will," said Carey, nodding to her. She held Anneliese on her hip and was adjusting the child constantly.

"Could I ask you to watch Anneliese for a few minutes?" she asked. "I need to stir the stew, and I'd not want to take her near the fire. She likes to leap from my arms."

Carey glanced to and fro, searching for a member of the Reinalz clan not currently engaged in work. There was none. He turned back to Isola without an excuse as to why he was unable to hold the infant.

Isola grinned and handed Anneliese over. Carey took her as if she were made of glass and attempted to hold her as he had seen Holt carrying Isolde previously.

"She likes to look around," Isola said, holding herself back from laughing at the awkwardness of the tall man. At Isola's patient direction, Carey righted Anneliese and held her on his hip, allowing her a wide range of views. She talked to him pleasantly, now at the age of burgeoning curiosity and many questions. Thinking that Anneliese would like to see more of the scene around them, Carey walked among the gathered families, allowing the small child a view of every intricacy. He found a mouse poking around the base of the table under the tent and crouched quietly before it, explaining how the creature lived, what it ate, and where it burrowed.

Anneliese laughed brightly, drawing a similar reaction from Carey.

Continuing his rounds, he showed Anneliese the design of the sycamore bark not yet peeling from the large tree in the center of the green. Ants crawled up and down the bark in little trails.

Treu ran up to his master, flopping down in the grass and panting heavily. Carey set Anneliese beside him and crouched with his back against the tree. Anneliese giggled and flopped over Treu, causing his tail to flap happily. She buried her face in his coat and grabbed handfuls of his soft fur.

Holt called everyone to attention, loudly announcing the start of the meal. He bowed his head and removed his cap. His prayer was ended with a blessing over the food.

A line formed by the fire, where Farmer Knappen shaved pieces of brisket off with a large knife and placed them directly onto plates with a long-handled fork. Eliza poured gravy over the top of this and added a potato for each adult and youth, half a potato for each child. Isola had loaded platters with vegetables and placed them in the center of the long wooden table, where they could be divided at will.

Farmer Welch wandered around with a canteen of cordial and filled steins to the brim. When those were finished, dark beer was served before Mr. Basch could bring out his un-sieved mead. He was placated by the comment that his mead was only for truly special occasions, and so decided to reserve it for further notice.

After replenishing the vegetables, Isola reclaimed Anneliese and found a seat beside her husband. The rest of the Reinalzes were spread out among the families gathered at the table. Lieselotte and Ada practically clung to Carey, watching him with awestruck eyes, though they seldom spoke.

Carey was given a two-fold measure of beef, two potatoes, and an overfilled cup of cordial. He held his head up and shared conversation with those seated near him, trying in vain to banish his spirit of unwelcome. It seemed to find difficulty in latching on to him when he was surrounded by happy people who endeavored to engage him. For now, he was not an onlooker of joy, but rather a partaker.

36

The First Welcome Spirit

Carey's only lesser feeling was his search for Nonny, who had yet to arrive. He scanned the crowds constantly, looking for the wild brace of hair, the shining eyes, and the bright smile that would mark her presence. Of all the features on the people surrounding him, it was hers he knew best, having made detailed study of their design. He found nothing but perfection in every aspect of her and often found himself mulling over the curve of her cheek, the shape of her lips, and the dark rim of lashes round her eyes.

In searching for her, his reasons were two. First, he simply wished to see her (he always wished to see her, so this was not new). His second reason was inspired by Mrs. Reimenschnell's chatter; that of her possible engagement to the butcher. He thought it a very unsuited match for someone so bright and lovely as Nonny Von Stein. The butcher was no champion of thought, nor touted as a good fellow in any sort of way. Not that Carey considered himself a better suitor—he did not think of himself as a suitor at all, but rather considered himself an admirer and one who had reasonable concern for Nonny's health and happiness.

Looking over the top of Mr. Kinderkopf's head, Carey finally spotted her. She was dressed in her usual blue—a periwinkle frock with cobalt sleeves, and a cerulean ribbon in her hair. Her eyes were bright and skin flush with color. She carried a magnificent cake on a stand, calling out to any in front of her, demanding that they split apart to allow her through. Delivering her cake to the tent, she set it upon the table and heaved a relieved sigh. She dusted her hands and turned towards the table at last.

The Weeping House

Carey moved to stand and greet her but was stopped short by a figure approaching Nonny quickly.

The butcher.

Carey sat back down so firmly the movement spilled beer from the rims of nearby steins. He inhaled a deep breath and set about reclaiming his feelings of goodness, which had all fled at the sight of the butcher. He sought to ignore the two, who were now engaged in amicable conversation. The butcher spoke, Nonny laughed. Carey gripped the edge of the table.

The butcher stepped closer to Nonny and produced a small package from his pocket. He took Nonny's hand and placed the package in her palm, then rolled her fingers around it. The lady's brow drew together in unmistakable confusion, although Carey interpreted the drawing together as something pleasant to the butcher and felt his chest crack.

Mrs. Reimenschnell was rarely wrong, Carey thought. No one had any room to wonder at the closeness between the butcher and Miss Von Stein.

Averting his gaze, Carey ate sparingly of beef, poked a hole in the side of his potato, and took a small sip of cordial.

"Why, you changed spirits quickly, Mr. Alsch," remarked Mr. Basch, seated across the table. "Has something soured your palate? Would you like some mead?" He lifted a jug that was apparently hidden between his knees under the table. Carey shook his head and took another sip of cordial.

"I'd say something's tuggin' on his 'art," said Mrs. Froel, who had enough hair to weave two rugs from her locks and still have enough to tie back with a cord. "What's got yer 'art, Alsch?" She had an endearing, albeit abrasive, manner.

"Nothin'," Carey said, taking a bite of potato, peel and all.

"'Tis not nothin'," said the lady. "Likely, 'tis the butcher and 'is lady, I'd say."

"But the butcher—" Mr. Basch started to say but was interrupted by

Mechthild Reinalz.

"Leave Mr. Alsch alone," she said. "'Tis unkind to pry so."

"Ye have a defender, Alsch," Mrs. Froel remarked. "Not surprised it's a Reinalz; they tend to be little warriors, the lot."

"I just think we should leave Mr. Alsch alone," Mechthild said. "He stays out of gossip. I think it's a good thing."

"Gossip?" said Mrs. Froel whilst looking askance. "My dear, that's quite smart of ye to say to an elder. No wonder ye haven't got a husband yet."

"It's not a wonder," Mechthild said simply, "when there are no young men worth having for fifty kilometers. Any I meet are regurgitations of the word unremarkable or fuddled by town. I'll wait."

Mrs. Froel laughed raucously, slamming her cup against the table. She was clearly fond of the eldest Reinalz and usually engaged in conversations of a similar style when the girl was present. Mrs. Froel had a penchant for witty banter.

"'Tis only right to wait, to be sure," Mrs. Froel said, wiping spilled beer away with her sleeve. "Alsch,"—she looked directly at Carey—"sorry for prying. I'm schooled by a girl more'n half my age again, and I'm not too old and cross to admit it. Yer a fine man, and I'll leave ye be."

"I'd not meant to bother ye, Mrs. Froel." Carey ducked his head.

"No bother at all," said she. "In fact, if any were botherin' any, I'd be botherin' you."

"But she's got the suit of the butcher, Carey." Mr. Basch leaned forward, rejoining the conversation.

"Alsch is a fine, sturdy man, Konrad," Mrs. Froel said. "If 'ee be competing for Miss Nonny's 'art, 'e'd be sure to win."

"But hasn't the butcher proposed?" Mr. Basch asked. "I saw him give her a gift a moment ago. Rather peculiar, I'd say."

"Engaged isn't married," said Mrs. Froel.

"It certainly isn't," added Mechthild. "Carey, I know you and Nonny are friends. It would be so lovely if you married her!"

"Marriage!" Carey leaned back, gripping the edge of the table to retain some semblance of security. "I don't even think of suitin' her!"

"Why not?" asked Mrs. Froel. "Yer handsome. And ye got a house. Got a dog, too." She handed Treu a dripping piece of brisket beneath the edge of the table. "Ye have a fine craft a' leathermakin'. Yer a treasure, Alsch."

"A good man with useful knowledge, helpin' those Reinalz girls was fine indeed," said Mr. Basch.

"Are you sweet on Nonny, Mr. Alsch?" asked Lieselotte, who sat close beside him.

"Sweet?" Carey's brow drew together, and color blossomed in his face. "Why—I'd not." He cleared his throat. "I need more drink," he said, moving to rise to his feet. Mr. Basch had his mead out from under the table before Carey stood. He topped the empty stein off with thick, cloudy mead and grinned brightly at his seatmate.

"Sit, Alsch," commanded Mrs. Froel. He seated himself once again, itching to spring up and run away from the interrogation. "If yer sweet on ' er,"—the lady leaned forward, resting her elbows on the table and looking at him very seriously—"you should tell ' er."

"How can I do that if she's gone and accepted Wistom's hand?" he asked. "Wouldn't be right."

"Aye!" said Mrs. Froel, slapping the table with glee. "So ye are sweet on ' er! Ye got to fight for ' er, man."

"Yes, Mr. Alsch! Do!" said Mechthild with a hopeful expression. "Please do!"

"You have to, Mr. Alsch," Lieselotte whispered. "Cousin Nonny is the best. Mr. Wistom works with blood and guts all day; his house smells like stomach. Nonny can't live there! She must marry you!"

"'Tis not a thing I can do." Carey stared at his plate. "I'd not impose, and she doesn't think of me like that, I'm sure. My house is nothin' fit for a woman, either."

"Why,"—Lieselotte sat straight—"your house is not all that bad. It needs cleaning."

"We can help!" cried Ada, who had been sitting silently up till now and stood up on the bench seat to offer her aid to Carey.

"I couldn't—" Carey held up his hands.

"Oh hush, Alsch," Mrs. Froel tut-tutted, taking a sip of cordial, then hiding her mug from Mr. Basch, who could not be prevented from sharing his mead. "Take 'elp where 'elp comes and it'll work out good for 'ee, Mutti used to say to me. She was a wise woman, like me."

"Well," Carey said, appeased with the new direction of conversation. "If ye have a time free, perhaps we can clean a bit." He smiled at Ada. She clasped her hands together at her heart and smiled brightly. Carey forgot his lesser feelings, finding himself laughing amicably with neighbors who had been there his entire life. He had never known he was a person with whom they might find friendship, having hid himself away for so long. He was struck by the ease with which they spoke to him, and to one another. With a warm spring breeze and evening shadows drawing in, Carey Alsch felt a welcome spirit.

Red-Breasted Nuthatch
Sitta canadensis

37
No Unsightly Will

Smoke drifted lazily into the twilight sky, framing the dark edges of the trees and scenting the air with the crisp char of cedar and spruce. Lanterns were lit in a circle round the table, posts stuck deep in the ground. Their flames flickered and danced, seeming to move with the sound of the vibrant zither and violin. Oscar Reinalz sat on a half-log and beat a drum to a rhythmic melody.

Couples rose from their seats and moved about the grassy field. They danced in the emerging starlight. A lively tune lifted, increasing in tempo and volume. A great crowd formed, moving with vigorous footsteps. Laughter rang and beer spilled from the edges of tin mugs.

Carey watched the festivities, tapping his foot along to the beat and humming under his breath. Treu sat beneath the bench and licked his hand. The hound's tail thumped happily against the earth.

"Is there room?" a familiar voice asked. Carey turned to see Nonny standing with a full plate of uneaten food. A girthy shadow stood behind her. The butcher.

"Ho, Alsch," Fritz Wistom said, pushing Lieselotte and Ada aside, banishing them from the table to go and frolic among the flowers. He sat down heavily in their place, spilling gravy and beer on Carey's arm.

Nonny grimaced and watched the Reinalz girls hurry off toward the sycamore tree, Treu at their heels. After a few minutes they had fashioned a necklace of daisies for the hound and danced gleefully around him. Nonny was appeased by their dancing and seated herself at the table. She greeted Mrs. Froel, who scowled openly at the butcher.

"Had a good evening?" Fritz asked.

Carey nodded.

"I made a fine cut of this brisket, I must say," the butcher mused, tearing into the beef. "I really should've been in a larger town. Slaughter season is already nearing its end, and I've only just plied my trade. I suppose I'll have more bratwurst to make; that'll take a few weeks. You'd like that, wouldn't you, Miss Von Stein?"

"Would I?" she asked, poking her food with marked disinterest.

"Do you not like bratwurst?" a shocked Mr. Basch asked.

"Of course she does," said the butcher, patting Nonny's hand. She dropped both hands into her lap and did not look at Fritz. Carey sat upright and stabbed a fork into his potato. Mrs. Froel seemed the only one to notice this motion and watched him closely.

"What do ye like, Nonny?" asked the elderly lady. Her words carried weight, and her knowing eyes jumped back and forth between the two men sitting on Nonny's right.

"I like—" Nonny said, lifting her chin for a moment. She caught Mrs. Froel's eye and saw something there that swept a wave of embarrassment over the girl.

"Do ye like Alsch?" Mrs. Froel asked. Nearly all seated in the general area went silent, staring at Nonny, waiting for an answer. Carey Alsch did not look up; he stared intensely at his plate and did not move.

"I'll say," the butcher interrupted, "what a question. Of course we like Alsch. Carey's a great friend to us all."

Mrs. Froel scowled at Fritz Wistom but held her tongue at a sharp nudge from Mechthild.

"Mr. Wistom," Nonny said, taking a deep breath, "will you please join me for a moment over by the linden tree?"

"The what?" The butcher had no interest in trees.

"That tree." Nonny rose to her feet and pointed to the linden shading a bit of ground near the fence that ringed the town hall. She stalked over to it and waited with her arms crossed.

"I suppose I'll be back momentarily," Fritz said. He smiled broadly to all and excused himself.

"Well, Alsch," said Mrs. Froel, "I'm afraid I've put my foot in my mouth. Looks like 'ee's claimed 'er."

"Likely," added Mr. Basch. He nodded to the linden where Nonny and the butcher were engaged in animated conversation. She produced a small package from her pocket and placed it in his hand. Evening was too far gone to be sure whether it was the same that the butcher had placed in her hand shortly after their arrival.

"Don't get discouraged," said Mechthild, leaning against the edge of the table. "Mr. Wistom is a bother and Nonny knows it."

Farmer Knappen stood at the far end of the table. The music died down and conversation fell away. Nonny and Wistom worked their way back over to hear what the farmer had to say.

"I thankee all for help and spirit," Knappen said, holding his mug aloft. "Welch and I are always grateful for any help, and when threshing comes round, we'll be the first out on the floor turnin' the wheat. It takes a village to make the world run. My wife an' I are proud to be part o' this one." Everyone cheered and drank deeply of dark beer in toast to the season.

"Now," Farmer Knappen continued after wiping his chin with a loose linen sleeve. "I'd like to hear a song or two. A sonnet? Poem?"

Several young maidens were pushed forwards by their siblings and mothers. They produced pretty tunes and smiled endearingly beneath the flickering flames of the lanterns. Several boys cleared the table and danced on one end, showing their particular fondness for clogging. A passage from *Hermann and Dorothea* was received with much delight, resulting in an enraptured crowd.

Carey leaned on the wood grain of the table, listening to but not watching the oration. His gaze wandered across the yard, studying swaying trees, their pattern and bloom, and how they moved in the roll of sweet spring wind. Mechthild Reinalz clung to Nonny's arm near the far end of the table. The girl whispered effusively, nodding her head up and down. Nonny shook her head abjectly. She was eventually convinced of whatever Mechthild was vying for and stepped up to the makeshift center stage.

Her voice started small, though it grew with each word. Taking a breath, Nonny spoke into the silence. Her voice was sweet, rich with life and warmth.

> I know not time nor when,
> he will put his foot upon my door.
> Until this rich and blessed friend
> will come upon me poor.
> For wretched nights, abated soon
> bring some truth delights,
> arriving with the slated moon.
> He deftly steals my tearful blights
> and hides away all pain and gloom,
> so neatly tied in silken show,
> bonny, yet worn, from laborious loom.
> He will strike upon the lintel 'fore the snow
> and begging rest aside, I lend,
> For warming there, his wealth abounds
> and by some fire, gladly mend,
> my resting place, for the hare and hounds.

A few seconds of silence followed her voice. She smiled and dipped her head and shoulders in a sweet curtsy. The table erupted in cheers. She moved back to her seat amidst raucous attempts to draw out an encore and repeat of the poem. Shaking her head, she laughed but stayed firmly planted.

The festivities carried on for another hour, ranging from songs to re-enactments of famous battles, and an acrobatics performance by Ada Reinalz and Marie Basch, who had both just learned to cartwheel. Their act devolved into giggles, and eventually, the girls were carried off-stage by their respective mothers.

Having reached his limit of social interaction, Carey excused himself from the table and searched out Treu, who was cavorting around the edge of the park with Wolfgang and Miff Reinalz. He crouched and called the hound to his side. Treu rolled onto his back and wagged his tail happily.

"Does Treu like people?" Miff Reinalz asked, crouching beside Carey at the foot of the sycamore tree. Amalie chased Wolfgang past the tree, yelling something concerning the nonsense that oft goes on between siblings. Music picked up, and those gathered around the fire cheered loudly.

"He does." Carey smiled, scratching the long hairs at Treu's chin. "More than I, probably."

"Do you not like people, Mr. Alsch?"

"I don't know people," he said. "Their ways, their faces, their words. They take over me and confuse me in ways I can't fix."

"You know me!" Miff said, standing tall. "Will you be my friend, Mr. Alsch?"

"I will." He smiled. "I think I've not met a family kinder 'n' you Reinalzes. I think I can be friends with 'ee." Treu was off again, baying loudly into the night as he tore after the children across the yard.

Miff laughed brightly and was not long for continued conversation, being the age at which young children are very easily distracted by loud noises and fun. Carey watched the children from several families chase one another through the park, fighting over a long ribbon that had originally been tied in Inge's hair. One of the boys took hold of the ribbon and tore off under the cover of several alder trees in full bloom. He ducked and wove between the trees, taunting his sisters with the ribbon all the while.

He was thwarted by Mrs. Kinderkopf's eldest child, Heinz, who popped out from the last tree and snatched it from the enemy. He presented it to Inge Reinalz with a flourish, like a noble knight returned from a quest.

38

Engagement

Retrieving his hat from the table, Carey whistled for Treu. The tone was sharp and direct, cutting through the lilt of the violin. Treu emerged from the shadows on the edge of the park and pressed loyally against his master's leg.

Carey watched the flickering flames of the bonfire, thinking of brighter things than he usually thought whilst staring into his own fire in the hearth of his home. His head was lifted, no longer studying the tread of the earth or the shape of his boots. He observed the faces in the crowd and the colors dancing on their happy faces; ochre, amber, aureolin, and the warmest gold reflected by the light of the fire.

He found Holt Reinalz with baby Isolde cradled in a swathe against his chest, a sleepy Anneliese on his shoulder, and an exhausted Ada leaning against his leg. Anneliese's head was buried in the crook of his neck, arms hanging limp by her sides.

Isola danced round the fire, holding hands with Inge, Liselotte, and Mechthild. Mrs. Kinderkopf was being propped up by her husband, having consumed beer beyond her limit. Beyond the line of the fire, Mr. Basch was sneaking his mead into mugs that were not properly guarded, giving proper taste to the silt-heavy drink.

Mrs. Froel sat aside on a low bench consisting of two oak rounds bearing an uneven strip of hand-milled lumber. She caught Carey's eye and lifted her mug in salute. He dipped his head and turned to leave.

"Carey." Nonny approached him, silhouetted by the fire. She took hold of his sleeve and quickly turned him to face her. "Are you avoiding me?"

"Avoiding?" he asked, taking a step back and not meeting her eye.

"Yes!" She crossed her arms. "You've not said one word to me. I thought—you're not even being friendly."

"'Tisn't friendly to be in company? Do 'ee always have to speak?"

"What's the matter?" She stepped forward and reached for his arm.

"Meant to congratulate ye," he said. "Blessed thing, engagement is." He nudged a rock with his booted toe.

"Engagement?" She was incredulous.

"To Mr. Wistom." Carey ducked his head, running his thumb along the brim of his hat held tightly at his hip. She did not speak, only continued staring at him. "Mrs. Reimenschnell said—" he continued.

"Mrs. Reimenschnell?" Her voice was direct, colored with hurt. "Carey? That woman? She is a rumormonger!"

"But Basch and Froel also said the butcher was keen on ye."

"If he is," Nonny said, crossing her arms over her chest, "it's something Wistom will have to deal with on his own. I've made myself clear."

"What do ye mean?"

"I don't like Wistom," she said. "He won't leave me alone. I've been trying to avoid him all week, Carey. I am not engaged to him, nor will I be. He's slightly insufferable, in case you haven't noticed."

"But the gifts he's given ye." Carey looked at her.

"I gave it back." She narrowed her eyes. "I give everything back. He's certainly good at imposing his will. You saw how he interrupted me. Oh,"—she ground her teeth—"I can't stand him. It can be rather hard for a woman to tell a man no. They tend to not understand the concept."

"Oh." He looked up at the night sky. Something lifted in his chest, and he wondered if the stars had always appeared so radiant. Nonny was quiet. She stood beside him, nearly touching his arm with her shoulder.

"Carey," she whispered. "Would you have been terribly upset if I was engaged to the butcher?"

He cleared his throat and shifted his weight from foot to foot, not daring to look at her in the darkness.

"Why were you upset?" she pressed. "Carey? Are you listening?"

"I'd not want ye engaged to a man like Wistom," Carey said, putting his hat back on and tugging it low over his ears. "He's not good enough for 'ee." He turned to go, desperate to escape before his heart spilled over. It thundered in his chest, making it difficult to breathe, think, or speak.

Nonny stepped in front of him to block his way. "Will you speak plainly with me?" she asked, taking his hand.

"If ye come to the woods tomorrow," he said, "I'll teach ye about the shape and design of fly agaric. Pretty mycelium. It's poisonous, mind ye," he rambled, lifting her hand, running a thumb over the top of it, studying the way it rested in his. "Ye have pretty hands," he said under his breath. His eyes widened as if he realized he had spoken aloud.

"Carey." Nonny took a step closer, her cheeks reflecting the light of the bonfire. "Do you—"

"Ho, Carey!" Mr. Basch called out, walking toward the two figures standing near the edge of the yard. He was intercepted by Mrs. Froel, who grabbed him by the muscle between his neck and shoulder. Pinching hard, she steered him away.

"I need to go," Carey said. "My chickens—they'll miss me. I mean, I have to fill the well." He shook his head, drawing his brow together. "I have the lye, the leathers. An' clear the straw in the barn. Lots to do."

"Right now?" Nonny asked, cocking her head.

"Aye, right now." Carey backed away, then whistled sharply, calling Treu to heel. He turned and walked quickly into the night. The distance he put between himself and Nonny Von Stein did little to still his heart. Every step echoed in his mind. Following the path up to his home, he wondered if Nonny thought as often of him as he did of her. In his heart, he felt a great pull towards her; a tugging, wrenching, and binding which fixed him in place. He was sure that no matter the length of his life, if he died the next day or lived for a century, hers would be the only face he saw. He would have no recourse, no changing, nor deviation from this feeling, though he still left it unnamed. Nonny Von Stein was a fixture in his heart, and no machination of man nor spiritual devilry could remove her.

Standing on the top of the hill before his home, where nighttime winds distilled the silver-stalked grasses, he listened to the call of a reed warbler. He considered the cry of that songbird, studied the range of stars overhead, and felt the chill mountain wind brush past his clothes. There was beauty to his home, he noticed. He had always sought to know the lay of the land but had never felt any surge of affection for it. Now, his heart was stirred by that lady, and he seemed to feel clearly how beautiful the sky was.

It was not, however, due only to Nonny that he felt the first fruits of unknown love. Although it seemed plain cause-and-effect to Carey, this metamorphosis of the heart had originated elsewhere. Its beginnings were laid near the edge of Lautersee, foundations set in place in the home of the Reinalzes at Christmas dinner, beams built by eleven children who played with his dog. The sturdy edges of this feeling were constructed by community. Brick by brick, and despite his protestations, the kind people of Mittenwald had pulled forth the heart of Carey Alsch.

39

Of Liking Things

A heavy fog settled just above the hills, not daring to touch the ground for fear it might lose any appearance of cloud-shape and become water only. The sun rose behind these misty morning drifts and passed through like reaching fingers of pure light to touch the early morning earth. In other places where the fog was not so thick, amber sunlight colored the vapor in lighter hues. Beyond the rolls of fog, a melancholy loon called out from the pond. His lilting melody carried across the still water, where the mist hung heaviest. Amidst the damp of dew and the sad notes sung by the water-bird was the taste of morning. It was that particular scent on the air of newness, as if sunlight itself was tangible in the air and could be consumed.

Carey crouched beside the pond and studied the unmoving surface of the water. The pond was small, only about two hundred paces in circumference. The shallows were filled with reeds, the deep with algae and lilies. Hundreds of tiny frogs poked above the surface of the water near the edge. They sang a concerto, notes overlapping with varying depth and power.

Considering the shape of his heart, Carey dipped his hand into the icy water. The orchestra changed tune, sounding the alarm. The change only lasted for a moment and returned to regular tone when Carey was still.

Carey looked into the depths of the pond and saw the spectral shape of his mother floating face down, having given up on him and life. He recalled the pull of water at his feet, then knees, and hips, the weight of her body altered by death as he dragged her to shore. His heart had changed form that day. Any reconstruction would require work. Work to fend off the darkness that threatened to make him numb, the kind that said he had been forgotten.

"I'm not forgotten," he whispered, stirring the mud near the edge. "I'm more 'n a rose. Ye be a weeping pond." His voice was firm. "And that is a weeping house. I'll see it cast to earth, Mutti, and I'll burn out the badness ye left in it. I'll tear down the gate that Father left through and warm my new house with the wood. Ye'll see. Ye aren't my curse. My curse isn't so heavy, and it'll soon leave."

The frogs altered their chorus, allowing his voice to echo off the surface of the pond. On the far shore, the loon stirred, taking up his tune again. His song seemed to describe the grief hanging on the shoulders of the man.

"I'm not the measure of my father's wrath," Carey whispered. "Mother's despair is not my despair." He stood and rubbed his face, having spent the night pondering. Wandering across the yard, he climbed the steps to his house, passing Treu curled up on the doorstep. The hound followed him inside and lay back down on the furs spread by the cold hearth. Stripping off his clothes, Carey fell into the bed and slept, but did not dream.

Loud knocking woke him from his sleep half a day later. He lay still for a moment, slow-blinking in the afternoon sun. His mind moved sluggishly, stuck halfway between sleep states.

"Carey?" A familiar voice carried through the door. Carey frowned and stretched, struggling to comprehend reality.

"Carey, are you sleeping?" the voice sounded out again. "Carey, I'm coming in!"

He sucked in a sharp breath and leapt from the bed. He slammed into the door whilst half-naked to keep it closed.

"So, you are awake!" Nonny Von Stein said from behind the door. "Were you ignoring me?" She pushed on the door, attempting to open it and enter.

"I bain't dressed!" Carey nearly shouted.

"Dressed …" Nonny repeated, then paused. "Oh!" she exclaimed. One could hear embarrassment in her tone and almost picture the way her face colored.

"Give me five minutes," he said, resting his forehead against the wood grain. "I'll be out."

"I'm sorry," she whispered on the opposite side of the door.

"No worryin'," he said, then quickly pulled on a clean pair of trousers and a loose linen shirt of a deep blue color. He opened the door and found himself looking straight down into Nonny's face.

"Why were you sleeping in the middle of the afternoon?" Nonny asked, holding a basket in front of her with two hands.

"I didn't sleep last night," he said, running a hand through his hair.

"Why not?" she asked. "Filling the well and talking to your chickens? Were they as lonely as you said they would be?"

"Sorry?" he asked, nervously stepping around her onto the porch. Treu followed and began to show his excitement at the visitor. His tail thumped against the door frame.

"You said you had to leave last night because your chickens would miss you." She arched an eyebrow. "Were they happy to see you?"

"I s'pose." He nodded. "What d'ye have in the basket?"

"Supper," she said. "I thought we could picnic after talking about mycelium, like you said."

"Right," he said, walking down the steps into the yard. "This way, then." He jerked his head towards the woods ringing his yard.

The Isar portioned off his home from the woods, spanned by a makeshift bridge of stones. He walked up to the edge and glanced at Nonny. "I usually jump the stones," he said, stuffing his hands in his pockets.

"I can do it," she said, "if you'll help me."

His eyes widened when she handed him the basket and held a hand out towards him. He stared at the proffered hand.

"Hold my pretty hand." She looked at him with that peculiar expression.

He grimaced, recalling how he had spoken the previous night. Meeting her eyes, he took the basket in one hand and her hand in the other. Treu crossed the river just upstream, where the water ran thin before it bunched behind the stones and swelled at the edges.

Carey stepped onto the first stone and waited for Nonny to follow. He crossed each stone with sturdy feet and did not stumble. Halfway across the river, Nonny joined him on one slightly larger stone, so they stood chest to chest. Carey gulped, still holding her hand, but now looking down into her face and standing very close.

"If you keep looking at me like that, I might fall from this stone, Carey."

"The water is cold," he said, not minding his words. He was instead studying the perfect shape of her lips as she spoke.

"Should I not fall in?" Her eyes lit up with good humor.

"No," he said, "ye can stay like this."

"But isn't the goal to cross the river?" she whispered, continuing to look at him. He blinked twice, then glanced toward the bank on the far side.

"'Tis." He nodded.

"Shall we cross?"

He nodded again and stepped over, turning her hand so he held it against his back. She followed closely, guided by his sure steps. They crossed with little difficulty, although the gap between the last stone and shore was so large that Carey had to wade to his ankles in the frigid flow and lift her across. He did not mind in the least.

The woods beyond the Isar were illuminated with a mid-afternoon glow. Sunlight streamed through the trees, catching on particles in the air so all the darkest parts of the wood seemed stark against the shining rays of light.

Carey stuffed his hands in his pockets, his right hand burning with the memory of how perfectly Nonny's seemed to rest in it. He sighed deeply, tasting the sunlight filtering through the trees.

"Fly agaric likes to grow beneath pine, spruce, or birch," he said over his shoulder.

"What do those trees look like?" She grimaced in embarrassment. "I can only differentiate a willow from an oak, or a deciduous from an evergreen. Or a linden; I know that one by its flower."

"If ye look at the leaves," Carey said, "the stalk where they attach is woody and reddish colored in a spruce, and the leaves are like wax. Pine has longer needles that grow in clusters, rather 'n each leaf from the stem. Birch is easy." He smiled. "Skinny, with white or varicolored bark."

"Varicolored?"

"Like it has patches of white 'n' black, or reddish when it peels. Leaves look like an egg and turn yellow. Male catkins come 'fore the flower."

"And what is a catkin?"

"'Tis a little petal-less flower pollinated by the wind. Stain your hands yellow and gets all over everything in spring."

"Can we find some?" She quickened her step, coming up alongside him.

"Of course," he said, "I'll find ye anything ye like, Nonny." His words were light, but there was something in his expression that made her miss her step and stumble over even ground. She caught herself and continued in confident stride, face flushed red.

Beneath their feet, the detritus ground thumped, each step echoing with years of layered decay. Roots twisted and rolled over one another, creating mazes of complex networks, both above and below the crust. Spring was active, so the layers of leaves were latent material from the previous fall. On the left, a hog run cut through the dense underbrush. The earth there was overturned from rooting. Clumps of dirt and leaves were pockmarked with holes the size of snouts.

"The leaves overhead don't want to touch," Carey said, pointing towards the canopy. "Trees are polite … mostly. They want to let light in for the little things that grow. We call it 'crown shyness.'"

"I think you have crown shyness," she said, pursing her lips.

"How can I?" He laughed rather loudly.

"You always move away to let light shine on other people," she said simply.

"Am I a tree?" He smiled a broad, full smile, one that seldom appeared.

"You are a bit like a tree." Her eyes narrowed. "Tall, sturdy, not easily moved, deep roots."

"D'ye not have roots?"

"I don't like my roots," she said. "I wish to pull them up and put them back in the ground where I desire."

"Replanting is difficult for things," he said. "Plants don't always survive. Has to be done right."

"I think I can do it," she said. "I'm doing it."

"I'm glad ye chose these woods to set new roots," he said. "My woods are lovely."

"Oh,"—she grinned—"your woods, are they? I thought they were just trees and sticks. When did you start actually liking them and claiming them?"

"Last night," he said. "I started liking things and claiming them last night." His voice took a momentarily serious tone. His eye held a particularly keen intensity, rivaling the depth of his voice when he spoke.

"Oh," she said, walking faster and jumping over a log. He stood for a moment, watching the way she moved through the forest. She was a bolt of light; a periwinkle vision; seeming more like fable than reality for how lovely she was among the pines.

The Weeping House

Eurasian Red Squirrel
Sciurus vulgaris

40
Mushroom Talk

"Tell me," Carey began after passing under a low-hanging branch hanging with moss, "where is the birch and where is the spruce in this copse?" Nonny joined him amidst a clump of trees of varying color and height. One near the center had a portion of bark torn away from the middle trunk. Weeping sap spilled over the wound, forming a sticky mass.

Nonny stopped in the center of a little circle of trees and put her hands on her hips. Narrowing her eyes, she peered at each tree and inspected the leaves swaying in the slight breeze.

"That is a spruce," she said, pointing to one. "It has needles and thick stems."

"Very good." He smiled.

"And the birch is there?" She pointed at a cluster of narrow trees with oval leaves of a bright green. "It seems very birch-y to me."

"'Tis," he said. "And here is our prey." Taking a few steps past her, he crouched beside the group of young birch trees. Several red caps peeked through the humus. Most were wide, strawberry red caps with white stems, having fully opened only recently, although a few were still round polyps. Little white spots covered the tops, peeling away from the smooth surface.

"Fly agaric?" she asked, squatting beside him, making sure her skirts covered her knees fully.

"Amanita as well," he said. "Amanita Muscaria."

"It's poisonous?"

"Aye," he said. "Though some use it for pagan rituals. Makes you see things."

"It's so pretty." She placed her hands in her lap. "Why does it look so tasty, Carey?"

"Lots of things in nature are pretty and dangerous," he said. "It's a warning sign."

"Male birds are pretty." She cocked her head.

He smiled and pulled layers of bark from the birch tree and stuffed it in his cross-body bag.

"Why are you collecting the bark?"

"Tannins," he said. "I'll make tannin with it for the leathers."

"May I help?"

"Ye may do anything ye like," he said. She ripped off a large portion of bark and passed it to him, dusting her hands on her skirts.

"Do you collect the agaric?"

"No." He shook his head. "I'll collect boletus if we find more spruce, and chantarelles, shaggy manes, and blewits. Shaggy manes are my favorite."

"I'd like to know them by sight," she said. "I do love to eat mushrooms."

"Ye will." He nodded, "I'll teach ye."

"These here are very different looking," she said, "but I've found white mushrooms that look just like other white mushrooms and one is poisonous, one is edible."

Carey smiled. "Blusher amanita looks like this,"—he held up the red amanita—"though 'tis edible."

"How can you tell which is which?"

"Can test the spores," he said, "or cut into it. Or look at the gills." He pulled a single amanita up, root and all, then took a small knife from his pocket. Cutting into the cap, he showed her the variation of the gills and the red stain of the cap. "Boletus bruises blue when ye cut it. Though spore patterns are the surest determination. We put it on paper and tap it to knock spores loose, or let it sit overnight. The pattern of the dropped spores tells us what it is."

"And if you're wrong?"

"I spend a day sick in bed, and Treu passes condemnation on me." He laughed, sitting back on his heels.

"Let's collect every kind of mushroom and make spore patterns!" she said, climbing to her feet after passing an agaric cap to Carey.

"There's not enough room in my bag for every type." He followed her out of the copse.

"After we eat supper," she said, "we can fill my basket with more." A small bird flitted to an overhead branch, singing out a bold call.

"What is that?" she asked.

"Crested tit," he said. "When he sounds alarm—like now—he sounds like a red-throated pipit. 'Tis an imitation call."

"How can you tell the difference?" she asked. "Is he sounding alarm because of us?"

"Practice," he said. "And aye. One bird takes it up, passes it to another, and another. Soon, a hundred meters of forest area knows where we are. 'Tis a bit like the postal system, only with birdsong."

"I want to draw it," she said.

"Do 'ee have—" He paused, seeing her take a leatherbound notebook, inkpot, and quill from her leather satchel. "Oh, ye do."

"I'm going to draw the agaric, too," she said. "It'll only take a moment." Crouching, she set the notebook on her knees and squinted at the bird, tracing an outline on the blank page. Her movements were precise and clean, not spilling a drop of ink. After a few moments, she had a near-exact rendition of the little bird. She held it up for Carey to inspect.

"'Tis very like," he said. "Only, how're ye to show his red eyes?"

"I'll paint it when I am home," she said. "And perhaps next week I will bring my supplies. Plein-air is one field of artistic study I have seldom ventured into. I shall soon!"

"Plein-air?"

"Painting outside," she said. "Making study of living things."

"Do ye like to paint?"

"I do," she said. "Very much. Although I left some of my most vibrant colors at home, so now I must make do with fairer shades. It can be hard to make contrast and definition on a canvas with little variation of hue."

"Are ye finished with the likeness?" he asked, leaning over her shoulder to further inspect the page.

"I am," she said. "Let me see the agaric."

He withdrew the mushroom and held it for her perusal, explaining all the parts, including how mycelium lies just beneath the soil, connecting one to another in a massive tangle. Before she finished the first drawing, he retrieved two other mushrooms in various stages of growth. She copied each of these on the paper, neatly annotating his comments beneath the drawings with perfect penmanship.

"Saw chantarelle on the way in," Carey said, tugging his hat low. "Didn't know ye wanted to see it."

"Can you find it again?"

"Course," he said, whistling for Treu to heel. The hound came barreling out of the woods and leaned against his master's leg, pleased to be called.

"He seems to be feeling better." Nonny scratched Treu between his ears.

"Has good days 'n' bad ones." Carey said. "Doesn't like town near as much as the woods."

"So he resembles his master in more ways than one." She held a hand out towards Carey.

"Am I like a hound?" Carey laughed. He took her hand and pulled her to her feet. "I thought I was like a tree."

"You are like a tree, your dog is like you, so your dog is like a tree, but you are not like a hound."

"And what are ye like, Miss Nonny?"

"What do you think?"

"A flower," he said immediately.

"Which flower?"

He thought for a moment, still holding her hand. "Cornflower," he said finally.

"Show me one." She smiled and reclaimed her hand, albeit slowly.

They wandered back the way they had come, searching for white, grey, and brown caps peeking above leaf layers. On several fallen logs were large bracts of fanlike mushrooms, porling, reishi, and various blushing brackets arrayed in shelf-like patterns horizontally across the bark.

Chantarelle was found in the underfall nearest Carey's home. Branching from there, they followed the upward slope of the Isar. Carey rolled logs and described the insects scattering in the dirt there. A stag beetle had made its home beneath one log. He let it crawl over his hand whilst Nonny drew it in her notebook. He explained how the large horn at the top of the male beetle's head was used for wrestling during mating season, wherein the victor would claim a mate.

Mid-afternoon passed and dusk slowly overcame the forest. Shadows ran long from the bases of trees, mixing into one large shadow as darkness crept in. An owl hooted, claiming territory and warning predators—Nonny and Carey included—to stay far away. Nonny was attentive when Carey described the varying ululations, which increased in volume and speed, and the interposed kip and kew, signaling this owl as a Tengmalm's again, likely the very same they had seen in winter roosting in the dead oak. He showed her how to hold her hands to create a similar call by adjusting the flow of air between her knuckles.

Nonny, though she listened attentively, was fascinated by the quiet, shy man who lived alone in the mountains, who had never been among noisy, bustling streets and stone landscapes. When he spoke, her gaze never strayed; she was always studying his face and expressions. Although she had a vested interest in natural science, she found herself continuously asking questions merely to keep him talking, finding beauty in the way his eyes brightened when he described mushrooms and beetles, how he spoke quickly of tree identification, and the way he could expertly mimic any bird call, whether male or female. She resolved to soak in every bit of knowledge from him and not stray far from his side, so long as time and respectability allowed.

She could not, however, sense how his heart pounded when she was near, nor how every look on her was lingering and dear. Nor could she surmise that he held his breath when she spoke for fear he might not catch every word from her lips. She would entirely miss the fact that every word from his mouth was a gift to her only and not likely to be shared with anyone else.

41
Life Will Be

When foraging was near done, Nonny found a pleasant hill on which to spread her lavender blanket. She weighted the edge with the basket and emptied its contents, placing four links of sausage on a plate. She rested thick slices of Emmental cheese against these, cut a thick piece of rye, and piled several pickled vegetables on the edge.

Sitting there, she looked out over the ridge edges of distant mountains, cut across with smooth green slopes, bald peaks, and low tree-lines creeping up the inclines. A clear sky hung over the peaks, making distant mountains seem monochrome in shades of blue. Nearer foothills and crags bore distinct colors—varying tans, browns, greys, greens, and patches of white, where glaciers clung. Moraines and culs were carved between mountains, marking the path of ancient glaciers slow-crawling down the valleys.

"The world is so broad," she said when Carey sat beside her on the blanket.

"'Tis wide and full of things." He nodded. She handed him the full plate, and he gratefully accepted.

"You have lived here always?"

"Never wandered away," he said. "'Tis not far I've ventured, either."

"And is your life full?"

"Full?" he said, "I don't know your meaning."

"Are you pleased with life." She rested back on her hands, studying the landscape.

"Life is life," he said. "Lot's gone astray. Lot's wrecked. Wasn't much special about it, till—"

"Until?" She looked at him.

"Just—" He searched for the words. "Lot's seen as wrecked. Not much found to be lovely."

"I heard about your mother," she said. "And they said your father ... he left?"

He nodded.

"I don't mean to pry," she said, sitting upright and fiddling with a portable kettle and cup.

"I don't mind," he said. "Holt says I should hold my head up. Feels heavy, but I'll try."

"Holt is right." She rose to her knees and grabbed his forearm, looking into his face emphatically. "Hold your head very high."

"If ye tell me to," he said, "then I will."

She sat back on her feet, releasing his arm and placing her hands in her lap. "Am I some grand determiner of truth and trust?" She laughed.

He nodded, as if it were not a difficult answer. Regarding his steady gaze, she looked toward the mountains, unable to meet the intensity found in the man. "My mother loved the rose more 'n' she loved me," he said.

"Rose?" She frowned.

"The one I burned." He watched a kestrel yaw in the wind, then dive behind a craggy peak in the distance.

"Your mother's rose," she whispered.

He nodded.

"Your mother placed her love ill," she continued. "You are more than a rose."

"She was vain and hated life," he said. "I nearly hated life, but not anymore."

"There is so much to love in everything, Carey!" Her eyes brightened.

"Sometimes, when you speak of the woods and the workings of the world, I feel so—so overcome that I can barely speak. It is all so wonderful I can hardly stand it."

"I see that now," he said. "Though I wandered half my life in a darkness. I see it."

"I want to know all the things you know." She fell back on the blanket, so her hair splayed outward in a fan around her head. "Until my head is so full of trees, insects, and birds that I can't think normal thoughts."

"D'ye now?" He laughed, petting Treu, who leaned against his side, begging for scraps of cheese.

"I am the last daughter in a wealthy family," she said. "My parents have a grand house, two carriages, two horses each, and a home in the country. I am nothing more than a person who breathes in my family. They forget I exist and do not notice when I am gone. I told you I would have turned to stone if I continued in that way."

"Was it hard?" he asked.

"It was so easy, it turned terrible in my heart. I think it made me terrible, for a time." She sighed. "I want to climb mountains, Carey. I want to scratch my knees on stones, tangle my hair in branches, drink honey mead, and dance around a fire. I want to use my mind, my hands, my heart for real things in a real world."

"Overworked hands'll fall off," he said, "don't 'ee wish to keep 'em?"

"No!" She held her hands up, spreading her fingers as if she could grab handfuls of sky. "Take them!"

He took one. Clasping it in his, he held it gingerly, as if it were some grand treasure he might lose. Nonny took in a small breath. She continued looking into the sky, her face coloring brightly. She covered her face with her other hand, partially hiding herself from view.

Carey said nothing, scared to move or even breathe for fear she might run from him.

"Carey," she said quietly, "why am I a flower?"

He gulped, heat rising into his face. "Ye are lovely. Like nothing I've seen in life."

"Oh," she whispered. "But flowers don't bloom for long."

"Nay," he said, "but flowers come about to sow life. And ye are a woman, not a flower. Ye are more lovely and will live far longer than a flower."

"Why am I a cornflower?"

"Blue," he said. "Can be a medicine for the sick and weary." He rolled her hand over, interlacing his fingers between hers.

"Will you bring me cornflowers?" she asked.

"I'll bring you anything," he said. "I'll fill your room with 'em, make 'em burst through the windows and break the frames."

She laughed, a pure, unrestrained laughter that carried through the woods. "I'm not so sure cousin Holt would appreciate his house being destroyed by flowers."

"Do you want any other flower?" he asked, tracing over the top of her hand with his thumb and studying the shape of her face, noting how her nose scrunched when she laughed.

"Anything blue." She smiled. "I dearly love the color blue."

"I know," he said. "I'll bring ye blue flowers every day, Nonny. Till ye are sick o' the color."

"Shall life be better for the both of us, Carey?"

He was quiet. For a moment, his life of despondence seemed but a whisper, a haunting shadow in the corner of his eyes. Something that fled in the face of light, but never left entirely. It was there, always demanding he pay full price for the sins of his father, for that man's faithless abandonment. For the curse laid upon him by his mother.

He had only begun to look up, and the faces he saw were bright and smiling. Even so, he did not feel worthy of any face he saw, nor of bearing a lighter feeling. Stones are not so easily cast off when the strings binding them are tightly knotted. Inside his chest, he was pulling at the bonds, struggling to the surface of the water where his mother had dragged him to the bottom amidst rot and decay.

"Life will be," he answered her simply.

She echoed his words, squeezing his hand. He breathed deeply of mountain air and found temporary relief from his shadow.

The Weeping House

Barn Owl
Tyto alba

42

Tannins

It had been a chief request of Miff Reinalz to be included in the tanning process of all the hides Carey had obtained from Farmer Welch and Farmer Knappen. In the bright, earliest morning of the next week, Miff waited on the edge of Carey's property. His elder brother, Wolfgang, waited with him, hands in his pockets, studying the shape of Carey's old cottage. The shingled roof was weary in places, and the lefthand wall seemed off-kilter, unless one tilted one's head to the side upon inspection. Layered shingles were in need of repair round the windows. Several shutters were missing entirely.

"What does he do if it storms?" Wolfgang whispered to his little brother.

"He's a man," Miff said, "has no fear of storms."

"I don't fear storms either," Wolfie said. "I was just wonderin'."

"A real man can survive any weather, any storm, anything!"

"I know," Wolfie said, crossing his arms over his chest. He kicked stones buried in the dirt there. Neither of the boys took the tentative steps required to reach the threshold of the house.

The door rattled and flung open. Treu leapt from the porch, dancing around the boys' feet in exultant joy. He rolled in the dry leaves and barked loudly, announcing his chief pleasure at having two playmates come to his very house. The boys tussled with him in the tall grass growing on the far side of the fence. They raced to and fro along the edge of the river until they were weary and winded.

"Ho!" Carey called when they were quite finished. "D'ye want breakfast?" He stood on the porch, holding a steaming mug of coffee.

"Mutti gave us breakfast already—" Miff began to shout.

"We will!" The elder brother pushed past the younger, climbing the steps into the house. They creaked loudly in the cool morning breeze. Miff followed, eagerly accepting three eggs fried with bacon and thick rinds of sausage.

They sat on the porch, legs hanging over wild-run weeds and old heirloom flowers gone to waste. Treu waited in the bare, well-worn grass spread over the yard, pacing back and forth until he was thrown a morsel of meat.

"Do 'ee have an interest in tannin', Wolfie?" Carey asked, setting his plate aside.

"I'm going to work leather like you, Mr. Alsch," Miff interrupted, mimicking Carey's relaxed posture.

"Not entirely sure, sir," Wolfgang eventually answered. "I don't want to work inside, like my father. I want to be outside."

Carey nodded. "I learned leatherwork from my father, and he from his, and so forth. I don't have any sons to pass it to, ye know. I'd like to do it right, not like my father did." He rubbed his sleeved arm, where marks of angry lashes crisscrossed over one another beneath the cuff.

"Would you mind greatly if I tried it, even if I find I don't like it?" Wolfgang asked with a tentative spirit.

"Ye both can spend a summer learnin' with me," he said. "An' if at the end, ye don't like it, I'll harbor no grudges."

"Thank you, sir!" Both boys stood in excitement, eager and ready.

"Call me Carey." He took the plates to the pump to clean and wash them in the ice-cold flow. Miff took over, forcing Carey to stand aside as he scrubbed the plates thoroughly and without complaint.

When breakfast was finished, Carey showed the boys how to drape the hide over a post standing in the middle of the yard and use a fleshing knife to separate any remaining fat from the skin. They took similar hides, though smaller and lighter than Carey's, and draped them over the fenceposts.

Miff had to stand on the bottom rung to find the best angle to lean over the rail and work the fleshing knife downward. When these hides were scraped, Carey dragged a barrel from the shed. He pulled soaked hides from the barrel and draped them over the fence and fleshing post. The unsoaked hides were stuffed into the barrel and left to soak.

"We mix lye in with water," Carey explained, dumping white powder into the barrel and mixing it with the end of a shovel. "Sits for a few days. When it comes out, the hair comes right off." He pinched a tuft of hair on the topside of the soaked hides, and it sloughed off without much effort. Taking the fleshing knife again, he demonstrated how to draw the horizontal blade downward to push the hair off.

They mimicked his movements, struggling to find a smooth rhythm like Carey. He finished three hides by the time theirs held any similarity to his smooth pieces. He rinsed the hides three times over each, then dropped them into another barrel half full of water. Taking a pail filled with a dark brown liquid, he emptied it into the barrel.

"Tannin," he said, nodding to the brown water. "Made from tree bark, which has sap an' bitters that stain the hide. When it's stained all the way through"—he pulled the lid from another barrel and showed the stain of the hide, which had permeated through the thickest portion of the skin—"it keeps it from breaking down. 'Tis much stronger 'n' hide, tanned leather is. These have sat for three months," Carey said, dropping the brown hide back into the barrel. "Today, we'll take 'em out, let 'em dry, and rub 'em with mink oil. Keeps the leather from cracking."

"And then?" Miff asked.

"Then,"—Carey took a deep breath—"I'll teach ye leatherworkin'. Afore that, I'll show ye how to make the tannin."

The Weeping House

He led them to the back wall of his shed, where cupboards were stacked overhead, almost like chicken roosts. Each was filled with different specimens of herbs, mushrooms, spices, birds' nests, seeds, and an array of clays, silts, and dried fruit. A ladder rested on the wall, set aside to reach to the top shelf, where myriad tree barks were stacked on top of one another.

"Fetch some bark," Carey said. Miff climbed the ladder with alacrity, descending a moment later with heavy chestnut bark. Wolfgang retrieved dark spruce bark and picked at the edge of the wood, pulling off a bit of lichen that had gathered there.

"Did you collect all of this?" Wolfie asked, somewhat awestruck by the mere size of the collection.

"Aye." Carey nodded. "'Tis sparse, now." He grimaced. "Used a lot in winter."

"This is sparse?" Miff was incredulous.

"'Twill be full again by the end of spring." Carey shrugged noncommittally. "The woods are full, 'tis only left to be collected and used."

"This is like a treasure trove," Miff said. "Where is the dragon?"

"Treu is the dragon." Wolfgang laughed, tossing a stick out of the shed for the hound to fetch. He bayed loudly and retrieved the stick almost immediately.

"He is a dragon." Carey nodded. "He fearsome likes to guard, though he seldom breathes fire."

Taking the bark from the shed, he showed them how to build up the fire in the yard, then let it burn to embers and hot coals. He placed a metal pot on the iron bracket set over the coals and dropped the chunks of bark in. Miff poured water over the tops of these.

"The water changes," Carey said, poking the coals with a stick, "based on the amount of tannins in the bark. Birch, alder, 'n hemlock has more, 'n older bark that grows close to the ground has the most."

"Should I have taken a different bark?" asked Miff, peering into the water that had yet to turn colors.

"No," Carey said, "ye should test different barks, see what ye like best."

"Which one do you like best?" Wolfgang crouched beside the fire and tossed a leaf into the coals. It lit up with flame immediately, producing a spiral of pretty smoke.

"Birch," Carey said, "easiest to collect. Though oak 'n' alder works just as well."

"Chestnut smells good," Wolfie said, pressing his strips of bark against his nose. "I love to eat roasted chestnuts at Christmas."

"You love to eat anything." Miff rolled his eyes. Wolfgang grinned sheepishly. They bickered almost constantly, occasionally throwing a stick across the yard for Treu, until the hound found a soft patch of grass to rest until lunch.

Wolfgang stirred the slightly darkening tannin with a large stick. It rolled in a low boil, bubbles of air escaping from the surface. He whistled a tune while he worked, and looked up in surprise when Carey followed suit, taking up the melody with ease. When the song was finished, Carey demonstrated his whistling prowess, perfectly imitating the calls of three different birds perched nearby. The boys were awestruck and spent the rest of the day attempting to twitter like birds.

Working in the light of the day, Carey did not notice how light his burden had become, nor how easily he talked with the Reinalz boys. Birds sang from the trees ringing the property, and a hawk circled high overhead. A warm breeze filtered through the yard, carrying the promise of a warm summer. He was contented with the day and felt no pull of despondence. He was light in his heart.

Eastern Meadowlark
Sturnella magna

43

No Poor Opinions

Someone called from the bottom of the hill leading to Carey's cottage. Isola and Nonny carried a basket each and were followed by a posse of children. Baby Isolde was cradled in a sling against Nonny's chest and Mechthild carried Anneliese on her hip.

Lieselotte and Ada ran forward, greeting Treu with open arms. The hound threw himself at them. They collapsed in a heap at the top of the hill. Amalie lay down on top of the heap with her arms outspread to envelop both sisters and the dog. Hearty laughter and a game of chase ensued when Treu freed himself.

"We've come to see how you fare!" said Isola when she reached the top of the hill. Looking around the yard, she saw the ramshackle appearance of the little cottage, the dead, tangled state of the garden, and the dilapidated fences hung with leather hides, but made no change of expression. As a mother, she saw the position of Carey's heart reflected in his house and home. To herself, she said, this truly is the face of Carey Alsch and shall have to be mended. She knew, however, that for mending to be done, Carey would have to begin in his own way. No insistence from her or her husband would cause change in a man, especially one who had lived so for the majority of his life.

"Mutti!" Miff shouted, running to her in the throes of pride and accomplishment. He carried a sopping-wet piece of hairless hide aloft, claiming it as his greatest achievement. "I learned to use a fleshing knife!"

"How wonderful." Isola stared at the sheet of skin flapping in front of her face. "Shall you break for lunch?" She leaned around the hide and addressed Carey, who had drawn another cowhide over his fleshing post and worked quietly.

"'Tis not required," Carey rumbled in a low voice. "Had planned victuals myself. Ye had no need to come all this way. Lookin' on my house in this state"—he did not look up—"'tis bad for the eyes."

"Oh hush, Carey," Isola said, entering the yard by way of the half-rotted gate. Nonny followed, cooing softly to Isolde, who had begun to stir. Mechthild placed Anneliese in the yard and went to help her mother set things out on the large picnic blanket they had packed away in the bottom of one of the baskets. The second eldest, Corinna, followed Lieselotte and Ada to the edge of the water, minding them in case they happened to fall into the icy flow. All three girls pulled off their shoes and stockings and played in the shallows, holding their skirts in bunches above the water.

Wolfgang and Miff paused their labor to throw stones and were joined by Amalie and Inge in a feat of strength, challenging one another as to who could throw the largest stone the farthest.

Nonny stood on the edge of the garden, softly rocking Isolde back to sleep. She met Carey's eyes and smiled. Kissing the baby's forehead, she continued to look at him, and he at her. Her presence in any vicinity near to him was enough to soften his countenance, enough to lead him to lay down his work, enough to bring a smile to his normally sullen face.

Although Nonny lifted his spirits, he still worried that Isola would notice the lingering ghosts and dark spirits who lived in the pond, at the gate, and beneath the roof of his cottage. Nonny already knew the shape of those spirits, so he did not mind her seeing the state of neglect. He feared that Isola would see the darkness and remove her family from his presence, that she would not allow him to remain an extension of her family, for fear he might spoil her perfect brood of children.

"Hello, Miss Nonny." He was unsuccessful in hiding any form of smile when he spoke to her. He took off his hat, holding it in two hands before his waist. "I missed ye," he whispered, when he thought no one could hear.

"Missed me?" she said, taking a step closer. "Why, Carey, it has only been two days."

"Can I not miss ye however many days I do not see ye?"

"Where was this bold spirit in the face of the butcher or Mrs. Froel?" Her eyes sparked with humor.

"'Tis not a bold spirit." He shook his head. "Only … I wish to be honest with 'ee. I miss ye when ye leave. Even if 'tis only a minute."

"Well," she said, blushing red. "I do, too." She turned away sharply and hid her expression behind Isolde's thick, black hair, where the baby slept soundly in the sling on her chest. Carey took a deep breath, then laid his work aside and joined the family on the edge of the Isar. The younger Reinalz children played among the stones scattered against the shore, where fallen trees were lodged between shores. They were wholly forbidden from crossing the river on the logs, warned against possible death, though it was likely they still dreamed of forbidden crossings and would have attempted if there were not so many watchful eyes.

Lunch consisted of stuffed pies filled with beef, pork, assorted beans, corn, and thick gravy. Nonny sliced tomatoes, carrots, and cucumbers and laid them in a pretty pattern on a plate. Several cheeses were arrayed beside them, although these disappeared minutes after their debut.

It was a casual affair, lasting nearly an hour and a half. The children played, ate their fill, then played again, then ate an additional fill, and so forth. Carey sat beside Nonny on the edge of the picnic blanket. His hand lightly brushed against hers when he thought no one was watching.

Isola and Corinna were always watching. They looked at each other knowingly with each occurrence. Theirs was the mindful connection of mother and daughters, able to communicate silently with only the eyes. Mechthild was also skilled in this language but was busy teaching Amalie to skip stones across the smoother portions of the river.

"How goes the work?" Isola asked Carey whilst handing Nonny a plate of fresh raspberries. "Are the boys any good?"

"Good for it." Carey nodded. "They listen well. No arguin' with me."

"And Miff pays attention?"

"Very much. He has keen interest, I think."

"It was the animal you made him," she said, "the lion. He will not touch it for fear of ruining it. Though it's a toy," she said, laughing, "he treats it like a royal treasure."

"It won't spoil." Carey smiled. "Cured the leather myself."

"He won't be persuaded," Isola said.

"It would be fine to have an apprentice," Nonny said. "Don't you think, Carey?"

"Aye," he said. "Only, I don't know if I'm fit to teach. He should apprentice in München."

"There's not a leatherworker there to rival your work," Nonny said. "I've seen the whole of it, and I'll not be swayed by any other leathercraft. Alsch or nothing for me."

"And us." Isola was in wholehearted agreement. "I bought Corinna shoes from München for her birthday when she was younger, and they fell apart within a month of use. Carey made her a pair four years ago that are practically new."

"Do ye never have poor opinions of me?" Carey laughed. Nonny's hand rested beside his on the colorful blanket and he absentmindedly traced his fingers over it. Her eyes widened, meeting Corinna's, who fought against laughter, somehow maintaining a reasonable expression.

"If there's a poor opinion of Carey Alsch in the world," said Isola, "it doesn't come from the Reinalz family, you can be sure of it."

"Mutti would silence any who spoke of such a thing." Corinna laughed. She uncovered a cake layered with fruit and cut thick slices, plating them and handing them to each adult first. When they were all served, she cut smaller pieces and called her siblings one by one. Sticky sugar was soon spread on fingers and mouths. When they were done, Mechthild scrubbed each of the younger children's faces and hands in the shallows of the Isar.

"In this town," Nonny said, "it is practically a crime to dislike Carey Alsch." She finally placed her hand in his, and, in full view of the Reinalzes, laced their fingers together. Carey hiccupped loudly, nearly choking on a piece of cake. He tried to subtly remove his hand, but Nonny would not release him. He sighed, both captive and captivated.

Isola laughed heartily along with Corinna and Nonny, who seemed to find great amusement in Carey's vain struggle.

"We all know, Carey," Isola said after a bout of laughter. "It is not a secret in this household."

He stared at each of the women, unable to speak for half a minute. "'Tis only—" He seemed to have forgotten the nature of language. "I had thought Miss Nonny's hand was cold. 'Tis so pale and light."

This produced another round of laughter. Defeated, Carey dropped his head into his free hand and could not meet any of their eyes. Eventually, he was persuaded by their good humor and joined in the laughter with full heart, though still held captive by Nonny.

Barn Swallow
Hirundo Rustica

44
The Chair

When his visitors had all gone, Carey sat on the porch and filled his long pipe with tobacco. He lit it with a small stick left in the dying embers of the tannin fire and pulled deeply of the pleasant smoke. Darkness fell over the angle of the tree-line, where dusk silhouetted the tops of the pines. Stars emerged from their curtain of black, preparing to shine for the whole night. Constellations sprayed the vault of the heavens with myriad pale colors.

Somewhere deep in the alpine woods, a wolf howled. His sad cry carried across the mountains and was taken up by a similarly mournful wolf on some distant hill. Treu added in his own portion of worldly grief and sorrow. It was a hypocritical howl, as he was not a partaker in burden, unlike his distant wolf cousins who roamed the mountains, having been well taken care of since his birth.

Carey ruffled the hound's velvety ears and leaned against the railing on his porch, which was beginning to show its age. Reclining there, he surveyed his cottage and its failing lines and beams. The roof sagged; walls angled in; foundations sank into the soft earth. On the far wall, the old walnut was partially grown into the side of the house, lifting the foundation on that side. Already a few rotten branches had fallen from the tree and damaged his eaves.

Ivy grew around the edges, swallowing the once stylized shingled paneling done by his grandfather. Shingles were dropping off, piling around the lower trim, where several thorny briar patches grew, tangling with the ivy and discarded lumber. Carey had planed the lumber himself, hoping to repair his house many years ago, but had been caught by that spirit of apathy and never finished the project.

He sighed and finished his pipe. Dumping the ashes out against the wooden railing, he turned to go inside, calling Treu to follow. The hound went faithfully to his spot by the hearth but seemed disconcerted when he was not joined by his master. He sat and whined softly, watching Carey with an attentive eye.

The man stood in the middle of his house and stared at his chair by the hearth. A cool breeze filtered through the open windows, begging for a fire to be lit there, drawing him toward that familiar nightly routine of mindless staring.

Though he was still and quiet, Carey wrestled greatly in his mind, feeling the weight of all the dark corners of his house and the poison of curses laid over him throughout his early life. His pulse thrummed in his wrist and a wild feeling danced across his chest. Taking in a sharp breath, he took hold of the chair and dragged it out the door, across the porch, and down the steps into the yard. He threw it aside and took up his axe.

With a loud cry, Carey descended the axe upon the chair. He swung again and again until it was only pieces. Each movement of his arm was a turning of darkness in his mind, and he attacked it with renewed vigor. Each strain, each brutish cry, each reckless stroke of the sharp blade. Treu sat aside, cocking his head at the odd behavior of his master, who was not prone to loud noises, aside from occasional bird calls.

Sweat beaded on Carey's brow, and a knot worked in his chest, though it was slowly unraveled by the strength in his arms. It was undone when the chair lay in pieces.

Taking the shattered pieces of wood, he cast them on the fire, and watched it engulf them fully. His face reflected the flames, angry red—crimson like blood—poison drawn from his very skin. He crouched before the fire, skin beginning to grow hot from proximity. He did not move, letting the heat wash over him as if it could burn out all the parts he hated most.

"D'ye wonder at me these days, Old Treu?" Carey whispered, not looking at the hound. "I'm not behaving like myself. Or—not the self I thought I was. Who am I, Treu?"

The hound padded towards the fire, wary of the height of the flames ravenously devouring the remnants of the chair. He rested his large head on Carey's leg, looking up at him with great, sad eyes.

"My weeping house." Carey still spoke quietly. "Should I burn it all? I can't seem to get the stain out. What should we do, old boy?"

Treu continued looking at him. If hounds could speak with their eyes alone, Treu would have been a master of the language.

"'Tis more than that, though," he mused. "I have a family. They want to visit! To see how work fares, how the day goes, and the like. 'Tis likely they do care for me, Treu. Not a one is vain, nor deceitful. A family. My family. I'm part of one now." He set his brow low. "Means I have to care for and protect it. All of them. Especially her."

The wind howled through the trees, making the leaves shiver and dance. A bat ripped through the yard, flying in static patterns until it disappeared in darkness. Treu continued to listen in silence, looking sweetly at his master.

"I couldn't have her live here." Carey sighed. "I couldn't. Ye can't put life itself in such a dirty place. An' with so many curses, why, I think even the shutters heard all utterance of cruelty from Father. An' the beams are surely weighed down by it. Ye can see 'em, all curved an' sagged."

The fire crackled and popped, consuming all the wood like a starving man given his first meal. Soon, all memory of the chair was ash and ember. The glow was softened, almost to the colors he knew chiefly from memory, as he had seen them reflected on Nonny's face. He loved those colors, finding them overlaid with visions of her face in his mind. Lovely and bright.

"I think I shall be dashed to pieces," he whispered. "I can't seem to find any sense within me these days. Only her, old boy." He studied the breath-like glow on the largest ember. "Only her."

Wind passed through the yard, dragging across the embers. They flared brightly, sending sparks upward in a spiraling dance. Carey sat back on his heels to avoid being singed. He laughed.

His laughter was loud when accompanied by the wind. For nearly the first time in his life, Carey laughed for the sake of laughter. He laughed because of the feeling buried in his chest. He had not noticed its placement, nor the portion it had filled, only that it was shaped like love.

He was confronted by the unusual appearance of such a thing, having decided long ago that it was strange and foreign and thus kept it apart from his life. Staring into the night sky, where stars spanned from horizon to horizon, Carey weighed the measure of love in his chest and found it substantial, but not heavy.

45
A Wilderness to Some

Whether the woods are regarded as a howling wilderness or a comforting fold of green is entirely dependent on three things: degrees of darkness, one's familiarity with nature's depth and breadth, and marked alteration to the senses affected by variations in the first two. When darkness is deepened, so are the senses of touch, smell, and hearing. Conversely dampened is the sense of sight. When familiarity of flora and fauna is increased, the woods seem to be less of a howling wilderness and are often considered more comforting than home and hearth. Those who do not understand the heights, hills, dells of nature will often find it devoid of comfort. They will seek solace behind bricks and stone.

In this way, the two perceptions are usually kept separate. They find amusement at the appearance of silliness in the other. A woodsman will find a gentleman silly when the latter cannot determine stick from stone, nor tell forage from fodder. A woodsman laughs at a gentleman wandering in the woods like a babe, unpracticed, unskilled, and uncouth.

To a city man, genteel in character and bearing polished speech and dress, a woodsman will appear wild. An unintelligent man, ragged from work, touched by filth, not understanding (nor withstanding) societal convenience, behaving in all appearances entirely antithetical to the status quo. The gentleman will mock this creature, claiming sophistication as the mark of a true man.

The true mark of a man, however, is the matter of mind he possesses when confronted by the most natural state of the world. His most honest prowess is residing along with, and surviving, the greatest storms, coldest winters, famine, plague, and war, all whilst retaining a good heart and pure soul. A heartless woodsman derides the gentleman as much as the polished gentlemen disdains his counterpart. Either may be a man, but not truly a natural man, unless he battles the world and does not lose himself entirely.

Carey Alsch was not a natural man, being thoroughly good despite having ample reason to detest the world and everything in it. He made no mockery of any man, nor did he cast derision at those who knew less than he in fields where he had made mastery. This was due in part to having a poor view of himself. He greatly deprecated any supposed success in his life and thought his strengths were his weaknesses. Indeed they were, as any weakness becomes a strength in good light, and any strength eventually becomes weakness if brought into darkness.

A month into the full swing of summer, Carey minded the flow of a small tributary. He breathed deeply of the scent of forest loam that hung heavy on the summer breeze moving between trees. These trees were old, with ragged bark, broad branches spanning wide gaps overhead, all hung with moss and patches of lichen. Mistletoe suffocated several branches, stealing nutrients the tree reserved for its periphery.

The woods were surprisingly quiet, full of bright gladness and midday cheer. Treu had been left home due to the hound's disdain for silence when espying birds. He had made known his great displeasure, and his cries were heard far beyond the crossing of the main Isar.

Just returned from München after a week's absence, Nonny studied a pheasant moving through the woods just opposite the creek. It had yet to register their presence and poked absentmindedly at the ground cover in search of bugs. Sketchpad upon her knees, she drew several variations of the bird, including its long, ornate tailfeathers, variegated pinions, and round breast.

They had spent the last three months studying local birds, and despite the interruption of her short trips to München, she had nearly filled her entire notebook with miscellaneous sketches. Carey regarded her warmly as an intelligent pupil and seldom had to repeat descriptions of any specimen they encountered. She learned to mimic bird calls with some success, although she did not yet have the ability to differentiate male and female calls, as that was more difficult.

"Now," she whispered, "why is it regarded as a regular game bird if it is so stunning?"

"Tastes good," Carey mused.

"Is game primarily decided by taste?"

"Some make game with foxes and squirrels." Carey shrugged.

"You don't?"

"Couldn't kill a fox for living," he said.

"But a pheasant?"

"There are many more pheasant than fox, and a fox is so clever 'tis almost human. If a fox is minding my chickens, though, I'll kill it. Foxes are wily."

"Wily," she said, making a note in her book. "Can we see a fox?"

"I'll try," he said. "I know where a den is, but they're very elusive."

"Let's go!" She closed her notebook and stood abruptly, causing the pheasant to startle and disappear in a flurry of feathers. "Oh, sorry." She grimaced.

"No 'arm." Carey smiled. He stood and gathered his foraging bag in one hand and her hand in his other, pulled her up, and started off into deeper woods. "Foxes live in the next valley over. Can ye make it?"

"I can!" She came up close behind him and smiled brightly.

"Ye are very lively today." He returned the expression.

"It is good to be alive," she said, passing him and walking with quick step down the hill.

"'Tis." Carey frowned. "I s'pose." Thinking it was good merely to be alive was not a naturally sprung thought in him and clearly originated from the part of his mind dominated by thoughts of Nonny.

"You suppose?" She turned to look at him with a curious expression when they reached the top of the hill on the far side of the little valley.

"Dunno." He shrugged. "Never really considered it good. 'Twas just livin', sometimes easy. Most times hard."

"Indeed." She nodded, sitting on the edge of a log grown over with moss. Leaning forward, she studied the bracts of brown fungi growing along the edge. "I think some days are hard, others tiring. So much is busyness, with no actual living. All for desires that mean nothing. People in the city are always moving, and no one is living. I find it wearying."

"There's lots of weariness to find in the world." He nodded. "'Tis weary sometimes just to live."

"You think so?" She frowned. "Are you weary to live?"

"Not like I used to be." He shook his head. "I like it more now."

"I'm so glad." She turned her face towards the sunlight streaming through the trees.

"Are ye weary to live, Nonny?"

"No!" she said, "I want to live and keep living. I don't want to stop, ever."

"Well, we all stop sometime." He was a very serious man.

"I should stop when I've done everything," she said. "When I've felt everything and expressed all my feelings. Then I'll die." She rose from her moss-covered seat and followed him under a broad oak, where mistletoe choked out the upper branches.

"Why talk of death?" he said. "I don't like to think of it. For another thirty years, at least."

"Shall we still be friends in thirty years, Carey?"

"I'd never not want to be friends with ye," he said. "Anything else sounds miserable."

"We are the dearest of friends, aren't we?"

"We are." He nodded. "Better friends than ever was walking, would, or will walk."

She laughed, allowing him to lift her from the log. He set her down in tall grass and looked down at her, hands remaining on her hips.

"And when I die," he said, "I'll lay down in the meadow, and wait for 'ee to lie down beside me when ye go on."

"Do you assume to go first?" She grinned.

"I'll have to," he said. "I can't be here when ye aren't."

"You did before." She continued on through the woods, inspecting the leaves on nearby branches. She decided they were oak and released them back to the underbrush.

"Well," he said, "my life before was mindless and numb. I didn't like anything about it, aside from Treu."

"Was it really so bad, Carey?"

"It was." He nodded. "Though I think that was the place I put myself in, not the way it truly was. Holt helped me realize that. I was a miserable sop. He's a good man."

"I am sorry." She was very still. "I'm sorry you were alone, regardless of whether you made yourself alone, or you truly were."

He looked at her, then continued walking. When he had gone a little distance he spoke softly, so she had to strain her ears to listen. He described his childhood fully as he had never done before, speaking of lashes and wrath, of pain, misery, and solitude. In an effort to meet her expectation of feeling all and expressing all feelings, he told her of the moment he found his mother, face down in the water near the center of the pond, how he had waded in to reach her and dragged her lifeless body to shore.

Nonny was quiet, utterly attentive and fixated on the man as he spoke, taking every word captive. Holding his words close to her chest, she felt his grief in a wave, though he spoke as if it were all a simple matter to discuss. She listened while he explained how his father cleared the house of personal effects and left him with an empty hearth. How, in lieu of tears, Carey made himself completely alone for half his life.

When half an hour of walking and revelations was done with, he stopped and looked at her again. "I would've continued on in such a vein for my whole life," he said, "but for the Reinalzes, of which ye are an extension. All such good people. I should hope to be as good as ye, one day."

"You are a good man, Carey," she said. "The best. Truly. Holt speaks highly of you, unlike any other man."

"He is a good man." Carey smiled.

"Cousin Holt is a very kind man," she said. "My father was very upset when I came here, but Grandfather convinced him to leave me alone because Cousin Holt was here. I think he is my savior as well. Isola, too. And you."

"I'd not thought a father could be unhappy with his daughter."

"What difference is a son to a daughter if they rebel?" Nonny shrugged. "He does not like my ways. Nor does my mother. She hates me, I think."

"Ways?"

"I don't want to—to stay there, I don't want to marry a withered man and then die, feeling all alone for all my life. They wanted me to marry a man who was twice my age, so I came here. Father nearly tore the house down."

"Don't ever marry another man." Carey pulled back on her hand to turn her towards him.

"I would never," she promised. She found a splintered stump still attached to the recently felled tree and knelt beside it, finding a seat on a portion of its broken branches. She looked at Carey closely.

"And when ye go back to München?" he asked. "Are they unkind to ye? Do they speak darkly to ye? How can ye go back, when yer parents are so horrible?"

"My grandfather requires me." She hesitated before speaking. "He's a good man, and I can't often say no."

"I worried ye wouldn't return," he muttered.

She rose and took his hand, continuing to wander through the virid scene. "And what if I couldn't return, one day? What if—"

"If ye are held there as prisoner,"—he was very serious—"I would take ye out of that place."

"But if I—Carey, there are some things." She took a breath. "There are some things that can't be mended by rescue."

"Well, if there is a way to rescue ye," he said, thinking about each word before he spoke, "I will do it every time. Ye belong here, Nonny."

"I do." She nodded. "I belong here, and I want to stay here."

Red Fox
Vulpes Vulpes

46

Fox Dens and Foxes

Reaching the edge of the valley, Carey worked his way down a gentle slope covered in daisies. Wind sent shivering whispers through the petals, making the hill seem alive with movement, a white sea buried beneath the cover of tall trees. Three elk stood on the far slope, headed toward a fell field higher in the range. They watched the strangers, movements stilted and tense, noses twitching, ears alert and shifting side to side.

Nonny followed Carey into a wet meadow cut through with oaks, alders, and tall chestnuts. Silver lamb's ear grew thick among the white daisies, whose yellow sepals looked up into the crown of the forest like little suns spread out across the forest floor. Tree-shade was spread in patches, leaving small portions of the meadow bright with dripping sunlight. In mid-afternoon, any touch of sun was warming and spun like liquid gold between oak leaves.

Drops of dew clung to a neatly crafted spider's web stretched between a sapling spruce and hollow oak, where age had carved out the center of the tree and left it empty until it was wholly taken by decay. The dew in the web shone like spotless glass, purer and more refined than any pane filling a window. It seemed to sparkle when the sun caught there, marking the weaver's handiwork as a delicate and precise craft.

"Fox's den is nearby." Carey scanned the meadow. "Believe 'twas between the far clump of birch, there." He pointed. "See, markings of fox."

"You can see markings from here?" Nonny was incredulous.

"Branches broken, ground pressed from passage." He shrugged. "Scat just outside. Not to mention, I can see the den."

She frowned, peering in the same direction as him. "I don't see it."

"Well," he said, "ye aren't lookin'."

"I am looking," she sniffed, "my eyes are open, and I'm seeing things. Is that not how one looks?"

He grinned. Stepping behind her, he pointed over her shoulder. The ground sloped slightly upward on the far side of the meadow, where globe sedge and rockfoil clung to a scattering of boulders fallen from the abrupt cliff-face extending upwards from the meadow. The cliff-face presented a stark contrast here but melded into sloping grasses flush with primrose, sandwort, armeria, and penstemon on either side, forming one portion of the sloping valley edge.

"'Tis beneath the globe sedge," Carey said, still pointing over her shoulder so she could follow his direct line of gaze. "Beneath that shrubby rhododendron and silver fir, where the globe sedge creeps along the edge of the boulders. There's a den there. D'ye see the shadow?"

She squinted, focusing not on the plants, boulders, and supposed fox den, but rather at Carey's proximity, the tickle of his breath on her ear, and the deep tone of his voice.

"Shadow?"

"Aye," he nodded, "'tis a fox den."

"Shall we go look in it?"

"No." He stepped back. "We wait." He doffed his forage sack and sat down amidst the white flowers. Lying back, he rested with his arms behind his head.

Nonny sat beside him, pushing the forage sack aside to sit very close. "We wait? For how long?" she cocked her head, dark hair spilling over her shoulders.

Carey squinted, opening one eye to look at her. "Foxes are elusive," he said. "Won't come unless we wait, and if we go and look in the den, we'll never find one."

"Very well," she sighed. Taking out her notebook and quill, she sketched birds that landed nearby. Carey named them all: nuthatch, starling, sapsucker, and, diving for a mouse further afield, an osprey. He described their calls, imitating each in perfect succession. Nonny listened attentively to the numerous places they made den, what materials they spun nests from, and in what season they were hatched and bred.

An hour passed in similar fashion, lessons on natural specimens being the foremost conversation. Hands weary from sketching, Nonny lay back beside Carey, supporting her head with one hand, the other plucking absentmindedly at flowers and grass.

"I wish we had planned for a picnic," she sighed. "We were not expecting to come so far in search of foxes, I suppose."

"Are ye hungry?" Carey asked, sitting up quickly and leaning over her to reach his foraging sack. He paused there, one arm outstretched, the other pressing into the soft grass near her shoulder. Nonny blinked. Smiling, she looked up into his face, hair spread around her head like a halo, tangled in among the daisies and edelweiss. Carey was still, a statue frozen in time, studying the shape of her lips and the color in her eyes. He could not hold her gaze for any length of time and had trouble forming complete thoughts when she looked at him in such a way. Taking a deep breath, he grabbed his foraging bag with a stiff hand.

"Aren't you going to kiss me, Carey?" Nonny asked, her voice nearly a whisper blending into the soft breeze filtering through the meadow. Her eyes were filled with bright humor.

"Kiss—" Carey stared at her. In a brief striking of time, he only saw her, not sky, nor ground, grass, tree, or leaf. He did not see the flowers framing her face, nor hear the caw of ravens overhead. In her eye he saw the beauty of her entire person, both within and without, and his heart poured out a full measure of his feeling. Releasing his foraging bag, his gaze fell to her lips. His heart was not still when he touched her cheek and kissed her.

All sights and sounds—any sense of the world aside from her—were forgotten, discarded, and found wanting, inconsequential when compared to the true feeling of living he felt in that moment. He held her, brushing aside dark tresses and tangling his hand in her hair. His other arm was framed against the grass and flowers, so he was close, but not crushing her.

Her hands found the back of his neck, gingerly touched his face, and passed over his ears. She kissed him with the same portion of tenderness pouring out from his heart. Unlike him, she claimed her own feeling, naming it the most right, honest, and good love.

Carey sat upright. "Wait, Nonny." He took a breath. "What if someone saw. I'd not want to—"

"Who will tell, Carey?" She laughed. "The trees? A tree is truthful witness but will not speak on what it has seen. And if the trees know"—her voice a was quiet again, though full of good sense—"then the memory of this will last far longer than either of us. It shall be memorialized for the life of a tree, which is long, longer than ours."

He hesitated, gazing at her with that continuously serious look. "How is it that ye have lips like strawberries?"

"Strawberries?" She laughed, covering her face with her arms.

"Sweet," he said, "like strawberries."

She sat upright and kissed him again. "Strawberries." She laughed with a bright sound.

He nodded, holding himself upright with one arm. "The foxes," he said, turning to look at the den, "we need to watch—"

She pulled his face back to hers and kissed him again, so he forgot entirely of fox dens and foxes.

47

Away and Awry

"I need to tear down my house," said Carey when Holt opened the back door of his house. Another month had passed, and he had thought of little other than Nonny. At the first bloom of summer cornflowers, he retrieved a nosegay of the blue flower for her. She had been gone in München the previous week and returned only three days prior, so he had yet to see her.

"Tear down?" Holt Reinalz was not often confused, but his face was a mask of befuddlement when he looked at Carey. The quiet man from the mountain held a bunch of cornflowers against his chest and gripped his wide-brimmed duster hat against his leg. His words were unusual, and his face quite serious.

"Aye, tear down," Carey repeated. "Needs to be gone, and a new one built."

"What brought this revelation on?"

"Not a fit house. 'Tis falling apart. The roof leaks, foundation crumbling. I let it go, to be sure."

"And you want to just tear it down?" Holt stood straight and gestured for Carey to come inside.

Carey nodded stiffly. "Tear it down and build a new one."

"I ... think we can manage," Holt said as he led Carey into the Blue-Rue and seated him in the great chair facing away from the door, where light streamed in from the morning sun and colored the floorboards in a rosy hue.

"When can we start?"

The Weeping House

"Well." Holt sat on the edge of the hearth, elbows propped on his knees, chin propped on his palms. He was deep in thought. "If you don't mind, we'll get half the town on it, make it a day."

"I don't mind," said Carey, "if they do the buildin', but I'd not want them to see it still standin'."

"Very well." Holt nodded. "How about a Reinalz demolition crew? We can come tear it down in a day or two, and then do an old-fashioned 'raising' to build it back up?"

Carey nodded. He looked down, realizing he still held the bunch of blue cornflowers, which were now shedding seed on his clothes and the edge of the armchair.

"Holt," Isola said as she pushed into the room, not realizing Carey sat in the about-facing chair. "I couldn't find you. I walked past Nonny's room about an hour ago, and I heard the most—she was sobbing, dear."

Holt lifted his head and met his wife's gaze with a slight look of alarm. Carey leaned forward so Isola could see his face.

"Carey?" Isola's eyes widened more than her husband's. She clamped two hands over her mouth. "Oh, please don't tell Nonny I said anything. I did not know you were there."

"Where is Nonny now?" Carey stood abruptly.

"She went for a walk," Isola said.

"Which direction?"

"Towards Truwald; there's a flat meadow of birch and aspen she likes to walk in."

"Thankee," he said, then quickly left, being the kind of man who did not find practical use in pointless explanations. He was so used to solitude, he never gave thought to giving reason for any of his actions, as he was beholden to no one but his dog.

Treu met him at the door and began leaping about his heels. The hound saw the deepening of Carey's brow, how he pulled his hat low over his ears, and the swift manner of walk in which he descended the front steps of the house. He kept close to his master, understanding his mood but not knowing the reason for his urgency.

Carey turned toward Truwald, the next town over on the way to München, and descended the rocky path. It was well worn, with ruts dug by frequent wagon wheels. He passed a man driving a mule yoked to one such cart and did not stop to look who it was. Veering from the main path, Carey found a simple foot trail leading between dark spruce and silver fir. He followed this trail, listening for the call of meadow birds: redpolls, finches, chickadee, and other tits.

Birch began to replace the darker trees, and the underbrush became looser and softer in variation. Trollius, columbine, and white thistle grew in patches throughout the meadow, and white birch became the mainstay, not yet set to peeling, and bearing a green cover overhead.

Carey stood silently for a moment, casting his senses broadly and detecting myriad bird calls, crickets, chirps—and quiet weeping. He followed this last sound, searching among the trees for a familiar brace of hair.

Nonny sat on a moss-coated log on the far side of a dense clump of young birch trees. Her form was hunched over, and she held a letter in one shaking hand. Her soft lament struck Carey, and he could not move. She took a deep, shuddering breath and raised her eyes to inspect the crown-shy trees overhead, recalling Carey's description of the politeness of trees. In the midst of her sorrow, the memory brought forth a smile. Cheeks wet with tears, she saw him standing there, Treu by his side, hat held tightly in his hands at his waist. For a moment, his presence seemed more fictitious than reality and she frowned, considering the scene set before her.

"Why're you crying, Nonny?" His voice was steady.

"Carey?" Hers was not so sure. She turned, hiding her face from view as she wiped her tears. It was in vain, for any tear she wiped away was quickly replaced, until she seemed to find difficulty forming words, or even taking in breath.

Carey was by her side in a few quick strides, kneeling in the damp, cool earth beside the log. He did not touch her, only set his hat aside and waited. Treu dropped his great head into Nonny's lap, demanding attention. Nonny continued to hide her face from view.

"I don't want you to see me like this," she whispered, voice altered from tears.

"I'm not seein' anything," he answered, equally as quiet. "Consider me a blind man."

"How did you find me?"

"I listened to the birds," he said. "Isola said ye'd be in a birch meadow. I listened. Heard redpolls an' the like."

"What are redpolls?" Her voice had regained some of its color, though she still did not look at him.

"'Tis a red-brown songbird who loves birch trees." He slowly took her hand, turning it over in his. Her other hand still tightly held the letter, filled edge-to-edge with ornate handwriting. He waited several long minutes before speaking. "I've asked Holt to tear down my house. I'll make it new, so ye can live there. We'll have our shared sorrows, but the house won't have the weight of a lifetime of 'em."

"Tear it down?" She finally looked at him. Her eyes were red, lashes brimmed with tears.

"Aye. All down," he said, scooting closer, till he held both of her hands in his.

"Live there?" she whispered, "together?"

"Aye. Together." He smiled.

"But I can't—at least not now." Tears spilled over her long, dark lashes, tracing down her stained cheeks. "Carey, I have to go away …"

"Away?" He looked up at her, brow drawing together. "But ye'd just gone away. Does your grandfather need ye?"

"Yes." She nodded.

"But why does that make you cry?" He reached up and brushed her tears aside. "'Tis not like parting makes a difference; ye'll come back."

"But I—I might come back." She sucked in a deep breath but it seemed to fill no space in her chest and was just as quickly expelled.

"Might?"

"There's things I have to do. I don't know if I can come back. But if I do, it will all be better."

"What do ye have to do? What makes ye cry, Miss Nonny?"

"It will all be better, Carey." She shook her head. "And maybe the new house will be done when I return. We can only hope."

"But why does it all make 'ee cry?" Carey came even closer, so he held her face in his hands and wiped her tears. "I'd not see anything make 'ee cry, and if it's family, ye can leave 'em all behind and be my family. Me and Treu, we'd be good family for 'ee."

"I have to," she said. "It will all be so much better if I go, Carey. The only way I could come back permanently is if go now. I promise." She cupped his face gently and kissed him. He kissed her back, not fully understanding the reason for her tears but understanding the expression of them. Kneeling in the dirt, he held her in his arms, and she wept.

The Weeping House

Ermine
  Mustela erminea

48

The Felling of the Weeping House

Four weeks after Nonny's return to München, the whole Reinalz family helped tear down Carey's house. After spending the morning emptying it of all contents, they took axes and hammers, and dismantled it roof to floor. A great heap of burning lumber was arranged in the next meadow over, carefully maintained by Mechthild and Corinna Reinalz, who also watched the youngest children. Michael and Amalie dragged tarps laden with broken frames, beams, and shingles between the two clearings.

Carey said little, though that was not unordinary. The difference was that this silence stemmed from the heart, rather than personal mannerisms. He worked with an axe, tearing apart the corners of the house he hated. Holt Reinalz labored beside him, along with Wolfgang, Oscar, Inge, and Isola. They saw Carey's heart expressed in each swing of the axe and ached for him, since he was so unused to the physical manifestation of his own aches. As a rule, he typically found apathy and despondence to be the cure for any feeling, but now, he worked hard to avoid those pits of numb despair.

Holt expressed his sympathy, and his equal level of confusion and surprise, at Nonny's abrupt and supposedly lengthy return to München. Neither husband nor wife could explain Nonny's emotional reaction to the journey, but they left the topic undiscussed out of respect for the lady.

When evening fell, they gathered around a smaller fire, constructed in what was once the front yard, although now there was no front or back, nor house to delineate yard position, so it was just a yard.

Two days were reserved for demolition, and a week for the raising of the new house. When the house was leveled down to the foundation, Farmer Knappen and his family, Farmer Welch and his, Mr. and Mrs. Basch and kin, Mrs. Froel, and the Albrights appeared at the top of the hill. Even the butcher blessed the group with his presence, speaking about his father's notoriously keen woodworking craftsmanship—a skill that had been genetically passed to his son, of course.

Trees were felled in the forest, primarily spruce, cedar, and pine, then planed and prepared for raising. A rising stack of clean lumber steadily grew on one corner of the property, and framing decided upon on the third day. The gardens were cleared, the rotted walnut felled, replaced by an oak sapling far enough from the foundations of the house to not cause future damage.

On the fifth day, they set to framing out the beams of the house, forming walls from fresh lumber. Farmer Knappen surprised the gathering with a wheel of cheese, and his wife and Isola presented their dark rye loaves, so a meal of cheese, bread, and forest berries was had by all.

When the sun settled low at dusk, Carey sat by himself on a discarded log that had been found wanting in the shape of its knots. Such a malformed tree was not suitable for building a house, and so it had become a seat of sorts. The rest of the group ate out-of-doors and without a table, finding any scrap of wood or turned stone to use as a seat.

"Where's Nonny gone?" Mrs. Froel asked, sitting beside Carey on the log, which he thought was clearly too small for more than one person.

"To München," Carey said without looking up from his small piece of bread and cheese.

"And she's abandoned you?"

"Not abandoned." He frowned. "She'll be back."

"In the past," Mrs. Froel mused, "she'd only be gone a week or two; it's been three, hasn't it?"

"Four," he corrected.

"Are ye so sure she hasn't abandoned us all? I thought ye had a chance, my boy."

"A chance?" Carey finally looked at her, showing keen anger and frustration in his face.

"Aye," said the lady, "it seemed like ye liked her, and she liked ye. But now she's gone, and who knows if she'll come back."

"Why are ye talkin' so," Carey grumbled. "Best leave it, 'tis not to be discussed."

"But you do care for her?"

He was quiet, picking at the thick crust of rye. "I do."

"And did ye ever name it? Did ye tell her?"

"No—"

"Whyever not, son?" Mrs. Froel was astonished.

"I hadn't the time," he said. "She'll be back."

"Sounds like ye are betting on an uncertain future," she said. "If I were you, I'd go find her in München and tell her everything. Ye lose things ye don't claim, otherwise."

"'Tis not uncertain between me and Nonny," he said.

The woman sniffed. "I know I speak it plain," she said, "too plain sometimes. I'm a coarse woman, Alsch. But I care for ye, and I'd not see ye lose it and have it all fall to shambles. Find the lady, love the lady, and bring her back!"

"I'd not know how to speak in terms of love," Carey said.

"What a silly thing to say!"

"Silly?" He frowned at her, taken aback by her candor.

"Aye, 'tis silly." She faced him. "Ye need no special license nor understanding to speak of love. Lots is love, lots is true, and full of good feeling! If you feel it, tell her!"

"I feel a great deal for her, but is that love? A feelin' alone?"

"Never!" said the lady. "Ye 'ave to choose to love, my boy. 'Tis through life and death, and more than a promise, I swear on the soul of my late husband. And 'tis the strongest stuff ye got inside. Love has good feelings, and hard ones, and long days, and sad nights, but 'tis always mighty, and in honor, always right. Outside of honor, there's ruined love and poisoned love. But in honor, the truth of love. 'Tis solid stuff."

"You speak plainly, Mrs. Froel." Carey smiled.

"I do, I do." She nodded, laughing deeply. "Tired of the fluff, tired of the custom of society for mindful interaction. I like a good, stout conversation like I like good, stout beer."

"I like how ye speak of love," he said. "In honor."

"In honor," she agreed. "The worlds full o' dishonorable things, and it's like a creepering darkness."

"I'd know of darkness." He nodded.

She looked at him, deep in thought. "We all do, Carey," she said finally. "All of us has a great deal of darkness in us, and everyone has some kind of pain. That's why we should bear up and love one another, for it'd not be on me to sow more darkness where darkness already lies."

"I doubt ye have darkness in ye, Mrs. Froel," Carey said. "Ye speak so brightly of love, it can't come from anywhere that has soured spirit in ye."

"Oh, but it can and I do," said she. "And so does everyone here. It'll soften the heart of yourself to know, and the heart ye see others with will be kinder. Ye are about as bad as the next man or woman, Carey; the difference is how you deal with the bad, and how ye protect the light and good things in life. A good man is one who knows there is a great deal of doom within his chest, and yet makes things bloom and grow. You make so much grow, Carey, even if ye don't know it."

"When ye sat beside me on this small log,"—Carey smiled—"I didn't know 'twas to teach me a lesson on life. But I thankee, Mrs. Froel. I don't know how, but it seems ye can see straight through me. I'd not often thought of myself as good, but these days, no darkness overtakes me, no doom escapes, and it's all dissipated so much in the light—and company." He gestured to the people sitting around the fire in his yard, laughing and enjoying one another's presence. "I think I was not a good man when I let it consume me, but now 'tis not the same."

"Then I am very happy, Alsch. And when ye think hard on it, I hope ye will go an' get that girl. She needs to come home."

Alpine Marmot
Marmota marmota

49

Letters from München

By the end of the month, a new house was raised along the upper portion of the Isar, where a small parcel of land had been carved out of the wilderness. The fence was mended, set in with a new gate that bore no ill will or curse. A garden for flowers wrapped around the porch of the house, filled with azaleas and white yarrow. Out near the old shed, a vegetable garden had been raised and planted with cucumber, carrot, potato, turnip, beetroot, and various dillweed, mint, sage, and thyme. In a mixture of loam and grit, rosemary grew by the porch, transferred with care from Mrs. Albright's own garden as a gift.

Carey sat on the porch in a new rocking chair, crafted by Mr. Basch's son, who was apprenticed to the local carpenter. The chair was the first of its kind. Though it was knobby in places and a little uneven in its rocking, it was a welcome gift. A second, similarly fashioned rocking chair rested beside him, empty for now, though he hoped to fill it soon. Treu was very fond of this new arrangement and laid his head atop his master's feet and looked up at him with only the most loving, warm gazes. These expressions were the kind only a hound could muster and could never be rivaled by a human gaze. There is something in hound which bespeaks the deepest of love.

Summer stretched on. Warm breezes filtered through the upper reaches of the mountains, beaten down by the remnants of spring storms. Green was in full display, evident in the arms of the canopies, grass, undergrowth, and passerine fields clinging to the sides of the hills. There was no limit to the color found in every place in the full range of virid shades.

By the end of summer, Nonny had still not returned from München, and a whisper spread through Mittenwald that she would never return. Some said a husband had been got for her, that she had a secret lover far away in the great stone town. Others said she was not fit for country life, and others still considered she was only delayed, and would come home soon.

Carey held the latter view, and though he missed her greatly had full faith that she would not be long for it. He had no script to write to her, nor paper and quill to be entirely legible, as his were scraped from charcoal and rendered from gall nuts, barely realized enough to be called ink. Nonny's absence was entirely silent.

Carey made lists of things he would show her when she returned and made note of amusing things that happened, thinking of how bright her laugh would sound at their mentioning. He had a different kind of anguish. This was different than the soullessness lingering with him through his younger life. This was agony in matters of the heart. He felt his heart might bleed and stain his clothes if she did not soon return.

Michael and Wolfgang came for their lessons each week and showed great enjoyment in the craft, though Wolfie still kept his reservations, being undecided in the direction of his future life. He liked to sit on the porch at Carey's feet and pet Treu, talking of worlds that spun in his head. Carey liked to hear the stories Wolfie told each week, as if they were installments in a local newspaper. Michael had little patience for such fiction and worked diligently at turning the leather, scrubbing lye, and fleshing the hair from the soaked skins.

The most affected aspect of Carey Alsch was that he was little disturbed by outward experiences and had found a peaceful forward motion in life, not relying on actions or wishes for inner resolution. He waited for Nonny, not because he found fault in himself at her prolonged absence, but because he wished to wait for her. He listened to Wolfie's stories and let Miff work, because he liked their company, and because he wished to. There was no other alteration to his heart—though he did not perceive it—than simply finding out what he liked and what he did not. He found a great deal of comfort in the company of any Reinalz and spent many summer nights in the Blue-Rue, surrounded by laughter, food, and family.

His heart did begin a serious aching by the first signals of fall's approach. Though leaves did not fall, nor cooler winds blow, there is a sort of sense one gets when seasons are like to change. Though Nonny held the utmost place of good feeling in his heart, it was now layered by separation and the pain that brought. He sighed a great deal.

On one such evening, he was sitting in the Blue-Rue and explaining—in detail—the difference between chickadees and finches. It seemed to him astonishing that one could be wholly unaware of the fact that chickadees were primarily local to North America, and finches widespread across the Americas, Asia, Europe, and Africa. Holt Reinalz was unaware of this significance and listened with full attention. Though he was required to access some of the skills acquired through the rearing of eleven children. He was a very good listener.

On the far side of the room, Corinna read a book in the window seat, where evening sun filtered through the panes in a pretty golden color. Her sister, Inge, was sprawled nearly in her arms, reading a similarly dark novel, a soliloquy or some dreamy epic.

Isola sat on the blue couch, mending scarves and minding Isolde, who had begun pulling on furniture to stand and wobble. While she worked, Isola hummed a soft tune with a pretty voice. Treu lounged by the hearth, chin atop a very soft corner of the rug. The feeling in the Blue-Rue was one of contentment and company, and clearly not to be disturbed.

The Weeping House

Mechthild pushed through the door into the Blue-Rue and leaned down to whisper in her mother's ear. Isola looked momentarily astonished, and then sat erect. She whispered something in return and glanced at her husband.

"Holt," she said, her voice filled with tense concern. "Mechthild's had a letter from Cousin Karoline."

"And?" Holt frowned. "Why do you look so stricken, Mechthild? Read the letter, if it's so serious."

"It's long," Mechthild said, "but she says—she says Cousin Nonny is sick."

"Sick?" Holt looked at his wife.

"She said she wasn't to tell me, but she had to," Mechthild took a deep breath, "because Cousin Nonny has been mentioning this place in fever, and she said a man's name, and was wondering if Nonny had a lover here."

Everyone turned to look at Carey, who held a pallor, a sick white sheen as had never been cast across his face before. He did not speak, only gripped the edges of the high-backed armchair and stared at Mechthild. Inge and Corinna had set down their books and were quietly listening. The window behind them darkened their bright faces in shadow. The feeling in the room was no longer lovely.

"Sick?" Carey only managed one word. He seemed unable to recall any use of language and was rendered quite useless.

"Cousin Karoline said Cousin Nonny's family has been completely silent and malicious, and Karoline only learned of it because she is friends with Nonny's maid, who is caring for her. She seems like to die." Tears sprung into Mechthild's eyes. She slumped against her mother, taking baby Isolde into her arms to hug.

"Die," Carey whispered. Then again, louder, "Die?"

"She said the doctor has stopped coming, and the family is trying to let her go quietly." Mechthild could barely speak for the tears that now flowed freely. "They stopped treating her, Father, why would they do that?"

Carey stood so abruptly that his chair was sent tumbling away behind him.

"Carey?" Holt stepped closer, reaching out to his friend. Carey brushed the hand away, his face colored by dusk and shadow.

"We're going to München, Holt," Carey said, striding from the room. "Now."

Lammergeier
Gypaetus barbatus

50
Likewise

Neither man said a word as the cart bumped and trundled down the lane. A sturdy black horse drew the cart along with a quick step, somehow sensing the urgency felt by those seated just behind. His large hoofs left behind deep tracks half filled with water. Rain drizzled in a hazy mist so they could not see farther than ten feet ahead. Night darkened the mist further. It coated everything like a blanket, though it seemed strung with haunting visions.

Mountains rose on either side of the lane. The pass broke on the far side, revealing a broader stretch of earth unbroken by Alps. Switchbacks wended back and forth into the broad valley, where the lower, wider portion of the Isar cut through München. Stars shone above, and a full moon illuminated the horizon. The rain-bearing cloud clung to the mountains and the mist was shirked off as soon as they moved below its swathe.

The cart bumped along through the night. They passed early through Krün, nearest town to Mittenwald, and later on in the night, Walchensee, Kochel am See, which is beside Kochelsee lake, and Grossweil. Twice, the heavy wheels ran aground in deep mud, and they were forced to slog through the muck and shove from behind. The horse, known as Mutzel, pulled against his yoke, aiding them in the way such beasts do, possessing a nearly human spirit.

When the road evened out past Grossweil, they drove Mutzel hard. He was a sturdy beast and did not mind, being accustomed to farm work and hauling logs from the mountains. Dawn rose, and still they pressed on. Carey did not speak. He tugged his hat low over his ears, showing only the lower half of his grim face. Holt pressed his lips into a thin line, reins held loosely but constantly pressing Mutzel.

Lowland trees grew wild here, hanging over the lane in a grand arch. Morning sunlight was dappling, making patterns beside the deep ruts carved by previous wagons. Then they were on a flat plain with low hedges, forming into farmland where several tributaries flowed down into the Isar. Several farmers working the fields in early light started at the sight of the wild cart bumping and jolting down the lane.

When the sun had fully risen, they stopped to rest Mutzel, allowing him to drink deeply from one of the icy creeks running between two green hummocks of moss-covered rocks growing richly with a variety of plain grasses. Two oaks twisted over the smooth surface of the water, splayed with branches nearly touching its unbroken, glasslike sheen. A dove settled there, cooing gently hoo-hoo-roo. On some distant farm, a rooster took up his ki-ke-ri-ki, telling the world that it was time to wake.

"D'ye struggle to do good, Holt?" Carey asked, kicking a stone down the side of the steep bank.

"Good?" Holt looked at his friend. "It is difficult, yes. There is quite a lot of me that is selfish and vain—most of me, to be honest. But good is what is required of me."

"Why?"

"Because I have received a full measure of goodness, and I know its power, so I must turn around and do likewise."

"Who gave it to ye?" Carey asked.

"My Father," Holt said. "The One who created those birds you love so. There is where true goodness is found. Only there."

"Then why did ye say ye think I am a good man?" Carey frowned. "If everyone is just as bad as the next. And how can ye find it hard to do? It seems so easy when ye do it. I'd not think any in the Reinalz family do 'arm."

"Oh, that is undeniably false." Holt laughed. "We are all quite rotten! I think most people spend their lives trying to hide just how bad they think they are from everyone else, and so everyone thinks they are so much worse than the next. There are those who think they are great and have no fault—silly, to be sure. But knowing we are capable of great failure does not mean we should burn from the inside, like you were; it means to have humility and seek forgiveness and truth at every turn, to shirk off all the darkness and walk in light. We as men must pursue something that we currently are not. We must have a striving—a holy pursuit—lest we wander." Holt paused, calling Mutzel back to the yoke. "To be honest, Carey, you really are one of the most humble and good men of my acquaintance, and always have been. I think that's why Nonny loved you so quick."

"Loved me?" Carey turned pale.

"She loves you, Carey," Holt said. "Now, are we going to get her, or not? Mutzel is watered. I think he is eager to continue."

They were off again, not stopping until the sun was fully in the sky and the distant horizon became jagged with the outline of buildings. The city was spread wide, with houses, farms, and churches clustered together in groups on the outermost reaches. The roads were still deep ruts, walled by stone on either side, with enough space for walking between.

Two towers rose high above the town, capped with green roofs, ornate windows, and a red shingled roof. Carey was incredulous at the sheer size of the cathedral, which Holt named Frauenkirche. They drew nearer, and the towers only seemed to rise higher and higher. Carey considered that they were more like mountains than any man-made structure he had known, and could not comprehend that they had been crafted by man.

München proper was crowded with carriages, horses, and bustling workers in drab gray, brown, and black dress. Their gazes were constantly shifting, lingering near their feet, then suspiciously away. Carey met several such eyes and found an almost empty person staring back at him, then shifting along noncommittally. He noticed birds fluttering in the streets, mostly dove, pigeon, and swallows. The smaller birds swooped in and out of the higher buttresses on the cathedral and hid beneath the eaves of the dark oak storefronts. The houses were all smashed together.

Holt directed Mutzel through the city, though the horse seemed to have some sense of direction and was avoided by the general populace due to his sheer size. He made every other horse look small in comparison.

Well-dressed ladies and men stared at the mud caked on the two men's heads, clothes, and cart, remnants of their wild flight through the night. They kept their heads down, focused solely on their tasks. Carey did not like the city and found the height of the buildings to be oppressive and stuffy. He understood more clearly Nonny's great desire for escape from this place. It was stone, and more like prison than anything else.

Holt brought the cart to an abrupt stop before a house set within a row of similar houses in a long stone promenade. Each had its own gate and porch and limited garden. This one had a frail jasmine and ugly green shrub. The stonework was elegant, supposedly rich, although Carey paid it no heed. He was out of the cart before it fully stopped and nearly at the top of the stairs before Holt joined him.

51

Another Kind of Center

Holt did not knock. He pushed the door open, to the great surprise of the servant waiting on the other side.

"Mr. Reinalz, sir," the servant said, bowing his head politely. "I did not know we were expecting you today." The servant's eyes traveled the length of both men, worn ragged from travel and caked in mud. He was not pleased by their appearance, let alone the mud they tracked indoors.

"I did not tell anyone I was coming," Holt said. "Is the family at home?"

"The Von Steins are out for half the day—but sir, if you wait in the study, I will tell the master you have arrived."

"No need," Holt said, "where is Miss Nonny?"

"My lady is not at home—"

"Where is she, Bernhard, I am not here to bandy words lightly or explain myself. Tell me now. I know she is here."

"Miss Nonny is unwell," Bernhard said.

"I am aware," Holt said. He began walking towards the steep mahogany staircase. Carey followed close behind. His grim visage caused the servant to hesitate. Holt looked up the stairs, then back at the man. "Where is she unwell?"

"I cannot tell you. I'm sorry."

Holt stalked over to the man. "You are a man who works here. In matters of morality, which do you wish to be? A coward? A man? Tell me where the lady is, Bernhard, or I shall tear this place apart, brick by brick. Or do you think my friend here will be less vehement than I? He will be quite wild unless we find the lady."

The Weeping House

"Upstairs," Bernhard said, his resistance diminished by Carey's presence alone. The quiet man seemed to loom, his figure made taller and broader by his cold demeanor. "Last door on the right. If it is locked, Miss Von Stein has the key."

"I care not for locks," Carey rumbled deeply, then turned towards the stairs. The front door opened, causing light to stream into the dimly lit hall. A lady with dark hair and bright eyes stepped through. Soft lines aged her face, but her countenance still held an elegant air.

"Bernhard—" she started to say but stopped short. "Holt?" Her gaze fell on the man in the hall, seemingly arguing with her servant. "And … a man?" Her bright eyes swung to Carey, who had one mud-caked boot on the first step of the stairs.

"Lina," Holt coughed. "We've come for Nonny."

"You have come to kidnap my youngest daughter?" she said quickly, taking her gloves off, finger by finger. She pushed past Holt and handed the gloves to the servant. "Anselm!" she called over her shoulder, "there's a situation."

"Carey"—Holt looked at his friend—"Go."

The tall, quiet man turned without a word and disappeared up the stairs. Voices grew loud below. Someone yelled Holt's name, a man with a deep, unkind voice. Lina Von Stein's voice grew shrill and seemed to pierce through every stone in the house.

Carey reached the upper landing and paused. It was dark, stretching long into shadows with doors punctuating the hallway at regular intervals. Juxtaposed between these were small, ugly paintings of flowers. None were accurately labeled.

Taking a deep breath, Carey took a step down the hall. It seemed to lengthen before him, each step creaking underfoot. His breaths were so loud he thought he might shake the foundations of the house when he exhaled. There was nothing lovely, nothing light, nothing bright about Nonny's house in the city. It turned people to stone, she had said.

Reaching the last door on the right, he rested his hand on the handle and steadied himself. He turned the knob and entered the room.

Light streamed in through a window on the far wall, illuminating the dust hanging in the air. A faint musty scent struck his nose, one of sickness and neglect. A bed was pushed against the same wall as the door. The covers were turned up, and a small figure lay there, enshrouded in white sheets and wreathed in unkempt, dark hair.

Carey came close, but she did not turn to look at him. He knelt beside the bed and took her hand in his. It was a familiar hand; the shape, patterns, and size were all the same, but it was lighter, frailer, and white like alabaster.

"Nonny, my love," Carey whispered. "Can ye hear me?"

The world was more silent than it had ever been in that single revolution. Though the earth spun around its axis, and the earth around the sun, and the sun around the galaxy, Carey did not mind such things; here was his axis, another kind of center.

The sheets rustled. She slowly turned to look at him.

"Carey?" she whispered. Her face had lost none of that pure beauty that is expressed in the form of goodness both within and without, but it was pale and wan. Her eyes, once bright and full of life, were like glass, as if she did not fully see him, though she looked directly into his face.

"I've come for ye, my love," he whispered, taking her hand and pressing it to his lips. Her skin was cold.

"Are you real?" Her lips were cracked and dry, blisters forming around the corners. She reached out and touched his cheek, his lips, and brow.

"I'm real." He cupped her face, leaning down to kiss her forehead. "I'm real, and I've come to take 'ee home."

"Home? Where is home? I don't know if I have one of those."

"Home's here." He took her hand and pressed it to his heart. "Home's here, my love. I've built it new so ye can live with me. I cleared out the badness, Nonny, and it's so light. The weeping house is gone. Will ye come and live with me?"

"But—Carey," she whispered, "I'm dying." She took his hand and pressed it to her abdomen, just below her bottom ribs. Her belly was swollen beneath her soft gown.

"What is—"

"Tumors." Her voice was the faintest whisper, as if speaking drew all the energy from her body. "Cancer. I'm dying."

"Can ye make it home, Nonny?" He could barely speak for seeing tears slip down her cheeks to stain the white pillow. "If ye must die, ye can't here. It'll turn 'ee to stone, like ye said."

"I don't want to be stone." She ran her fingers along the edge of his hand, feeling every scar, texture, and knuckle, knowing how each one was shaped, for she had studied it often. "I tried to come back, Carey. But Mother wouldn't let me, and then I couldn't find the strength to stand, and no one would bring me a pen to write to you. They want me to wither away and be unnoticed. They always did. It's the way I should have always gone, I think."

"No, my love," he said. "I'll take 'ee home where 'tis all in full bloom, and soon fall will turn the leaves. 'Tis the rosiest hue, all crimson and ochre and burgundy. Treu misses you."

"Can I make it, Carey? I'm so tired, tired even to breathe."

"If ye can't walk, I'll give ye my body," he said, "and if ye can't breathe, I'll give ye my breath. But not in this place, Nonny, not here in this stone prison. Why, 'tis more like a cell than a room."

"If you will do the taking, I'll go," she said. "Take me home, Carey."

He took her into his arms and did not move, letting her arms settle around his neck. They were still, holding close for one long breath, one revolution of the earth on its axis, and one of their own, round their own axis.

52
Weeds

"She will be leaving!" Holt gripped the banister, blocking the staircase with his body. "If she chooses to."

"My daughter stays," boomed Anselm Von Stein, who was not a small man by any means.

"She is not your prisoner." Holt backed up so he stood on the lowest step and stared down at the man. "Though we are kin, Anselm, I'll not let you hold her here. It is wrong. If she wishes to leave, she will leave."

"How dare you come into my house," Anselm raged, "with that wild man in tow, and take what is mine!"

"Nonny is not yours! She is a free woman! She may go where she pleases, and she'll not be held any longer, if she listens to truth. You are a cruel man, Anselm; I've always thought so, though I did not say it before now. If only I could pull you out like weeds. I wish I did not call you family, for how you have abused and neglected your own child." As Holt spoke, the older man made to interrupt but could not break Holt's stride. "And I know! She has told me everything. Everything!"

"An ungrateful hussy!" Anselm stepped close to Holt. "I've given her everything, and she left it all to tramp around in the woods and be wild. Do you know how people talk? She is a disgrace to the name Von Stein."

"Then I hope she will not be Von Stein much longer, and I am so glad I do not bear the same name. I would much rather be considered disgraced by you than abandon Nonny."

"Do not think we will be silent about your behavior, Holt!" Lina's shrill voice broke through the lingering silence. "I will tell Grandfather Elias everything you said. Will you be remembered when he dies—which will be soon—or will you become an island with that wild family of yours?"

"Elias will die soon, if you continue poisoning him," Holt snapped. "You are a leech. I do not care for this life; I have all that I need in my own. So does Nonny. Besides,"—he blinked—"I know Nonny is his favorite, so you are surely hiding all this from him. I think he will soon find a letter that might make him look upon your cruelty with less favor."

"If your mother heard you now!" Lina reached out to take hold of Holt's collar but was held back by her husband.

"My mother did not know what was true in life," Holt said. "A shame, surely, but we have never agreed, Lina. There would be no surprise there. Besides I neither care, nor even consider any thought you have for the way I and my friends live our lives." He turned at the sound of footsteps on the upper landing. "Ah, I think we will be going now."

Carey appeared there, materializing out of shadow. In his arms was a bundle of white, contrasted by wild black hair. He descended, standing beside Holt at the bottom of the stairs. Nonny was quiet in his arms. Though her skin was wan and the shadows under her eyes hollow and ringed, a fire sparked in her eyes, and she looked at her mother and father, challenging them.

"I will walk," she whispered. Brow knitting with concern, Carey set her down, holding out his arm for her to lean upon. She walked towards her father, who blocked the doorway, arms crossed over his chest. "Move, Father. I will make my own way."

"You will stay, girl," said the tall man. "I will not have you ruin this house by dying in some strange land."

"I will die where I wish!" Her voice had regained some of its power. He did not move. Nonny turned to look at Carey. She smiled softly. Carey nodded, then stepped forward and picked Anselm up by his underarms and set him down beside the door so it was no longer blocked. The man was so surprised by the action that he could not speak when Holt, Carey, and Nonny strode through the open door.

"Anselm!" Lina shrieked, "do not let her leave! A disgraceful child! She's never been good for anything. Cruel enough of her to scorn our family's name and respectability in the city to go traipsing about with dirty people, now she's bringing them here! She's always had a fondness for the lowly—a fascination with animals, I'd call it. Look at these filthy people come to steal her away. Creatures, they are! Holt Reinalz, you are no family of mine! My child is more like a forest witch now, practicing devilry in the mountains with wild animals! Anselm, tell her! After all I've done to make her a lady, still she curses my good nature." She leaned upon her husband and cursed them all. "I'd never call her my daughter again! It would be better for her to die quietly here at home, so no one will ask questions!"

Carey led Nonny down the stone steps to the cart where Mutzel waited patiently, dozing on three legs. Nonny leaned on Holt's arm while Carey laid her bed sheets and cover in the back of the cart. He crawled into the cart, and with Holt's help, they made a comfortable place for her to lie, half propped up on Carey's lap, though he was still caked in mud.

"Anselm!" Mrs. Von Stein's voice carried out into the street with an astonishing force of volume and shrieking pitch as she stood on the porch. "She is outside in her nightclothes! Of all things! What will the neighbors think? Oh, my daughter is harsh! She seeks to wound me. She is a wild woman now!"

Anselm Von Stein grabbed his wife by the waist and tugged her into the house. The door slammed shut and did not open again.

Carey whispered softly to Nonny, holding her in his arms. His hands traced along her face, ran through her hair, and passed over her hands. She looked up at him, seeing how his heart nearly melted through his chest. Laying her hands over his, she rested against him.

Holt leapt into the driver's seat and pulled the cart around. He went slowly this time, carefully minding his new cargo. The bustling sounds of the city were a cacophony, though neither person in the back of the cart noticed.

They were through the edge of München before much time had passed. At the outskirts of one of the counties bordering the larger city, Holt stopped to feed and water Mutzel, who did not seem fazed by the abrupt return to the mountains. He was a sturdy animal. Though their pace was slower, they reached the edge of farmland by evening. Holt drove them on through the night. Nonny slept, still holding Carey's hands in both of hers. He did not sleep and instead watched her, studied every movement she made, and assured himself countless times that her chest still rose and fell in an even pattern.

By dawn, they had nearly met the end of the valley and began climbing the switchbacks through the morning, after Holt had a brief nap and Mutzel rested. They were near Scharnitz pass by mid-afternoon, and through the pass by that evening. Holt had procured some fruit and bread in a town outside of München and they shared these, though Nonny continued to sleep and did not notice whether it was day or night.

Mittenwald came into view by midnight, and the cart bumped all the way to the porch of the white house. Isola came out to meet them and was soon followed by every Reinalz, though Anneliese and Isolde were carried by their brothers.

Carey brought Nonny into the house, laying her in the bed upstairs without a word. Overcome by exhaustion, he sat beside the bed and held her hand against his chest. He did not move from there for a day and a half and was more like a hibernating bear than any human.

53

Miracle Man

The three travelers slept for the remainder of the night and into the evening on the second day of their return. When morning came, Carey appeared at the foot of the stairs and was very hungry.

Oscar Reinalz met him in the kitchen, clearing away plates from the family's breakfast. Upon seeing Carey's exhausted mien, he turned quickly and reappeared with a plate full of food. Carey gratefully accepted and sat in the corner of the kitchen. Isola served him a mug of black coffee.

"When Holt wakes,"—Isola looked at Carey sharply—"I will make him give you a change of clothes."

"I'll be running back to the house today, shortly." Carey coughed, surprised by Anneliese's appearance at his knee. She demanded to be lifted into his lap and talked amicably with her fabric doll. "Got to feed Treu. He's been left to fend for himself."

"He hasn't," Oscar said, seated directly across from Carey. He finished his sister's half-eaten bowl of porridge. "Wolfie and Miff kept him here and took wonderful care of him."

Carey stared at the youth, whose head was bent over the porridge and heavy milk. "Thankee," the man said. "I am thankful for all that ye've done for me." He turned to look at Isola and tipped his head toward her.

"You are family, Carey," she said simply. "There is nothing difficult for family to do. And nothing left undone."

Holt appeared in the doorway, cast over with a sheen of grey exhaustion. His eyes were deeply hooded, and he stared blankly at the table. Yawning, he swept his wife into his arms and hugged her, kissing the top of her head. "Always hated the city," he muttered, then found a plate and piled it high with sausage and eggs. "But for such a brief visit, it was not terrible. You should have seen Anselm's face, dear." He sat beside Carey and began to eat like a man half-starved. "Carey clear lifted him up and set him aside like he were a gate! Lifted Anselm! Ha!"

"You picked Uncle Anselm up, Carey?" Oscar was astounded.

"He was in my way," Carey said, nodding, "and he'd not move otherwise."

Isola and Holt laughed heartily. She cleared away the dishes and threw a towel over her shoulder. Holt finished his meal and summoned Oscar to his side. They washed, cleaned, and put away all the dishes while Isola fed Isolde.

Mechthild and Corinna began lessons with the younger children, teaching them letters, reading, and arithmetic. They sang songs to memorize grammatical tenses and played games in the yard to learn spelling. Carey sat on the porch and smoked a pipe with Oscar and Holt. Not one of them said a word, as perhaps they were content to not have a word to share, being pleased enough to have a brief moment of empty quiet within. The kind of quiet a woman might not know, unless she is well-kept and loved. Isola was one of those women, and this morning, she was quietly gardening, as was her favorite pastime. She sang a song about lilies.

"Nonny is awake!" Inge leaned through the doorway and announced loudly to everyone outside. Carey was on his feet in a moment and up the stairs in two.

Amalie sat on the edge of the bed, holding Nonny's hand. She looked up when Carey entered. Nonny's face had regained its color, and some of its vibrance, though there was an underlying aura of sickness surrounding her. She smiled at Carey, and more of her familiar color returned.

"I want to come down to the Blue-Rue," she said. "Will you help me?"

Carey nodded, smiling back. Amalie watched the two, her face shining brightly with amusement. She had helped Nonny change into a pale blue dress with loose fastenings, plaited her hair in a long braid down her back, and brought her a breakfast of porridge and apples. The young girl cleared away Nonny's dishes and waited for Carey in the hall.

Nonny held out a hand to Carey. He took it and she pulled him closer. "Will you carry me? I want to be close to you."

"Ye can be as close as life itself." He smiled, kissing her hand. "I'd do anything ye told me to, Nonny."

"Well, then,"—she looked him in the eye—"hold me and kiss me, Carey Alsch."

He did.

Most of the family waited in the Blue-Rue, eager to see and talk to Nonny, but respecting her space and health. Ada, Lieselotte, and Amalie shared one window seat, while Corinna and Inge took the armchair as one, squished together. Michael and Wolfgang brought Treu into the house. The hound found his precious hearth-front cushion and curled comfortably on the floor.

Carey brought Nonny into the room and laid her on the blue settee, covering her with a blanket. Exultant joy at the reunion was the predominant feeling in the room, though there was an unexpressed sadness in the children's hearts. Nonny was clearly sick, seeming worn out by mere hugs and laughter. She leaned against Carey, holding his hand tightly against her chest.

When conversation ran quiet, the family looked at her expectantly, though not directly asking her to tell them about her prolonged absence, or her reason for going away.

Her face fell when she spoke. "I am somewhat terrible in my heart. Coming to Mittenwald was not to find a new place to start my life, as I had told Cousin Holt." She took a deep breath. "I have been sick for a long time. I came here to die. But I had not thought to love you all so much, and it became all the more painful. And then I met Carey, and—well, we all know how that went." She looked up, finding grins and humor on every face in the room. Michael snickered loudly, burying his face in Treu's coat.

"So," Nonny continued, "I wanted to try and get better. There's a doctor who knows my grandfather who treats tumors of the abdomen through bloodletting." Nonny rolled up her sleeves, revealing red marks on her upper arms. "When I returned home every few weeks this spring, I was being treated. It was an agreement between me and my grandfather, whom I love. He is also dying—from a bleeding disorder—and I promised I would try and live. But the last time I went back, I couldn't stay with my grandfather; he was too sick. I went to stay with my parents, and they would not let me leave. I got sicker there, and soon I couldn't walk, nor write, nor do anything. Please believe me, my dearest family, I did not want to stay away."

"You were kidnapped," Isola said firmly, "and now we are together again. We will help you heal, Nonny."

"I can't heal." Nonny shook her head. "The cancer is in my belly, and it's grown. That's why they stopped the treatment. There's nothing to be done. I just want to die in a lovely place among people who love me."

"Then will you stay here?" Isola took a deep breath, struggling to stifle the flow of tears. Lieselotte and Amalie had already succumbed. They left the room so as to not be heard while they cried.

"I've my medicine," Carey cut in, "at the house. 'Tis not hopeful it will mend ye, but it will ease pain and discomfort. Perhaps a miracle will work in ye. It has before." He looked at Ada, whose cheeks were traced with tears.

"There's power in hope, Nonny," Holt said. "And we will pray, night and day. But I am glad you are home."

"Shall I bring my medicine here each day?" Carey asked. "I'd not bring Nonny back and forth. I've room in my house for her. Perhaps Mechthild and Corinna could come stay as well, or Oscar, so it will all be proper."

"Oh, I don't care about proper!" Nonny declared. "If I'm to die, I will spend my last days with Carey in the woods, please. You all may come visit me; that would lift my spirits."

"Very well," Holt said with a tender smile, "Carey's it is, then. Perhaps he will work another miracle. He is our miracle man, after all."

European Bee-eater
Merops apiaster

54

All in Proper Manner

Nonny spent one more night at the Reinalz home while Carey went to prepare the cottage. He picked cornflowers and placed them in pitchers in the windows, on the table and counters, beside the beds (he had two rooms now), and brought clothes lent by the three elder Reinalz girls. He laid several books on the bedside table in Nonny's room and dusted one last time, so she would not be disturbed by any inconvenience.

Word of Nonny's return spread through town, meeting a mixture of surprise and excitement. Those who really cared were informed of her condition and set about praying and hoping for her body to heal.

After eating lunch at the Reinalzes' house, Carey helped clear away dishes and afterwards brought Nonny onto the porch. He carried her like she weighed nothing and seemed content to remain just as close forever.

They were greeted at the foot of the stairs by a small gathering of friends: the Albrights, Baschs, Reimenschnells, Kinderkopfs, and even the Tilfens, though the latter couple had stony faces.

Mrs. Froel stepped close and held Nonny's hand. "I'm glad to see ye with the man." She winked. "I'd almost given up hope that he'd go and rescue you. Had a feelin' ye needed rescue, I did."

"She did tell me to get ye." Carey laughed. "Glad I listened."

"As am I." Nonny smiled at the older woman.

"Be comfortable," Mrs. Froel said, "and be light." She stepped back and allowed the Albrights to leave their words of affection and encouragement, which were slightly longer-winded but no less appreciated. Fritz Wistom stood off to the side, staring at Carey through narrowed eyes.

The Weeping House

"We best be goin' now," Carey announced, and began down the trail towards his home.

"Wait!" a man shouted.

Carey stopped and turned back toward the small crowd. Mr. Tilfen and his wife had pushed their way to the forefront and glowered at the couple further down the road.

"Tilfen?" Holt stepped forward, resting a hand on the man's shoulder.

"I will not allow it!" the man snapped, brushing Holt's hand off. "It is not proper. Disgraceful, shameful, truly. They are unmarried!"

"Nonny's sick." Holt's face was grim. "How dare you."

"Is that a reason to defile the face of our town?" Tilfen said.

"What would you have us do?" Holt stepped close, dropping his voice to a whisper. "The lady is dying, Tilfen."

"They are not married." Tilfen was adamant. "An unmarried man cannot live with an unmarried woman."

"What are you going to do about it?" Isola stepped up beside her husband, Anneliese on her hip.

"Wait, Isola," Nonny said, sounding very tired. "I don't want to cause issue, I can't bear it. I will stay here. Carey,"—she rested her head against his chest—"will you take me back inside?"

"No," he said. The crowd was silent for a moment, struck with surprise by how simply Carey answered.

"Carey," said Nonny, "please. It's all such a fuss. I am tired. I want to sleep somewhere."

"No," Carey said again, more emphatically than before.

"What do you mean, Alsch?" Mr. Tilfen's wife spoke like a snake.

"Unmarried, we can't," Carey said. "Married, we can." He took a deep breath and looked at the woman in his arms. "Nonny," he began slowly, "will ye marry me? Will ye be my wife, and I'll be your husband? I will take ye home as my wife, if ye choose."

"Oh, but you can't marry me." Tears sprang quickly to her eyes. "I'd not make you husband of a wife bound for an early grave. I'd not be that wife, and I'd not see you tied to me."

"Why," Carey looked at her, almost in humor, "that's something I thought was understood. The entire point of havin' a wife is lovin' her before, until, and after she dies. 'Tis not for havin' a possession; not for years together, not for mighty names 'n' praise, nor for claimin' anything other than hearts. 'Tis for lovin' her as she is rightly to be loved." He looked very carefully at her face. "And I do love you rightly, Nadia Von Stein. Nonny. I love you in all the ways I could love."

"How could I?" She covered her face with her hands. "And leave you all alone when I am gone?"

"D'ye love me, Nonny?" His voice was very soft, so those nearby had to strain to hear the tone. Sweet, like honey; words full of meaning and hope.

"I do." She still covered her face. "Very much. So much, I think I will fall to pieces. I love you. I love you. I love you, Carey!"

"Then it is decided!" Holt was smiling broadly, surrounded by his children. All the familiar faces gathered cheered loudly, and plans were quickly made to have a wedding. Mr. Basch's daughter ran to the woods with Ada, Lieselotte, and Mechthild to gather flowers for a bouquet. Carey was commanded to bring Nonny back into the house, barring the door once he had returned to the porch empty-handed. Corinna, Inge, and Isola were a flurry of action in the house, finding a dress suited for a wedding, tying Nonny's hair in lovely plaits, and hugging her—nearly crying on her when they did so.

Holt took Carey aside and instructed him on the processes of weddings. Vows were written and the vicar was found. The churchman was slightly confused, not having time to adequately prepare, obtain licenses, and instruct the couple on godly ways of living. When the situation was explained to him, however, he gave his whole-hearted assent and was even seen laying wreaths out where the ceremony was to take place.

Oscar and Wolfgang were ordered to find the blacksmith and obtain two gold rings as quickly as possible. They raced towards the blacksmith's house, Treu hard on their heels. The hound sensed the tangible excitement exuding from his master, friends, and companions and bayed loudly as he ran.

The Tilfens stood in front of the Reinalz house, arms crossed over their chests, content to be the most dissatisfied and unhappy people in town.

Mrs. Froel was quite content to watch Isolde. She seated herself beside the child playing on the porch with a fabric doll. The older woman watched the family scurry to and fro, laughed at their antics, and talked quietly with the baby.

"I think this is a lovely day," she said. "We shall have a wedding, little Isolde, how perfect is that? Young love, so bright and hopeful, too."

Isolde said nothing, only continued playing with the doll. Playing consisted of waving it about and laughing softly. She was easily amused, and a rather delightful child.

Mrs. Froel continued talking as if she had a regular companion, "'Tis nice to see people havin' and claimin' their love. There's so much of holding it closely and quietly these days. They don't know how time runs out so fast, little one, so fast."

55
No End to Love

Just past the first curve of the Isar was a little wooded glen, full of bright flowers and hanging with moss. The greens found here were brighter, richer, and more vibrant than most others, contrasting heavily with the flowering linden trees growing in a natural semi-circle. The Reinalz boys had rolled logs and roughhewn wooden boards here, arranging them in makeshift benches. Flowers were draped everywhere, hung on the edges of the benches, from the trees, and laid about the ground just past where the seating was organized.

Mr. Albright sat aside, violin resting in his lap. He ran the bow through rosin and hummed pleasantly to himself. His wife reclined near him, fanning herself with a white lace fan.

Anyone close with the Reinalzes found their way to the glen and took up seats along the wooden benches. The only guests prevented from attending were the Tilfens. They were posted just outside of the woods and glared through the trees. Oscar Reinalz was set to guard duty and faced Mr. Tilfen with an immovable stance.

Farmer Knappen, Famer Welch, and their families had been fetched, as well as any other friend to Nonny and Carey, so the wedding party was about forty people. All had appeared dressed for festivities.

Carey stood at the forefront, dressed in one of Holt's suits, as they were nearly the same height and he had none of his own. Blue cornflowers stuck out of his pocket. The vicar, a man named Breck, stood just beside him. Breck was seldom found without a smile and a good word.

When all were seated, Mr. Albright took up his violin and played a graceful melody. The tune was soft at first, achieving the perfect combination of hushed melancholy and bright affection, a mood that was shared by most of the attendees. Though the occasion was enhanced by a beautiful sky and lovely location, the state of Nonny's health was not so quickly forgotten.

When the music reached the top of its sweet tune, Holt appeared in a dark suit at the edge of the woods. He carried Nonny in his arms. She was resplendent in traditional black, more closely resembling fairy or Waldleute than human. A white veil fell about her shoulders, drifting in the breeze like falling leaves. Delicate lace-trimmed edges brushed her cheek where dark locks curled under her chin and spilled down her back, wild and untamed. If she had wandered into myth, she would have had a place amongst legends of beauty from ages past. She whispered something in Holt's ears, and he set her down gently where the first bench was placed. When she was stable, he offered her an arm, which she leaned heavily upon for the entirety of the walk towards Carey.

When she stood before Carey, he took her hands, offering himself as a stanchion. In his face was the purest form of love, gentle and nearly spilling over.

It should be noted that neither groom nor bride heard a word that was said from that point on. Breck spoke of love, fealty, filial and romantic love, of God and man, of adoration, fidelity, and all things trial, war, and ease. Little heed was paid to his oration.

In the eyes of Nonny Von Stein, the only thing clearly visible in all the world was Carey Alsch. He was wholly real, good, and struck her as having the most affectionate gaze, unwavering and sure. She could scarcely meet his eyes for the overwhelming sense of devotion met there. There was no hesitant thought, nor wavering word in his mind. It was like a powerful wave of adoration crashed into her with each deep sigh breathed into his chest.

Ellie Johnson

Carey Alsch was no different, finding it difficult to breathe for how deeply he was affected by her mere presence alone. She had been parted from him by a cruel hand, now returned with pain and sickness, though she still held every grace, every soft feature, and otherworldly beauty to him. To Carey, Nonny was like myth, legend, and fable, a representation of all the good things in the world that had once been beyond his reach. He loved her in every way that love was possible. Filled with the fullest expression of each type of feeling, he was an unwavering, resolute man. Though death reached out a sickly, pale hand towards his love, he would fend it off with his body, spirit, and heart, determined to find her wherever she might go, and if he could not walk there, he would drag himself through any mire to be where she was. If she passed on from this life, he would find her at the end of his, where cosmos met earth, for such a love as he possessed was not barred by death, nor shortened by physical life; it was tangled in the very strings of being and could not be destroyed. He would be a traveler in any form of life or death needed to find her in eternity, where God had prepared a place for them both.

Such were the vows spoken by the quiet man of Mittenwald, leaving the guests awestruck and wondering how long such masterful words had spun in his mind, though he seldom spoke more than a sentence to most gathered. It was revealed in that moment just how deep the heart of Carey Alsch ran. It should be widely known that those who speak little, think often.

Though her voice was not strong, Nonny's spirit equally met Carey's with power and intensity, and she vowed to uphold a love unlike any other. Though her body may fail, and spirit arrive in the fold of Heaven, she would wait for him in that place. There was not any sadness found in her, only joy in the eyes of love.

They were married that day, professing their vows before a gathering so filled with filial affection and companionship as the Reinalzes had brought together. Before all, Carey took Nonny into his arms and kissed her, an action which invoked a cacophony of cheers and laughter in the glen. Not one person brought into that place felt grief upon leaving, bidding farewell to the couple and wishes for health, ever-increasing love, and all bright spirits.

Lifting Nonny from the ground, Carey held her close, speaking words of love quietly, so only she could hear. She laughed, taking his face in her hands and kissing him. Treu danced around their feet, delighted to see the two humans he loved most holding each other in such a way.

Mr. Albright took up his melody again, producing a tone even more cheerful than before. The procession made their way from the woods, passing a scowling Mr. Tilfen and his wife. Though they were appeased by the wedding, as everything was being done properly, they were the kind of people who were never truly sated and always found ways to be displeased. They were not aware that such a way of living has no point, and were quickly forgotten.

A wedding feast of sorts had been quickly thrown together by Farmer Knappen and his wife. In the yard surrounding the Reinalzes' white home, tables laden with food were decorated with flowers. Two dozen cornflowers had been specifically sought at Carey's request and covered the head of the long table in the middle of the yard.

As night fell, the company shared bread, drank wine and beer, and told affectionate stories concerning the celebrated couple. There was no shortage of the most delightful good feelings, and no end to love.

56

How Life Was

Nonny was astonished to find the little weeping house gone and, in its place, a handsome cottage, surrounded by gardens and flowers. Treu at their heels, Carey showed her the two rooms, windows, hearth, and chairs on the porch. She was delighted to find a home with good spirit, not the remnants of Carey's cracked and broken childhood. Although she would have been pleased to be beside him in either state of his heart and home, she rejoiced that his heart had been made new.

Time was oft spent on the porch, reading, watching evening birds and bats, patterns of rain and wind, and slowly dropping leaves as fall approached. Nonny requested that Carey teach her the intricacies of his annotated books and was soon quite competent at reading his unique script. He spent many an evening explaining how the desiccation of trees was vital to any biome, what the different tones of wolves howling in some deep part of the forest meant, and even collected moths in each stage, to show her how they transitioned from larvae to cocoon, and cocoon to delicate moth. She wrote everything down in a notebook, copying the shape of each creature, and quite extensively, asked Carey about every detail of them all.

When he worked in his shed, cutting, trimming, and scraping leather, she painted on the porch, rendering perfect likenesses of all Carey's treasures. There was devotion in her heart and a passion for creatures, though her passion for the man himself far exceeded any other inspiration. In the small cottage by the upper region of the Isar, Nonny was rejuvenated. Color returned to her cheeks. Strength returned to her body, restored by the tonics and tinctures prepared by her loving husband, who found great displeasure in any moment spent apart from her.

She liked to walk with Carey in the mornings, when the world was waking and all the creatures were calling to one another. Treu went wherever Nonny ventured, having declared himself her protector against all things unseen. He had that peculiar knowingness that dogs sometimes have about their masters, wherein he knew Nonny was not fully herself, and needed comfort and guarding. When she lay, he lay beside her; when she walked, he walked behind. When the mother sparrow started her day, going about all the trees in search of food, Nonny, Carey, and Treu followed. When the great boreal owl returned for the fall season, they were not far, measuring the span of her wings, counting her owlets when she was not at home, and winnowing owl pellets to discern her eating habits.

Nonny seemed so full of life that Carey could scarcely imagine how withered she had appeared when he rescued her. Though she liked to walk in the mornings, when evening came, she was often overtaken by a deep, terrible ache. She would lie in bed when she could no longer stand. With Treu's silken body beside her for warmth, she played with Carey's hair while he read to her. Sometimes, he would carry her to the porch, where they would watch the sun go down and imagine that life had no great pain. Treu liked these moments the most, finding comfort lying on the socked feet of the two people he loved most. Sometimes Nonny would paint the sunsets, depicting the scene from the cottage porch in the innumerable arrangement of colors it presented each day. Recalling her lament at the lack of vibrant paints, Carey foraged for suitable plants and clay to create whatever color she desired that was feasible to make out of wilderness supplies.

Treu was ever loyal, ever loving, and was even allowed to curl up in Nonny's arms on some days where she could not get out of bed.

In this manner, the depth and ability of Carey's love extended the life of Nonny Alsch far past what it would have been had she been left in the little room in the stone house in München. She lived more fully, more freely, released from the weight of secrets. As a woman, she was filled with peace and lived brightly in the sun. There has, perhaps, never been a man who loved a woman so deeply that her lifespan was made longer—until Carey Alsch loved his wife. Every aspect of her was fully met by him, and she did love him so. If a man were to be loved rightly, he would have to be loved by Nonny Alsch, for no woman has only one man, one person, one life to pour every bit of love into, unless she has already faced death and now may choose to live only so she might hold him close.

The Reinalzes oft visited, as did the Albrights, Knappens, and Mrs. Froel. Each came bearing gifts and company, sitting with Nonny while her husband made his living. He was not away long, returning often to show Nonny how the leather cured, how the new shoes were coming along, and to tell her how he loved her.

Corinna and Inge read books to her in the afternoon, sitting on the railing in the sun. There was passion and intelligence in the girls—as there is in any young woman—that was so well-treated and encouraged to make their laughter seem fuller and words deeper, clearer, and realized. Nonny loved them so, considering them closer than sisters. Mechthild, too, oft came to visit and was like Nonny's beloved sister.

Everything was so right and perfect, that before long the forest began to change, viridian to amber, gold, and citrine. Where yellow overtook the birch, aspen, and tallow, so came the brightest crimson red, like a bleeding heart.

When colder winds began to blow, Carey lit fires in the hearth and kept blankets in the house. The crisp scent of fall was mixed with pleasant smoke, warmed by fire and the comfort of the season. Treu liked this season best and found great comfort by the hearth, where Nonny lingered in the evenings.

By October, the only thing driving any memory of cancer and death was the striking pain Nonny endured. It was halved by her husband's devices, both of love and medicines found in the mountains. He was both lover and doctor, prescribing his patient many kisses.

Before long, Christmas arrived, finding itself celebrated in Carey's home, quite packed with family and friends. There was no end to bread, stollen, glühwein, leckerlii, and every Yuletide delight. A bonfire was lit in the yard for roasting chestnuts. These were dipped in sugar and enjoyed by all.

Though winter was cold, every heart was warm, for Nonny continued living. She was in great spirits, finding the purest joy in simple life. When spring came, she counted the days until flowers would bloom and caught the first cornflower poking up through melting snow. She claimed it as her flower and pressed it in a book. Before long, spring had fully arrived, shown by the emergence of flora and fauna alike. Elk traipsed in the woods, hog-trail was left behind, and foxes began to accost the chickens, though they were bravely defended by Treu.

In the full display of spring, all was calm and still. Life seemed to have found its mark upon the earth and set about causing things to bloom and grow. Such is the nature of the world; change is in everything, like winter melting away to spring. So also will one part of life melt away to another.

57

Beneath the Rhododendron

Spring days blended together, drawn like a curtain to shut off any remnants of winter. In those days, Nonny could not rise from bed of her own volition. This was not limiting to her experience of life, as she was not a burden to Carey. Instead, he employed himself entirely in assuring himself that she had ultimate enjoyment of every good thing. On days where she wished to be out among the wilds, he carried her. She was little weight to him, and he liked to hold her close.

In the spirit of spring tidings, they had made wreaths of ivy, woven with cornflowers were strung about all the rafters in the cottage, where drying bundles of lavender, sage, mint, and thyme already hung. The little cottage smelled of herbs, mixed with the warmth of the season.

By the end of May, Nonny was beset by sharp pains. Her skin had turned sallow over the previous month, and even the whites of her eyes had turned jaundiced. She had been visited that day by every Reinalz, conserving enough energy to kiss them all on the cheek, holding her dearest cousins in arms barely able to rise above the sheets.

When they had departed, Carey lay on the bed beside her, holding her close, so their bodies fit together perfectly. Treu had his large, velvet head resting upon the edge of the bed, watching Nonny with great chocolate eyes. Her breaths were shallow, the expiration echoing with a soft wheeze. There was still light in her eyes, but she was so tired.

"I am so scared to die," she whispered, shifting so she might look at her husband. "I have tried to be brave, my love, but what shall I do without you, and you without me? I do not want to go. I want to stay here with you.

I'm so scared."

"I will not be far." He kissed the space between her brows. "Ye need not fear, for there will be nothing lost. Whether in life or death, there is no change in our love. I would love ye for a thousand lives, a thousand deaths, Nonny, and if I might change places with ye, it would not even be a question needin' answering. If I could hold all the pain ye feel, so ye might be free of it, it would be so."

"I'd keep bearing this pain," she said, "so I might linger near you. There is no doubt you will keep me close. But I should wish to keep living here, with you."

"Ye have been all things right in my life, Nadia Alsch, and my wife. I'd n'er think to ask for more, for more has already been given to me. More than I thought would be claimed as mine."

"Do you know when I first loved you?" she whispered. "It was like the sun had come out. I remember it clearly."

"I'd not guess," he said, smiling, "for guessing wrong would be my folly."

"'Twas when the butcher cornered me at Farmer Knappen's." She smiled. "And you watched me. Then the clueless man sat between us at supper, and I was very upset. I had not realized how much I wished to sit close to you until he was in the way. And you were so very sweet."

"Oh," Carey said, looking away from her for a moment.

She laughed, seeing color fill his cheeks. His guess would certainly have been folly, it seemed.

"When did you love me, Carey?"

"When ye talked to the trees." He buried his face slightly in the white sheets.

"I talked to the trees?" Her brow furrowed, and the middle of her nose crinkled in the way he loved most.

"To get willow bark for Isola, who had just borne Isolde and was in pain. Ye wandered in the woods, dropping things ye had gathered, and talked to the willow tree. So, when I had met ye on the road, I decided to make ye a suitable bag."

"That soon?" Her eyes widened. "You saw me cut the willow?"

"I did." He grinned. "'Twas sat by, eating bread and cheese with Treu. Then ye appeared. I had decided against Christmas dinner with the Reinalzes—I had my unwelcome spirit with me and couldn't be burdened to change—and then ye appeared, and it was all bright to me."

"But you never said—" She laughed, reaching out to touch his face. He held his hand over hers, resting it on his cheek. It was pale and thin beneath his fingers and produced an ache in his heart.

"I didn't know the name for the thing until Mrs. Froel compelled me to find ye." He blinked slowly. "'Twas in me all along, I believe."

"You are wonderful, Carey. I love you."

"The love ye have has brought meaning to my life," Carey said. "And value to the things I didn't know I loved. I'd not vary from loving you. Ever."

She was quiet for a moment, then said, in the softest of voices, "You may vary, Carey Alsch. Your mornings might be bright, or quiet, or lovely, your evenings tired or sweet. Life varies; such is the contrast between sunrise and sunset. It's a good thing. You have been worthy of love since the day you were born. Had I died the day before I met you, you would've been no less worthy in all the world."

"But lovin' has made all the difference," he said. "I'd not change for all the world, 't'would be to lose my soul for changing courses. I see you. I've seen you, and that has made all the difference."

"I see you, Carey." Her eyes were tired, but still looking. "That has made all the difference."

Resting there, they were quiet for a long silence, matching breaths to one another.

"Carey." Nonny's voice was altered. "Take me where the foxes have dens that I can't see. That's where I want to be. I'll not be indoors, not now, not for eternity."

"But 'twill bring fever over ye." He did not move.

"I'll not die in a bed of blankets," she said, "but on a hill, beneath the sun, in a bed of daisies."

"Will it not hurt ye?" he asked. When she could not answer, he rose from the bed and descended into his larder, coming back with a tincture of wild poppyseed. "If ye wish to go"—his voice wavered for a moment—"I'll ease your pain." He placed a drop of opium on her tongue and hugged her close, gathering her up in his arms.

Treu at his heels, he carried her out of the house, down the porch, and across the Isar. Secure in his embrace, she rested her head back against his shoulder and looked up into the trees, where the crown-shy pines let rays of light slip between their leaves. The result was a myriad display of suns, like all the light fell from the heavens to kiss her skin. She was pale in the light, like wilderness fae, barely wisping between the living.

Carey brought her over the hills and into the meadow with the daisies, where foxes had made a den beneath the rhododendron, between the globe sedge that grew among heavy boulders. He lay her in the soft grass, where daisies encircled her head like a coronet. Treu waited patiently, a silent forest guardian. When Nonny was comfortably placed, Carey stretched out beside her, placing his arm beneath her head like a headrest. Treu rested just beside, so the edge of his coat was pressed against her arm.

"Though I fear death," she whispered, "it's less frightening in my woods, and I think I might find it beautiful, if it comes this way." Her hand gently brushed the length of Treu's smooth coat.

Carey did not speak, only held her close in the light.

"Every now and then I cry." Nonny's voice was less than a whisper, weary for breath and life. "But I'm not so sad when you hold me. I'll see you again. I think it's been perfect. Will you hold my hand?"

"I'll be the briefest moment of parting, my love," Carey whispered, taking her hand in his, fingers interlacing so she held his hand in return. He pressed it to his heart. "Like a light, ye'll wake in eternity, and then, when I have finished what needs finishing in life, I will meet ye there." He leaned forward, so he gently kissed her cheek. "'Twill be a moment for ye, though I will wait longer, for my life still begs livin'."

There was no more breath in Nonny Alsch. Her hand did not hold him back. She did not move again. Life had escaped her body.

Carey lay in silence, shutting his eyes against the world, then got up to his knees and wept.

The Weeping House

Tengmalm's Owl
Strix Varia

58
All Flowers Fade With Time

He visited that placed often—the quiet man of Mittenwald, who had known great suffering and even greater love. Owing to the real stuff of life, he delighted stranger and friend alike. Carey Alsch was a natural man, having kept his soul good and pure despite all trial and grief. There was now, where there had been despondence before, a brighter, keen sense of joy. While some may be struck by life and become stricken, Carey was instead given wholly to the memory of his wife, who had loved and loved well.

There was no shortage of filial love for him in town, and he spent many a night in company with the Reinalzes, and taught Michael leather-working for years on, though Wolfgang had given it up in lieu of becoming a writer.

Nonny was remembered in everything the family did, mentioned daily in loving memory, and kept close by laughter and good feeling. There was little of their lives unaffected by Nonny, and her passing. She was, perhaps, more honored and remembered there in that little town than in any hall in München, where the pieces of her former life turned to stone.

Once each year, every person who had attended the Alsches' wedding gathered around the wilderness grave growing over with daisies in that meadow. Inscribed on a granite stone were the words:

> Wife, who was loved, is loved,
> and will be forever.
> Nadia 'Nonny' Alsch did not die as stone,
> instead passed on like a flower fades with time.

Several months after her death, Holt knocked on Carey's door. Oscar was with him, carrying a heavy burden under each arm. Both men were grinning from ear to ear.

"You'll not believe this," Holt said, pushing his way into the simple cottage, still bearing the memory of the woman who had been the reason for its construction.

"I'm a man of faith." Carey arched an eyebrow. "Test me."

They laid their burdens down on the table and began to unwrap them with electric excitement. Encased in the brown postal paper were stacks of books, bound with leather and bearing the name *Of Mountain Woods*, Carey Alsch.

Carey stared at the books, not recognizing his own name imprinted there on the cover.

"She's written you a book!" Oscar said, unable to restrain himself.

"A book?" Carey was dumbfounded. He slowly lifted one of the books, turning it over in his hand.

"Nonny!" Oscar said. "She wrote it for you. It's all of your works, Carey!"

"I don't know when she did this." Holt shook his head. "Though I have reason to believe my wife had a hand in it. Mechthild as well. They walk about looking very pleased with themselves these days."

Carey turned the first few pages, scarcely able to breathe. Each page had a little drawing, done by Nonny's own hand, describing each notion he had shared over many months of wilderness lessons. He had seen her note-taking and drawings, and taught her how to read his annotations, but had not realized it had all been directed towards a culmination of his devotion to the mountain wilderness.

"Apparently," Oscar said, "Nonny knew people at the college in München, and they are using it there! It is a real book, a real textbook, Carey!"

"I've not written it." Carey shook his head. "It should bear her name."

"But it does," Holt said. He picked up another, flipping towards the front cover, where lists of copyright and official stamps were located. Near the bottom was a little line inscribed: Illustrations by Nonny Alsch.

"How did I not know?" Carey laughed. "It seems so obvious now. How quietly she worked! Truly,"—he looked at Oscar—"death is a little thing when Nonny loves me."

"I'm sure they will wish to speak to you," Holt said, "at some point. This is one of the most detailed books on natural history local to the area. Quite pivotal, in my opinion. What will you do? Will you go to the college?"

"I think any man or woman who wishes to learn about the wilderness," Carey said with a grin as he set the book down on the table, "should be out in the woods. If people wish to know me, then they must find me in my mountain ways. I'll not leave, not for their ease, not for any! How can a man know the sharp notes of a bee-eater unless he hears its call?"

"I'm sure." Holt laughed, clapping his friend on the shoulder. He presented an invitation to dinner, which was readily accepted. Carey took only one of the leatherbound books into his collection, giving it a pedestal made from all other, suddenly less important books of similar subject.

Together, he carried the remaining books back down into Mittenwald with Holt and Oscar. He was greeted by familiar faces, each begging for a copy. Carey happily gave his books away, refusing any payment and cheerfully expressing his delight at finding so many people interested in the design of all the creation they lived in.

On Sundays, he joined the Reinalzes in church, praising God for life and for the goodness he had been given. Regardless of the longevity of practical goodness, he felt each year in life now brought him closer to Nonny, and that, in and of itself, was goodness insurmountable. There was in Carey the complete change of character shown in those who—after much struggle—allow themselves to be loved. Being loved when feeling undeserving of any kind of affection seems at first a discredit or criminal action to those who are not used to the condition.

Love in its realest form, when guided by honor and truth, is that thing which mends, heals, aligns, perfects, and untangles any tightly bound cord of shadow tied to life. It endures all, hopes for all, gives strength, power, and ability where none can be found. Love is a table crowded, laid out with a feast, where there is always an extra seat. Love is in daily toil, in reminders to live well. Love is grace found in the absence of perfection.

Carey Alsch was a man who had endured fully the pain of life, bound for emptiness and apathy, expecting to carry an unwelcome spirit for his whole life. His unwelcome spirit was made welcome by that very real love found at a table where there is always room for one more.

Acknowledgments

Nothing must ever be said about anything worth something without first thanking my God for life, love, and liberty. No, this isn't a declaration of political and natural rights, this is an homage to the Spirit of the Living Word who has defined me from my infancy as living, loved, and free.

To go without thanking my mother, Alice Johnson, would be a crime. She is magnificent. One of her feats, it might be noted, was teaching a stubborn, weepy, firecracker of rage and no infinitesimal depth of feeling daughter how to write. Thank you, Momma, for putting in the work.

Second, I must thank my father, Brian Johnson, for teaching me the very real, very passionate love of language. Not cussing, obviously, but finding amusement in the construction of sentences, wit, banter, the words 'plethora', 'byzantine', 'somnambulant', and of course, the argument over the necessity of the word 'tergiversation'. How many times is too many times to include 'penultimate'? At least once per book, I have decided. Thank you, Dad, for taking me to see the world, and for lending me a glimpse into the beauty of knowledge.

Last detailed acknowledgement must be dedicated to my grandfather, Dr. Hans A Meinardus (everyone calls him Opa). He is truly one of the greatest people I have had the pleasure of knowing. It is also rare, I think, to call your grandpa a close friend, but we really are the best of friends. Thank you, Opa, for all of our long conversations about WWII, genealogies, history, Schrodinger's Cat and his equations, my disdain for sudoku, and tectonic plates all whilst sipping maté from a gourd with a bombilla. It must be mentioned that part of this story was inspired by life events, including the death of my grandmother, Corinna Meinardus, who died from cancer before I was born. I will include a quote that Opa wrote after her death which he sent to me upon finishing The Weeping House, "Personally, she has shaped my character like no other person, and so she lives on in my being." Elliemouse loves you.

In no particular order, I must thank Sophie Brantley, Mathew Lydy, Shannon Long, Brian Orser, Corina Wade, Amy Starnes, Ben Casey, and Elliot Williams for beta-reading The Weeping House. I really am so lucky to have such people in my life. All of you are partly responsible for The Weeping House as it is today. Though not a beta-reader, perhaps more akin to beta-listener, I'd like to thank Cosette Gentry for listening to the embryonic—albeit detailed and longwinded—plot summary for nearly all of my books. You're a real one. To my 'manager' Mathew Lydy, 'it's a draft as long as I want it to be a draft," is my hill to die on, although come May 25th, it probably won't be a draft anymore. To Shannon Long, manager of the hypothetical fandom, I could not have done it without support from friends like you. For some of these people, we've come a long way, haven't we? To have friends who will read my thoughts in their unedited, un-perfected(though no such thing as a perfect draft exists), and unorderly manner leaves me feeling rather vulnerable. I have a strange little mind, and letting people in can be quite frightening.

The Weeping House

Made in the USA
Columbia, SC
14 June 2025

4b1592b5-da65-4048-aff8-f45ba8a91374R01